Casta Diva

A NOVEL

IN LIFE, AS IN FILM,
FIGHT FOR THE ROLE YOU WANT

JAYE VINER

Casta Diva

Copyright © 2023 by Jaye Viner

All Rights Reserved.

This book is a work of fiction. Any resemblance to actual persons, living or dead is entirely coincidental. This work, or any portion thereof, may not be reproduced in any form or by any means including information storage and retrieval systems, or used in any manner whatsoever without the express written permission of the author. Thank you for buying an authorized copy of this book and supporting writers.

ISBN: 979-8-9878525-4-5

Cover Design by Damonza Designs

Formatting by Author Tree

Editing by Sarah McGuire

"I was thinking I wish you were an actor."

"Strange thought." Lucas turned the page.

"Not in my line of work." Quinn debated, then decided to say, "Your body is provocative."

"You say that because you think yours isn't."

There's no reaching him.

But now Lucas was pinching his finger in the book to hold his place and turning to face Quinn, his free hand a pillow under his head. *Those eyes.*

"Get down on your knees," said Lucas.

Heat flushed Quinn's cheeks. The command in Lucas's voice brought him halfway to obedience before he could even think about it. The book fell. Lucas's eyes glinted.

"Now crawl to me. No, not like that. Slowly. You're not hiding now, you're showing."

Quinn was on his hands and knees, frozen in the middle of the open square of rug between them. *Don't hide, show.* It felt incorrect, even silly. He'd given actors similar direction, and yet now it felt impossible to apply it to himself. How could he be hiding if he was here, choosing to sit under Lucas's withering gaze? But the voice had commanded him and so, though it felt wrong, Quinn started forward again.

Other books by Jaye Viner

Jane of Battery Park

Elaborate Lives

Terrible Love

––––––––––

The Afternoon Delight Shorts

Saucy Kaylee and her Stockbroker

Smart Jen and her Reality TV Star

Sweet Penny and her Tech Bro

Sour Marlee and her Sergeant

Casta Diva

"Everything in the world is about sex, except sex. Sex is about Power."
Oscar Wilde

Content Warning

This book contains Male on Male sexual assault in Chapter 24. There are mentions of terrorist activity, people disappearing, one faked murder, and one real murder.

Playlist

- Nur eine Waffe taugt from *Parsifal* by Richard Wagner
- Golden Slumbers by The Beatles
- Sukiyaki by Kyu Sakamoto
- Piano Sonata No. 13 in A Major by Franz Schubert
- The Blue Notebooks: The Trees by Max Richter
- Bad Reputation by Joan Jett
- Storytime by Nightwish
- Frost Upon Their Graves by CrimFall
- On Stirring Seas of Salted Blood by The Black Dahlia Murder
- Don't Look Back in Anger by Oasis
- Casta Diva from *Norma* by Vincenzo Bellini

Chapter 1

The Villa d'Umbras

Golden sun dappled the room in the most perfect light. Through the veils of his eyelashes, Quinn's heavy-lidded gaze absorbed the enchantment of gauzy curtains blowing in a cold citrus breeze, the leaves of potted plants clustered on the tile floor so green with life they seemed to glow. And in the chair not far from the bed, a man with all his edges softened.

Lighting makes the scene, thought Quinn.

Lucas wore satin harem pants and slippers. His button-down shirt was held closed by only the middle button, though the room wasn't exactly warm. On his lap, one of the notebooks of stories Quinn had written in high school, when he'd thought he'd be a writer instead of a director. Lucas turned a page, his gaze intent, as though he was reading an ancient text in Latin instead of the scribbling nonsense of an American teenager.

"You slept a long time," said Lucas without lifting his eyes from the page.

Quinn's awareness found his arms and legs. He was still wearing the sweater and slacks he'd worn to Larisa's family Christmas. The slipper socks sticking out from the end of the blanket draped over him were not his and, for a moment, this thought trapped his mind. Someone had put those socks on his feet.

"The weather has been unappetizing. I'm not surprised you waited until now." Lucas turned a page, frowned.

With difficulty, Quinn moved his tongue around his mouth.

It felt scratchy and thick and sour. "I wish you wouldn't waste your time with those."

"Why did you bring them?"

Quinn felt confused. He hadn't brought them, Lucas had. Slowly, he pushed himself into a sitting position, found a whole wall of pillows at his back, but he couldn't relax into them.

As though Lucas could read his mind, he added, "To Christmas with Gunter's family. Why did you pack these?" A self-pleased smirk curled his lips as though he'd already decided on Quinn's reasoning and found it cute in a childish way.

His mouth, thought Quinn, then quickly pushed the thought away.

"When you showed them to Larisa, did she sit you on a couch and ask about your daddy?" Lucas clicked his tongue between his teeth. "Daddy didn't want you, did he?" Lucas lifted his eyes from the page and gazed at Quinn, a steady, almost scientific gaze as though they were in a laboratory, and he was watching for reactions to stimuli.

"It's a good character trait," said Quinn. "The abandoned son grows up, never sure where he came from, never feels like he's enough. And there's the added conflict of watching his mom struggle and feeling like he's responsible."

"It's basic."

"It's relatable."

"What would actually be interesting is what it means for his sex life."

"Sex life?" whispered Quinn.

"Does he gravitate toward strong, caretaking women like his mother? Or try to compensate for the emptiness inside by being that figure to his lovers?"

"What if it's both?"

Lucas snapped the notebook shut and tossed it to the floor beside his seat. He rose and glided up to the bed where he came to a halt and looked down at Quinn with that same meticulous gaze. Quinn did his best to look up at him without flinching even though he was now fully awake and aware he'd agreed to come halfway around the world with this man, a professional criminal who'd probably killed people by proxy, if not by his own hands.

Beautiful hands, thought Quinn. They looked soft, the knuckles hidden in flesh, unlike his own skeletal appendages. And they were large, the kind of hands that played instruments, the kind that looked good on camera. For a moment, Quinn wished his first impression about Lucas being an actor had been correct. They could have done great things together.

Recent manicure, pristine cuticles. The observations crept in without warning. In his own voice, but with so much of Larisa's mind that he started. What must she think of him?

Whatever Lucas saw in Quinn's face, he took it as an invitation to sit down on the bed. With him came that smell that had been so powerful in New York, flowers and fresh-cut wood. Quinn thought, *Someday when this is over, I'll be out somewhere, and I'll smell this and think of him at this moment. The beginning.*

The beginning of what?

Quinn found himself leaning back into the pillows assuming a posture of relaxation he did not feel. Lucas's eyes traveled over him from head to ankles and up again.

"What do you see?" asked Quinn.

"You are an eighteenth-century courtesan. Not a trace of skin visible until the right person comes along. Then you might make an offering." Lucas took Quinn's hand, turned it over so his palm was facing up, then slowly pushed back the sleeve of Quinn's sweater, unveiling the pale moon of his wrist. Lucas lowered his head over that moon with his lips and branded it with the softest kiss.

It was one of the nicest and one of the most terrifying kisses Quinn had ever received. He froze. The heat that washed over him might have been excitement, but it felt like panic.

Lucas reached under the bottom of Quinn's sweater and set his hand in the valley of Quinn's belly just below his ribcage. "You're trembling." The hand beneath the sweater glided over

Quinn's skin as it rose and fell with his breath, not yet rapid, but not at all calm. "What has our fair maiden told you that you'd be frightened of me?"

This was what screenwriters might call an intertextual pandora, a question that looked and sounded like something ordinary, but in actuality was deeply endowed with significance. Lucas didn't just want to know what Larisa had said about him, he wanted to know if Quinn knew about Lucas's secret life. Which was confusing because Quinn thought they'd crossed that line of understanding at the bar in Minnesota. He'd also thought he'd been very clear about what he thought of Lucas's chosen profession.

Nothing about that scene felt clear now. Quinn had only drunk water, but it carried the haze of intoxication, the side effect of whatever drug Lucas had put in Quinn's water.

And now he's touching me.

Lucas's thumb had come to rest on Quinn's navel. The rest of his broad hand stretched around and cupped Quinn's side, a light pressure as it moved down toward the waistline of his slacks. If Quinn didn't find a way to put the brakes on soon, he'd have to make some even bigger decisions very quickly.

But his options felt limited. If he retracted, he risked pushing Lucas away. If he pretended he liked it, things might continue to progress, and he really wasn't ready to even think about what that might mean. Perhaps a part of him did like it. But they barely knew each other, and the touch felt so familiar, Quinn's signals were crossing. Larisa had touched him like this. So much like this that if not for Lucas's scent, Quinn might have closed his eyes and believed she was with him instead.

"Larisa said you were her college boyfriend. That you betrayed her."

Lucas stiffened. "How very simple of her. But then, she's incredibly dramatic."

"She's—"

"You're not really anything are you?"

The hand continued down, that thumb following the line of black fur below Quinn's belly button.

"You're not dramatic, or brave, or clever in any way. Quinn, the chameleon."

"What are you doing?" asked Quinn because he didn't think it was wise to say, *What are you doing with me?* and open himself up to questions about motivation and purpose.

"I'm looking for your soft place," said Lucas, as his wrist pushed against the top of Quinn's slacks. "That secret underbelly you keep hidden away. It isn't your parents. It isn't my darling queen."

"You assume I have one."

"Everyone has one."

That's what I'm here for also, thought Quinn.

The hand pressed still lower, almost to his groin. Any moment, Quinn's body was going to flinch or stiffen and ruin the mood in a way that Lucas wasn't likely to forgive.

"I'm an extremely slow chameleon." Quinn tried to make his face look apologetic instead of panicked, as he gently pulled Lucas's hand out of his pants.

Lucas's gaze narrowed with that prehensile interest, not a hint of disappointment. Because this seduction hadn't been about actual lust. It'd been about something else. Quinn would've given anything for it to have just been lust. He knew how to fail at that. But this, that gaze which wrote meaning onto every inflection, hesitation, and breath, held a purpose entirely altered.

"You're right. We barely know each other." Lucas drew back, but his eyes remained fixed on Quinn's face. "But Larisa and I have always shared everything. I feel like you're something she's sent me." He frowned. "Not a gift. Perhaps a puzzle."

Quinn pulled down his sweater so he was safely covered again. "That might have been true when you were together, but it isn't now. She would never share me with you."

A laugh burst out of Lucas's throat, so bright and startling

Quinn did flinch. "Your clothes are in the WC. Why don't you clean up, then we'll have dinner?"

Quinn was careful not to feel too relieved to be offered an exit. He didn't like the whisper of uncertainty in the back of his mind that pulled down all those moments since October when he'd been with Larisa and felt he barely knew her. In almost all of those moments, he'd thought of Lucas and wondered what exactly she'd shared with him.

There was a lock on the bathroom door. Quinn turned it as quietly as he could. Then, aware that movement would be visible through the crack between the door and the floor, he moved to the far side and stood in front of the toilet. He turned on the water for the shower and only then, under the cover of its waterfall, did he release all the taut muscles that'd held him together. The breaths came in jagged gasps, none of them satisfying. He allowed himself a full two minutes of this galloping panic, then he took in the room, trying to ground himself in details that felt either neutral or positive, an exercise his therapist had taught him.

Not that Quinn knew anything about architecture or interior design, but the bathroom seemed a work of art, with creamy textured walls, shelves that seemed to grow organically out of the floor, an aesthetic of earth tones so soothing in its harmony he couldn't pick it apart to see how it worked. In the center, a dressing island with vanity mirror. Folded on the island, the clothes Lucas had set out for him to wear. Quinn stared at them, his mind drifting almost to a standstill as it tried to absorb the implications. *Lucas dressing me instead of Larisa dressing me.* Then he moved on. There were windows, which he found alarming. Two small ones, without glass or screens, in the wall of the shower, and a large one he was surprised to discover was a door that opened onto a patio with a vine-covered pergola and a fainting couch sheltered from view by a half wall and a row of cypress trees. The shock of green and blue out the door was like a painting hung on the wall, too perfectly framed to be real. Dazed by the beauty of it, Quinn began to undress.

Lucas had brought him to a villa in the Tuscan hills named Villa d'Umbras. Apparently, it was a very old villa, even older than most of the other things in Tuscany, which were also very old by American standards. The architectural provenance of the villa could be traced back to the early days of the Renaissance when it had been built by the Duke of Umbras, a distant cousin of the famed Brunelleschi family, and was once the winter seat of a German duke. The German's family crest could be seen on every building along with the family token, a fox with a split tail. All this Lucas narrated as he walked Quinn down the hallway, around a corner, down a short flight of stairs, and into the central part of the house, which was modeled after the urban palazzo style which had been added on by a Polish owner in the eighteenth century.

As near as Quinn could tell, this meant that the drastic change in style from the textured walls, earth tones, and hard tile flooring in rooms that felt like caves to a romantic-era room full of giant windows, smooth walls, a wrought iron staircase, and parquet floor had been intentional and an absolutely absurd idea.

"His designer tried to talk him out of it," said Lucas. "There's virtually no visual appeal in imposing a palazzo into the middle of a villa. I would have simply refused the work, but here we are." He waved his hand at the fountain in the center of the room and the nine potted fruit trees that stood around it.

"If you don't like it, why do you live here?"

"Because it's the best house there is unless you want to live out in the campagna north of Lucca and drive an hour to get anywhere. Besides, how strange would it be, Lucas with a house north of the village of Lucca?"

"But easy to remember if you're giving directions."

Lucas paused as though Quinn's nonsense had thrown him off his spiel. It only lasted for a moment, then, with the light pressure of Lucas's hand on Quinn's back nudging him forward, they carried on, across the palazzo full of bright light, then back into the cave hallways of the villa on the other side.

"There have been four known murders, two suicides, and ten bodies discovered on the grounds. This sounds like a lot, but the grounds are extensive, and I believe that many more have yet to be found."

I've been awake less than two hours and he's already talking about bodies, thought Quinn.

"There is, of course, a family cemetery. And there are two History of Florence tour companies who focus specifically on Tuscan painters. They bring people up here to see it because a noted master of frescos was one of the first to put the Tuscan sun on the map, as it were."

Quinn nodded as though he was interested, but his mind was still back on the dead bodies. He wondered if Lucas had buried some himself.

After several more turns and a bewildering amount of history that quickly began to feel apocryphal, they passed through a set of what Quinn would have called French doors, though they were authentic to the villa so he doubted that was the right adjective, and stepped out onto a stone patio overlooking a baroque-style garden sculpted into the hill that sloped down from the house. Quinn decided in this case baroque meant topiaries and rigid, unnatural hedges marking out geometric designs. There was even a hedge maze down the hill.

At the patio table, a couple both wearing evening dresses, one black, one red, took turns sipping from the same orange cocktail. In the lounge chair behind them lay Larisa's traitorous cousin, Hannah, wearing a sweater dress but splayed out as though dressed for sunbathing.

No bodyguards, no easily visible security cameras.

"Luca, amore mio, you kept us waiting," said the woman in the red dress. *An Italian*, Quinn thought, with big bones and even bigger earrings that he thought were probably real diamonds.

"You're not coming out with us tonight?" said her partner in the black dress. Not an Italian, though she was working hard to pass as one. "Francesca's singing."

"I'm not going to sit through five hours of German for an understudy," said Lucas. He motioned for Quinn to take the seat beside the woman in the red dress. Lucas sat beside him. Hannah came over and sat down on Lucas's other side, filling the last seat at the round table.

"But you love her," said Black Dress.

"Maybe he just loved what she'd do in bed," said Red Dress.

"I'm not going to watch German anything in Italy," said Hannah, even though she didn't appear to be included in the invitation. She glanced at Quinn from across the table, a nervous look that was almost an accusation. As if playing spy under Lucas's all-knowing gaze wasn't hard enough, he also had to withstand Hannah's silent speculation.

"What about you?" Red Dress looked at him. "Does Luca's friend like German opera?"

It came as news to Quinn that German opera was the topic of conversation. His first and only association with German opera involved fat women in Viking helmets on *Looney Tunes*.

Lucas was smiling at him like he knew exactly what Quinn was thinking.

"I've never been, so I can't really say."

"Never been?" said Black Dress. "Have you taken on a new acolyte, Lucas? He looks a little old."

"I like fresh meat," said Red Dress. "Shall we try and guess what caught our generalissimo's eye?"

In a panic, Quinn looked to Lucas as though expecting to be rescued or discover that the women were joking. But Lucas's face was a smooth pane of bland interest.

"How many languages do you speak?" asked Red Dress.

Seriously? thought Quinn, his panic tilting toward the banked embers of his temper. He tried to answer like a normal person, someone who didn't feel attacked when asked personal questions about his education. "One and a half, neither of them very well."

"Me too."

"What instruments do you play?" asked Black Dress.

"None."

"Do you paint?"

Quinn shook his head.

"Sit in an endowed chair?"

"Cook?"

"Stitch?"

"Solve unsolvable mathematical equations?"

Quinn felt the heat rising on his face. Across the table, Hannah smiled into her drink, which provided the final straw that tipped his embarrassment into irritation. He wouldn't be here if it weren't for her.

"How old are you?" asked Black Dress.

"Thirty-one."

"And what have you been doing with your life all this time?"

"Working."

Both women looked at him, waiting for the rest of the answer.

"I drove a forklift in a warehouse until last year. Now I make movies."

Red Dress tilted her head at Lucas to help interpret this apparently confusing answer. Perhaps she believed her English had failed her.

"Is he any good at it?" Black Dress asked Lucas.

"Quinn is an undecided creative," said Lucas, as though it was a reasonable answer to the question, as though Quinn was a fickle amateur.

Hannah snorted into her drink. The two women exchanged a look. Red Dress leaned over and patted Quinn on the knee. "When I was young, I thought I would be extraordinary. But then I learned it's much easier to be the person who *appreciates* rather than the person who *creates*."

"My latest film is getting pretty good reviews, actually," said Quinn.

"Ah, the critics," said Black Dress. "What do they know about art? Who are your influences? I love Antonioni. He was a poet with film. Every frame held meaning."

"I'm biased to say that all my favorite films are Italian," said Red Dress. "But I've watched every Julia Roberts movie."

"You've pleasured yourself to every Julia Roberts movie," said Black Dress.

"And you haven't? She's wasted on men."

"What about Fassbinder?" asked Black Dress.

"Ach, Germans again. Is dinner coming?" Red Dress looked at her delicate silver wristwatch, then at Lucas.

"Ah, yes. I forgot to tell them we're ready." Lucas stood, walked to the patio door, waved at some unseen person, then came back.

"Forgot to signal dinner." Red Dress shook her head. "He must be very interested in you." She peered at Quinn. "But I cannot understand it. Tell us the secret, Luca."

"It's abstract."

Three uniformed waiters filed through the patio doors, delivering steaming dishes of food which they set before each person. Quinn's stomach rumbled, but when he looked down at his plate, the head of a fish stared back at him. One eyeball, half a divot in the skin where the mouth had been, and scales.

Fuck.

Out of the corner of his eye, he watched Red Dress select a small fork from the line of serving utensils beside her plate, but his field of vision wasn't wide enough to see what she was doing with it. His hand went to pick up his own small fork. Two prongs. *What the hell?*

"Mio Dio, the little orsacchiotto doesn't eat the fish."

Quinn looked up to see everyone watching him.

"Abstract in what way?" asked Hannah with a smirk, like she expected Lucas to dig himself into a hole trying to avoid explaining that Quinn had come to Italy to hide from Lucas's ex-girlfriend. Quinn couldn't imagine Lucas saying anything like that. Even the word ex-girlfriend seemed below him. Still, he found himself listening for the answer. *What does Lucas think I'm doing here?*

"I'm freeing Quinn from his delusions." Lucas picked up his fish fork and a knife and began to efficiently remove the scales from the fish flesh beneath them. "He believes he's a submissive. This isn't true. He won't be capable of anything noteworthy until he understands what he is."

Silence.

Quinn's face burned, though now it was dark enough maybe no one could see. Did it matter if they could? He was humiliated anyway. In what was apparently an established habit of Lucas bringing interesting and talented people into his home, he'd brought Quinn for the sex. Not just for sex, for teaching him what he apparently couldn't figure out himself. What could he even say in response? That his work had nothing to do with his sexuality? That he didn't believe a person was always one thing or another? Any protest would make him seem even more of a fool.

Hannah lost her smirk. Red Dress studied Quinn as though his true sexual nature was written on his face if only one had eyes to see. Black Dress thoughtfully worked on her fish, then said, "All lessons in dominance should begin at the opera."

"Perhaps we'll join you after all," said Lucas.

Chapter 2

The Smoke Remains

The only salon open the day after Christmas was in Bloomington, at the Mall of America. Larisa de France-Kahn's mother, Suzette, insisted Larisa come with her to get their hair fixed. The idea of returning to LA smelling of smoke with smoke-damaged cuticles, and who knew what else, had driven Suzette to a brain-freeze of stillness—her word for a non-clinical panic attack. This was how Larisa found herself in a mall, with a stranger's fingers massaging her scalp, twenty hours after Lucas had stolen Quinn away from her.

He chose to go. Her eyes burned as she stared back at the reflection of a woman who looked like she had her life together, who looked like the kind of woman other women envied.

"Doing some shopping today?" asked the stylist.

"No."

"Get everything you wanted yesterday?"

The burning increased. Larisa swallowed and told herself she was not going to cry in front of the stylist. "Sure."

Across the salon, Suzette was telling her stylist the whole story. Well, not the *whole* story, but the one she'd decided was fit for public consumption. Her daughter's vengeful ex had conned his way into the family Christmas only to set the tree on fire and abscond with one of the cousins. Quinn was not even a character. In reality, as defined by her mother, he didn't even exist.

"Aren't you going to tell her he also stole my current boyfriend?" Larisa angled her head so she could see her mother's reflection in the mirror. Suzette frowned, then continued talking as though Larisa hadn't spoken.

To keep herself from picking a fight, Larisa checked her phone. The group chat for her sorority sisters was busy. Krissy wanted a girls-only spa day to recover from holiday stress before New Year's. Kahleah and Jaden were still out of town, posting regular updates on the agony of extended family gatherings. Rosa sent pictures of her swollen feet.

> Rosa: Baby in 3 weeks, two days AND COUNTING!!!

No messages from Lucas, Quinn, or Hannah, the cousin who featured in Suzette's curated version of events. The silence from that particular corner of Larisa's phone stretched with each passing hour, looming like the cartoon shadow of a demon rising to cover a fantasy world. She sent a message to Quinn, then she added her own holiday update.

> Larisa: Please say something.

> Larisa: Nothing to report here in Minnesota except a small house fire. Flying home soon.

"I've never been that close to a fire," said Suzette's stylist.

"Hope you never do," said Suzette. "It was terrifying. Truly terrifying. And now I've lost all this time planning for my gala. The caterer says they can't get enough crab and want to serve imitation. The decorator has the flu and wants to send their assistant. It's like the world's ending."

"She doesn't care about your fucking gala, Mom."

A momentary silence that sounded like a ruffled bird. Larisa met her stylist's gaze in the mirror. "She doesn't like to admit that her daughter's a fucking mess. No healthy person has her boyfriend abandon her during a family event to hang out with her ex, right?"

The stylist's mouth opened, then closed.

"Right. That just doesn't happen to good people." The tears started to come, and Larisa was too tired to stop them. "Shit like that happens to the fucked-up children of celebrities who raised them in a media bubble, so they don't know how to have real relationships."

She was screaming into the mirror, at her mother's reflection, as though her mother could be touched. In actuality, Suzette was probably still thinking about the gala, working through the problems, while she told herself to give both stylists an extra-large tip to keep them from going to the press.

Larisa: Just tell me you're okay.

Gunter Kahn was on the phone pacing the aisle of his jet when his wife and daughter arrived. From the serious tone of the conversation, Larisa thought he was talking to one of his lawyers, trying to find a way to prosecute Lucas for nearly burning down Gunter's brother's house.

As soon as he hung up, Suzette tilted her head toward him. "I can still smell it. Can't you smell it?"

"You look fine, dear."

"Our staff will smell it the moment we walk in the door. We should release a statement before the press gets ahold of any rumors."

"Any luck?" asked Larisa.

Gunter shook his head. "He's already left the country. The damage isn't costly enough for an international lawsuit."

"But you must be able to do something," said Suzette. "All of us could've died."

Larisa took her seat, swallowed a Xanax and told herself she was going to survive this. She'd been thrown worse curveballs. This would be fine.

Fine.

Fine.

Absolutely nothing was fine. And it hadn't been fine for a long time. She picked up her phone to send Lucas a message, threaten him. Make him promise to treat Quinn well, or else.

But knowing Lucas, any direct contact would just further convince him that Quinn was important to her. It was wiser to trust Quinn to create his own narrative.

> Larisa: Whatever your plans, do them fast.

> Larisa: Lucas isn't safe.

She pressed her phone between her hands and willed the Xanax to take effect. Oblivion was her only hope for peace now. When it came, the high was uneven and troubled; her body relaxed but her mind still strained through hypotheticals, restless with entrapment. It couldn't accept the truth: There was nothing she could do. She couldn't accept it because there had been years when she'd had the chance to do something and failed.

She'd been crying again when the jet began its descent and parked at LAX. As usual, Gunter's assistant had ordered two hired cars, one for her parents and one for Larisa. Gunter's usual driver stood ready at one sedan, while a familiar blonde in a skimpy sweater and miniskirt stood beside the driver of the second sedan.

When she saw her, Larisa felt her throat clench, her body rushing ahead of her mind. She stormed forward, a moment away from grabbing the girl and shaking her. "What are you doing here?"

"Hi." The blonde smiled. "I'm Ana."

"I don't give a fuck what your name of the week is. How did you know I'd be here? What do you want?"

"I'm here to take you home." Another smile as Ana turned and climbed into the back of the sedan. With a glance back to make sure her parents hadn't noticed, Larisa followed her in.

"Is the driver working for you?"

"Not officially." Ana gave a little wave to the driver who put up the privacy barrier.

"He can still listen in, you know."

Ana giggled. "This isn't a top-secret meeting."

"But you work for Lucas."

"Sure."

"And why are you here?"

"He has a project for you. I'm here to help."

"No."

"I really love all the palm trees," said Ana. "And all the sunshine. It's so bright all the time."

"Did you hear me? Whatever it is, the answer is no."

"We'll talk when we reach your apartment."

"There's nothing to talk about."

"Is that true? Your friend is with Lucas now. And your cousin, right?"

Larisa swallowed a sudden rush of bile. "He wouldn't." She pushed back into her seat, the sedan suddenly too small, the air too dense as she realized it didn't matter if Lucas would actually hurt Quinn or Hannah. The threat was enough. She couldn't gamble with them. Whatever Lucas asked, she would have to find a way to make it happen.

The lights were on in Larisa's apartment. The front door was unlocked, but she didn't realize it until she thought she unlocked it with her key only to find she'd locked it instead.

Inside, Quinn's assistant, Sid, stood at the small kitchen island watching a movie on his tablet. Sabrina, the white Persian kitten Quinn had gifted Larisa that spring, sat on the island beside the tablet giving herself a bath. She paused when she saw Larisa, then resumed without interest.

"Hey," said Sid. Maybe Larisa was imagining it, but his voice seemed carefully neutral, the way one talked to an animal that startled easily.

"Hey," she echoed.

"Who's this?" Sid nodded at Ana as she hovered like a ghost at Larisa's shoulder.

"Ana."

In the corner of the kitchen, her electric kettle chimed.

"I was making tea," said Sid. "Want some?"

"Yes, wonderful," said Ana.

Sid gave Larisa a funny look that was ninety percent judgement, ten percent curiosity, then began to pull mugs out of the cupboard.

They took their tea over to the living room. The lights on the little holiday tree she and Quinn had picked out were on. Beneath it, the presents they'd planned to unwrap together. Sid pulled a flask out of his pocket and spiked his tea. When she held out her mug, he poured a shot into it as well.

"Did you talk to him on the phone or through text?" she asked.

"He called this morning."

"How did he sound?"

"Sorry if this sounds rude, but I don't feel great that you're asking about his feelings right now." He glanced at Ana as though she was the reason he didn't want to talk to Larisa.

Fair enough.

"It wasn't right, what you did. Keeping that stuff about the baby from him."

"I know."

"Then why'd ya do it?"

Larisa shook her head. In the moment, she'd felt she had good reasons. She was protecting him, trying to remove uncertainty from his life so he would have the energy for the things that mattered. Had that been her only reason?

"I didn't want him to leave me," she said.

Sid grunted.

"I didn't want him to feel responsible for a situation he didn't choose."

"Still not right."

"I know."

Sid slurped his tea down to the dregs and set it on the end table. Across from them, the tree looked sad, the unopened presents beneath it the relics of some unspeakable tragedy.

"You might as well take your gift," she said. "It's from both of us."

When Sid didn't move, Larisa got up and plucked one of her leftover gift card boxes from the small collection of presents and tossed it at him.

"What is it?"

"Dodgers season tickets with box access."

Sid whistled. "From the two of you, huh?"

"He said you enjoy large groups of inebriated people having a good time in arenas." She kept her eyes on the tree so she didn't have to meet Sid's disbelieving gaze. If she did, it would be too much. She'd break down and cry, beg his forgiveness because she couldn't beg Quinn's.

"I like sports," said Ana.

"Maybe I'll take him to a game when he gets back from wherever he is."

Larisa smiled. They both knew Quinn would hate being dragged to a sports stadium filled with people. "Florence," she said.

"Florence . . ."

"It's a city in Italy."

"How?"

"It's complicated."

Sid shook his head like it was all too much.

Imagine if he knew everything I knew, she thought.

"Oookay, I'm just gonna . . ." He stood, hesitated. "Quinn gave me a message. He said he believes there's a way to get back homeward."

For the umpteenth time in twenty-four hours, tears burned Larisa's eyes. She swallowed them back.

"Given the unusual syntax, I'd guess that's a reference to a Beatles' song, but he's immune to the brilliance of the Beatles so—"

"He said you had a Beatles phase in college. He listened to them with you every day." Larisa swallowed down a painful knot of something rising up her throat.

Why did you go with him, Quinn?

"It's just a thing I said once, about how I sometimes felt like the Beatles getting back together to do Abbey Road, even though they knew too much had changed for them, was—Oh God."

"What?"

"Fuck." She couldn't say it in front of Ana. And then, as the aftershocks of her surprise dissolved into dread, she realized she didn't even want Sid to be responsible for the truth.

Quinn has gone to play the spy.

Somewhere in the fast-descending brain fog, Larisa heard Ana say, "So, Sid, do you think you could help me score some crack tonight?"

Chapter 3

Daring a Devil

The opera ended in the middle of the night. During both of the twenty-minute intermissions, they drank champagne in the mezzanine. And both times, people approached to say hello. Italians, Europeans, and American expats, all of them displaying their wealth. But Lucas was also approached by less showy people. Men who wore suits instead of tuxedos, and women who wore pants and sensible heels. They were people who did business. And if it hadn't been obvious that Lucas had decided on this night out at the very last minute, Quinn found it easy to imagine these interactions serving as opportunities to covertly pass jump drives back and forth, or even slip an envelope into a pocket. He found himself looking for hidden earpieces like the scene in *Quantum of Solace*.

But this was his imagination trying to write menace into a situation that otherwise felt vibrant with innocence. People treated Lucas like he was a prince. Those who didn't know him watched him from afar. Quinn saw three different people take covert pictures of him, just in case he turned out to be a visiting celebrity.

What had he been like with Larisa at his side? wondered Quinn.

Larisa. She was like a ghost haunting the air. With any movement in his peripheral vision, he expected to turn and see her. He'd become so used to her presence at his side that now her absence felt like he'd left something vital behind.

She lied to me.

She doesn't trust me with my own life.

By the end of the opera, Quinn couldn't have said what the story was about, or if the singers were any good, but he knew he wanted Larisa with him, even though he didn't know where they stood, or how they were going to get past what she'd done.

Lucas's hired car dropped the women off at their home. Then he and Quinn were alone on opposite ends of a too small bench seat in the back of the car.

"What did you feel when the curtain fell?" asked Lucas.

Unobjectively angry, thought Quinn, then he realized Lucas was asking about the opera. It seemed a trap question, though Quinn wasn't sure how. He just knew it was harder to make up feelings than a fake evaluation. Of course Lucas wouldn't ask something as generic as, Did you enjoy it?

He plucked at the small white buttons of the tux shirt Lucas had loaned him. *I'm now a person who has gone to an opera.* "It was good. I mean, not really my thing, but—"

"Why can't it be your thing?"

Quinn shifted in his seat. The car was cold, but he was starting to sweat through his boxers. *I don't want to talk about feelings right now.* "I like movies."

"Fine." Lucas waved an impatient hand. "What did you feel at the end of the last film you watched?"

Out the window, an almost total darkness stretched beyond the half wall that bordered the road. So much darkness. And here he was all alone with the man who'd ruined Larisa's life, broken her heart, decided his work was more important than her happiness.

"Next time I ask you, have a better answer," said Lucas.

"Why?" asked Quinn.

"Because you're a person with a working brain."

"Maybe I just don't want to talk to you."

"Then what are you doing here?"

Trying to get you out of Larisa's life.

Our life.

Making a future. This last thought felt extravagant. What future? Were they even still together? Did he think if he managed to find evidence that would send Lucas to jail that Larisa would somehow see him as capable? Would it change how he saw himself?

"Jet lag can be challenging," said Lucas. "I forgive you."

Quinn glared at the headrest in front of him. *You forgive me, fucking great.*

"But if you're going to be here, you cannot just drift around like an amoeba, per your usual."

"How do you know what's my usual?"

"One notices many things when he's learned to see."

"Because you're just that amazing, huh?"

"Compared to you? Yes," said Lucas. Full stop.

The trouble was, Quinn agreed with him. Sitting side by side with this man, who made the curated stars of Hollywood look like washed-out showmen, Quinn couldn't stop wishing for another reality. If Lucas had been an actor. If Lucas had been just a little bit less of an asshole. If he was more open to possibilities, the three of them could have . . .

Quinn dismissed the thought. Immediately another took its place. *Does she still love him?* It was a question Quinn had asked himself so many times he couldn't remember the first time he'd asked it. What subconscious shift in Larisa's voice, in her word choice, in what it felt like she wasn't saying, had told him this man still held some part of her in his hands?

If I manage to do this, will she even thank me?

The villa felt quieter than before. Lucas led the way back to the bedroom where Quinn had woken up that afternoon. Quinn followed him, pushing down instincts to check the corners for the exits even though there was nowhere to run.

Lucas motioned to the bathroom door. "Use everything I've provided."

In the bathroom, Quinn again locked the door and took a

moment by the toilet to gather himself. *Whatever happens, you'll be fine.* But telling himself this didn't quiet his racing heart. *There's nothing to be scared of. You haven't done anything wrong yet. He's not going to kill you,* he thought, even though it felt like Lucas already knew Quinn had come with nefarious intentions and was pushing him so he'd trip up and reveal them.

On the bathroom island counter, an assortment of bottles had appeared during Quinn's absence. Deodorant, lotion, mouth-wash, toothpaste, and a toothbrush, all of them imported with labels in French or English, except for one bottle in Chinese with a man's pristine white face on it. Quinn opened it and sniffed it, a second kind of lotion, probably for his face.

No sex toys, condoms, or douche kit.

Okay. This is good. You're fine.

There was also a nightshirt that looked like something out of a costume drama, complete with billowing sleeves and a deep *V* of open chest with laces. It didn't quite reach the middle of his thigh, which meant his boxers showed underneath. Quinn wasn't sure, but he thought they'd ruin the look, so he took them off and prayed this would earn him points without making him seem eager.

Lucas stood a few feet back from the bathroom door. As soon as Quinn emerged, he looked him over, a brisk glazing that missed nothing. He closed the distance between them in a step.

"Open your mouth."

Quinn opened his mouth, too surprised by the request to do anything else. It felt so simple, so easy compared to the nameless things he'd anticipated.

Lucas looked down his throat, then ran his thumb along Quinn's front teeth. "Passible. You'll do better tomorrow."

It wasn't a question. Quinn might have laughed. Felt silly for wanting to say, *No, I won't,* because who argued about how well they brushed their teeth?

Lucas stepped back and motioned for Quinn to do a turn.

Quinn turned quickly; he didn't like having his back to Lucas, his legs exposed in all their pale hairy glory.

"What do you feel?"

Not this again.

"Right now?"

"Answer the question."

Objectively furious.

But not at Lucas, Quinn realized, which didn't quite make sense. At Larisa. At Larisa for . . . not being here to help him. Because underneath all that rage was something else. He was terrified of so many things. And for the first time in a long time, there was no buffer keeping them out of his mind. It felt as though everything Lucas said was meant to remind him of how very little he was worth to the world, to anyone who should have loved him, to himself.

"Nervous," said Quinn.

"Why?"

"I've found myself in a foreign country, half naked in a stranger's bedroom. This is a first for me."

A smile curved Lucas's mouth, and Quinn felt a small flutter of pride in his chest. He'd given a satisfying answer. He hated how good it felt.

"Have you had a nice day?"

"Yes." *But.*

"Have I given you cause to be nervous about something?

"No." *But.*

"Then what is making you feel this way?"

"It's just a feeling."

"Just a feeling," Lucas repeated to himself. He shook his head. "I cannot fathom what she saw in you. You're like a black hole of a person. You suck everything in without being touched by any of it."

Quinn knew when he was being baited, but it still stung. "What she *sees* in me," he couldn't help but say. "We're still together."

"Have you told her you're here with me? What do you think she'll do when she finds out?"

She'll break all her rules and come for me, thought Quinn, even as he prayed that she wouldn't. "I'm more interested in what you think," said Quinn. "And why you're so interested."

"I believe I just illustrated how terribly uninteresting you are."

"It must bother you. She would choose someone like me to replace someone like you."

Lucas's hand shot out and slapped Quinn across the face. Then he was up against the wall, Lucas's hand clenched around his windpipe with just enough pressure that if Quinn struggled, he couldn't breathe.

"You are a slug," hissed Lucas. "It's only a matter of time before she is embarrassed by you. She'll leave you behind when she goes out. She'll neglect to mention you in interviews. All of your sloppy, careless little habits will grate across her nerves until she despises you. And then she'll be stuck with you because you're too pathetic to be kicked to the curb."

Tell me how you really feel, thought Quinn. He focused on Lucas's face, told himself not to panic. This was a test. *No one's dying tonight.*

"So teach me." The words rasped from his mouth, barely audible.

"You're not a true submissive."

"Test me."

"What happens when you fail?"

Swallowing was painful, but the pressure building up meant Quinn couldn't stop himself. "Whatever you want," he gasped.

Lucas released his grip. "Say it again."

"Whatever you want."

"You'll regret this." Lucas eyed Quinn with a narrow gaze, then turned and walked out of the room.

Strangely, Quinn felt even more breathless after Lucas left than he had with those fine hands around his throat. He bent over, one hand braced against the wall as he waited for the oxygen to flow normally again. When the room stopped spinning, and his breathing no longer sounded like a hurricane, Quinn went to the door and stealthily turned the old-fashioned, gold-plated key in the lock. He took the key with him to the armoire where he found the bag Larisa had bought him for Jaden's wedding in the bottom. In it, his phone, magically not dead. He turned off the lamp. He took the pillow and the blanket from the bed and carried them to the far corner of the room behind the chair where Lucas had sat that afternoon. There, tucked up between the wall and the chair, Quinn made a new bed. Then, after taking a breath, he looked at his phone.

He wasn't sure what he'd expected, but it felt strangely anticlimactic. Larisa had sent him less than ten messages. She'd resisted the shouting temptation of all caps. The quiet, short phrases she'd sent into the void between them felt almost worse than if she had yelled at him.

With a glance toward the door to reassure himself Lucas wasn't about to barge in on him, he dialed. Almost immediately the line opened, but then there was a pause before she said, "I'm not alone."

Definitely not what he'd expected. He heard a warning in her voice he didn't quite understand. The only reason he could think of for her to say that was if she happened to be meeting with the CIA agents. But that seemed so fast.

"You're back in LA?"

"Yep."

"Any problems?"

"With what?" Her tone had turned frosty. "You know Lucas almost burned down my uncle's house?"

He hadn't known that. The surprise of it made him feel like an idiot. Not once had he thought about what had happened at Christmas after he'd made his panicked exit.

"Is everyone okay?"

"Yeah, sure."

Silence filled the line as they both took a step back, tried to reorient themselves.

"What about you?" asked Larisa in a much softer voice, like she was scared of the answer. "Are you okay?"

"Uh, I don't really know. But I went to an opera tonight."

"Did you?"

"Funny thing, we're in Italy, but they sang in German."

"Yeah, that happens."

"You didn't tell me . . ." He stopped because he didn't know how to finish his thought. "He's different than I expected."

This time the silence stretched so long Quinn looked at his phone to make sure the line was still active.

When Larisa spoke, her voice sounded husky. "I know you're angry with me. You have every right to be. But I need to ask you . . . I need to hear from you every day. Can you promise me we'll talk every day while you're with him?"

"Yeah, we can do that."

"Okay," she breathed.

"Until tomorrow then?"

"Tomorrow."

After he hung up, Quinn lay down in his makeshift bed and stared at the closed bedroom door until sleep took him.

Spa Day

Larisa slept with all three pieces of her Chanel luggage set pressed up against her bedroom door. When her mind reluctantly decided to draw her from the oblivion of sleep, they were the first things she saw. A reminder that she wasn't alone, and the nightmare was just beginning.

The suitcases felt too heavy as she moved them aside and opened her door. Ana lay sprawled out on the couch under the blanket Larisa had given her. In sleep, she looked more like a normal girl than an agent of blackmail. Across the living room, Sabrina jumped down from her tower and came to press against Larisa's legs. Time for breakfast. For a normal houseguest, Larisa would've been considerate. But for Ana, she took a vindictive delight in banging through the kitchen, startling the girl out of sleep.

"What time is it?"

"Nine."

"Fuck me."

"Don't like it? Get yourself a hotel." Larisa held two cans of wet food out for Sabrina to sniff. She opened the anointed can, spooned some onto a plate, then found herself spooning the rest into her mug. For a moment Larisa stared down at it, realizing it would never again not smell like cat food. She wanted to hurl it against the wall. Instead, she pushed it to the far side of the island and went to the cabinet for a new mug.

Ana wrapped herself in the blanket and came to sit at the island. "What's for breakfast?"

"I'm not feeding you."

"I don't have any money."

Larisa rolled her eyes. "Why don't you just deliver your message so you can leave?"

"It doesn't work like that."

"It's going to have to work like that, I'm very busy."

"Yeah?" Ana perked up with interest. "With what?"

Larisa opened her mouth to snap off an answer, then remembered it was the end of December. The only things on her calendar were parties she didn't intend to attend. "I'm having a spa day. And other things you don't need to know about."

"I love the spa."

"You're not going. We're not friends." Larisa felt her rage rising. She braced her palms against the island and leveled her gaze at Ana. "Why don't you just tell me what you're doing here?"

"I don't want to."

"Why not?"

"You won't like it, and I don't want you to freak."

"So you're what, stalling because you think at some point in the future I'm going to be an easier sell?"

Ana shrugged. "Can I have tea too?"

"Not until you tell me what Lucas wants."

"It's difficult to say."

"Try it."

"You know a man named John Hagan?"

Larisa stilled. In a split second, she understood what was coming. It beamed so clearly into her mind she barely heard Ana when she said, "Lucas wants him gone."

The laughter came first, a hysterical, overheated sound that cracked out of Larisa's throat like hardening lava, like she was suffocating. Ana's eyes widened with an almost comical fear. Then tears began to leak out of Larisa's eyes, and she couldn't see.

"I told you, you wouldn't like it," said Ana.

"Get out of my house."

"This is an apartment."

"Get out!"

When Ana didn't move, Larisa came around the island, grabbed the girl's skinny arm and pulled until the rest of her tipped off the island stool and followed Larisa out the front door. Larisa slammed the door behind her.

The yelling had startled Sabrina who was cowering in the cubby of her tower, ears twitching with cat-like irritation. Larisa took a few steps toward her, thinking she'd banished all the bad with Ana and could go about her morning. But at the kitchen island, her hand closed around the soiled mug. With a scream, she flung it at the wall.

One mug wasn't enough. Sabrina's little plate went flying, then even the fresh mug that'd been waiting for the water to boil. Larisa's fingers itched for new projectiles. She flung open the cupboards, scrabbling for whatever she could close in her hand. The rest of the small plates, more mugs. With nothing left that wouldn't require the work of both hands, Larisa sank to the floor and buried her head in her knees.

This is not happening.

This cannot be happening.

"That's going to be a lot of work to clean up."

Larisa turned and saw Ana standing at the edge of the kitchen, looking sadly at the shattered dishes.

"How did you get back in?"

"You left the door unlocked." Ana came forward, setting Larisa's phone on the table. "It doesn't look like the spa day is for sure yet? I told them you'd be ready by eleven. Jaden's coming to pick you up."

"How dare you." Larisa lunged for her phone as she tried to remember where it had been, if she'd left it in the bedroom or carried it with her when she'd come out. Ana, as Larisa, had joined the ongoing spa day conversation in the group chat almost ten minutes earlier with an enthusiastic vote for a recover-from-the-holidays spa day. Then she'd told her friends she couldn't drive because she was hung over.

> Rosa: You and Quinn do some private
> celebrating last night?

> Jaden: I can pick you up. NP.

> Kahleah: Since when do you overindulge,
> Risa?

The words swam across Larisa's vision. She'd never had any intention of going to a spa day. The only thing she wanted to do was lie in bed and cry. Now all she wanted to do was scream and cry, and possibly figure out how to murder Ana. Not that the absence of Ana would solve anything. She was just the messenger.

"We don't have a lot of time." Ana pointed to the oven clock.

"Lucas knows I won't kill someone for him."

"He said you'd find it challenging but rewarding."

Challenging but rewarding sounds exactly like Lucas, thought Larisa bitterly. *What the fuck is he thinking?*

This is a game.

A test.

A sick test.

He won't hurt them.

But did she really know that? There were so many ways for a person to be hurt. Neither Hannah nor Quinn were particularly safe in their minds, and Lucas was the king of manipulation.

"Do you mind if I borrow clothes? This is all I have."

Ana was wearing the same skimpy sweater and skirt from the previous day; her only other possession was a chunky purse that didn't appear to have much in it. Despite herself, Larisa felt sorry for the girl. Whatever circumstances had led her to this place, they hadn't been good.

"You've delivered your message, you can leave now. Go back to wherever you came from."

"I can't actually."

With a sigh, Larisa pushed herself up off the floor. "Why not?"

"I'm supposed to stay with you until it's done."

Larisa's stomach churned. The way Ana so casually referenced murder was chilling. It made Larisa think Ana had done this before.

"I don't need a babysitter."

"But you might need help. I'd love to help."

"Just to be clear. You're offering to help me murder Senator John Hagan?"

"Yep, but clothes first?"

"Sure. Maybe I have some old stuff that'll fit you."

They worked their way through a shared morning routine, taking turns in the shower, digging into the back of Larisa's over-stuffed closet. She found Ana a packaged toothbrush from the collection of spare toiletries she used to keep for when dates spent the night.

The activity gave Larisa space to think. There would be no way to get rid of Ana until she thought a murder had been committed. Logic said, Larisa had to at least make it look like the murder had been committed. But the only way she could do that would be to involve the CIA, and she couldn't contact them with Ana shadowing her every step.

"You look great," said Jaden. "I'm always amazed that you seem to gain vitality from the holidays. Unlike the rest of us who just look like strangled cats." She glanced in the rearview mirror of the Land Rover she'd purchased because Krissy had one and made eye contact with Ana.

"Hey."

"I'm Ana."

"Eyes on the road, please," said Larisa as Jaden nearly swerved out of her lane. Of the sisters, Jaden was the worst driver. It was a truth universally acknowledged that the possibility of dying in a car accident rose when one got in the car with her.

"So, fire in Minnesota?"

"It was nothing," said Larisa.

"Quinn impress the family?"

"You know how he is."

Jaden snorted. "Don't be offended, okay? He's not quite the guy you dream of taking home to your parents."

Larisa knew she should defend Quinn's qualities, but she couldn't think of any that wouldn't hit too close to the truth. And if that happened, everything else would unravel, and she'd have some kind of episode right there in Jaden's car. Which was terrible timing because they were almost at the spa and then everyone would see and maybe someone would take a picture, and really the last thing she needed right now was the world talking about how frigid bitch Larisa came back from Christmas heartbroken.

"I liked him," said Ana. "Even though he proved resistant to my invitations."

"So, you two are . . .?"

"Friend of a friend," said Larisa.

"I don't think Krissy knows she's coming. The reservation is for five."

"That's fine."

"So Ana, tell me about yourself."

Larisa clenched her hands together and dug her nails into her skin. On her lap, her phone sat with the saved phone numbers of two CIA agents who might possibly help her out of this mess. But she didn't dare call them. She didn't even think she could text. *Ana put something on my phone. She'll know.*

The other sisters were already at the spa waiting for them on the patio with little cups of fresh-squeezed wheatgrass juice.

"Risa, I love that look," said Krissy, then her gaze shifted to Ana. "Is that your Coachella 2005 outfit?"

"This is Ana," said Jaden like they were old friends. Larisa watched, alarmed as Jaden swung her arm around Ana's boney shoulders and drew her into the group. "She's from Kalinin. That's in Russia."

"Cool," said Krissy.

Kahleah, who'd become a totally different person since her husband decided to run for mayor, cut a suspicious glance toward Larisa. A mysterious, beautiful girl from Russia had certain geopolitical implications. None of which made any sense for Larisa's life from the point of view of her sisters, who had no idea that Lucas, the charming, sophisticated dreamboat who'd dated Larisa in college was an arms dealer.

"Let's all just pause and recognize that the holidays suck," said Rosa. "Especially when you're pregnant and find yourself trapped in a kitchen where the oven has been running for six hours."

"That's nothing," said Krissy, brightening as though nothing had happened. "My new stepmother from hell puts oysters in stuffing. Not even real ones, *canned* oysters."

"You're probably going to die of an uncurable disease," said Jaden.

"I know, right?"

"Next year, we should all just go to Disney World together."

"Are you serious? Do you know how stressful that'd be?"

"And expensive," said Rosa.

Larisa tried to picture Quinn at a theme park with his layers of long sleeves and his revulsion to crowds and chaos. But she would make a bubble for the two of them, a safe space where they existed beyond their environment while also reaching out to join it when they wanted. He'd walk with his head resting on her shoulder. They'd stay until the park closed, then walk the empty streets in the magic light. Without warning, her eyes began to burn.

"Risa, you okay?" asked Rosa.

"She looks like she has a secret," said Krissy. "Did Quinn pop the question?"

In her head, Larisa remembered an al fresco coffee tasting, the last stop in a whirlwind Italian Torrefazione tour. The Tuscan sun shining down around the shelter of the patio umbrella. Lucas, delightfully cheerful with two days of stubble growing on his chin, his eyes dark as he'd said, "What do you think about marriage?" And Larisa hadn't been able to stop smiling.

"We had a fight actually," said Larisa.

"A fight, or a *fight* fight?" asked Jaden. "Because you know there's a big difference."

Larisa looked toward Ana and wondered how much she knew. Probably almost nothing. "I just need a minute." Larisa stood up, thinking she'd call Quinn just to check in. It was evening in Italy. She just needed to hear his voice. Then she'd contact the CIA and solve her little problem with one phone call.

"I'll come with you," said Ana, like an enthusiastic child. She practically skipped beside Larisa as they walked through the spa to the pool deck.

"I want to be alone."

"You can be alone if you give me your phone."

"Absolutely not."

Ana shrugged. "I should probably call Lucas and give him an update then."

"Don't—" Larisa's hand shot out and grabbed at Ana's bag to keep her from her phone.

"I'd really like to have a spa day," said Ana. "You have nice friends."

Larisa sucked in a breath. "Fine. Let's go back."

"No secrets between friends." Ana looped her arm through Larisa's.

The group had moved into the salon. They were lined up in chairs with their hair pinned back getting facials, all questions about Larisa and Quinn apparently forgotten.

"I don't see why you can't just have it at a restaurant," Krissy was saying.

"Security," said Kahleah.

"Your life is weird now," said Rosa.

"Tell me about it."

"What's weird?" asked Larisa. She motioned for Ana to take the chair meant for her. Larisa didn't have the patience for a stranger touching her today. Besides, she thought if she was nice to Ana, pampered her as she was sure no one in her life had ever done, she'd be easier to work with.

"I'm giving a fundraising dinner Friday," said Kahleah. "Some potential big donors for Cade's campaign."

"Donors with *dietary restrictions*," said Jaden like it was a dirty word.

"Is this your first dinner?" asked Larisa, hating how much she sounded like her mother.

"I guess."

Kahleah's marriage, to date, hadn't been a hosting marriage. It'd been an invitee marriage, meaning she and Cade had been at a place in their ecosystem—mainly, Cade's law partners and clients—that they attended rather than hosted events. Now, with Cade's bid for mayor becoming a real thing, their status was shifting upward.

She should just call my mother.

But Suzette was busy with her New Year's gala for Saturday.

"There are companies that come in and do everything for you," she said.

"It's just a small thing," said Kahleah, her exasperation sounding strange as her esthetician massaged moisturizer into her cheeks. "Six couples, three courses, wine instead of cocktails."

Oh dear, thought Larisa.

"Honey," said Rosa, who'd played hostess for a short amount of time before she and Tate started having kids, or perhaps when he'd been fired, or something, Larisa couldn't really remember. "You can't think about this like a regular dinner."

"Who's doing your crystal?" asked Larisa.

Silence. Then a small explosion. "I don't care if we eat on paper plates! He doesn't deserve me, and they can all burn in hell."

"Whoa," said Jaden.

"And I thought pregnancy hormones were bad," said Rosa.

"Well, he deserves worse." Kahleah met Larisa's gaze, another meaningful look that Larisa couldn't interpret. As though the two of them were somehow in a shared place, somehow set apart from the other sisters. On a better day, Larisa would know what the look meant. Today, it barely registered as Larisa's brain searched for a way to get rid of Ana long enough that she could call the CIA. She'd probably need to use someone else's phone just in case Ana was somehow tracking Larisa's phone activity.

"Risa?" Jaden's voice broke through her thoughts, and Larisa realized the silence had been the rest of the sisters waiting for her to say the obvious thing.

"I don't want her help," said Kahleah. "Cade can burn."

"But you don't want to burn with him," said Krissy. "So unless you're getting divorced in the next two days—"

"Let's not escalate," said Rosa. "Cade's just going through a phase."

Kahleah didn't say anything for or against this assumption, so the silence settled again. Larisa considered Ana, whose eyes were closed as the esthetician worked on her face.

"You need to pull off a good time and get him a favorable impression, if not the funds." Larisa paused, her mind slowly chewing through logistics. Then it came out, words she hadn't even been aware she'd organized into a cohesive thought. "You know who's really great at these kinds of things? Senator John Hagan."

Chapter 5

A Nomos Beginning

Quinn knew he was dreaming, but it felt real. Larisa was telling him he was safe, that he didn't have to be afraid. She understood. Then a startling clatter of dishes jolted his system out of its fragile peace, dragging him back to reality. He'd spent the long night so wired he'd only slept a few minutes at a time.

An unfamiliar woman's voice muttered, "Porca puttana."

And Lucas's smooth as butter voice answered, "It's fine, Carla. It's time he was awake."

Dragging his eyes open, Quinn recognized that one of the wait staff from dinner the previous night had set a tray with an elaborate tea service on the small table at the far end of the bedroom. Lucas sat at one of the chairs at the table. He was dressed in a shirt and vest complete with a pocket watch, its chain linked to the vest's middle button. On the table, the gold key Quinn thought he'd used to lock the bedroom door so no one would be able to sneak up on him.

He'd gone to bed unhinged, and now he was waking up unhinged. Every part of his brain was scrabbling to find a way out, pushing back against his purpose, telling him he'd never be able to pull this off.

As Carla left the room she bowed an apology in Quinn's direction, which seemed excessive. The day was full light outside the windows. It felt like morning, but he was sure it was at least past noon.

"Come," said Lucas. "You're done wasting time with sleep."

Quinn untangled himself from the duvet he'd stolen from the bed only to remember that all he was wearing was the nightshirt Lucas had given him. Below its too short hem, his pasty-white legs were almost obscenely exposed as he crossed the room. As he went to sit, he tucked the back end of the nightshirt under his butt. It wasn't long enough. The backs of his thighs touched bare wood, cold and smooth, probably older and worth more than anything he'd ever owned.

"Pay attention. You'll do this tomorrow." Lucas began the service in full British tradition, tea leaves, a strainer over the cups, a kettle of hot water, a standard scene of British movies since the dawn of cinema. Only the egg timer and the absence of cream were different.

"What do you smell?" asked Lucas.

"Tea." Quinn's throat ached with strain even for the single word. His hand went to his throat and the tender flesh he was sure showed a bruise.

"Try again."

Quinn rubbed at his eyes, not quite awake, and wishing he was still asleep. Asleep, he lived in a world without Lucas, a world where Larisa understood why he'd left her.

"I smell trees. Plants? I don't know."

"This is eucalyptus leaf tea. Do you know what that is?"

"The stuff koalas eat."

Lucas turned over the egg timer and began to distribute cucumber sandwiches and open-faced bruschetta onto two plates.

"Isn't it koala food?" Quinn wondered if Lucas was looking at his neck, and if he felt guilty about losing his temper the night before.

"Providing an answer you learned in nursery school isn't cause for praise at this point in your life. Tomorrow you'll choose the tea, you'll present its taxonomy, ecology, and serving chronology."

"Why?"

"Because knowledge gained is never time wasted."

"It's just tea."

A dark look crossed Lucas's face. "Don't ever say that in my presence." He glanced up, caught Quinn's startled look, and softened. "What are we about here? That's what you're wondering." He smiled. "This is the first day of your life as a person of value."

"With tea."

"With nomos."

"The watch company?"

"I'm surprised you know them, but no. Nomos, for our purposes, is a Greek word having to do with custom. It's the art of behaving so you'll be impressive to the people you meet. It's the idea that, in certain settings, how you serve tea will decide what people think of you, and they are right to judge you for it."

"Audience expectations."

"More than that."

The last grains of the egg timer dropped from the top vial to the bottom. Lucas removed the tea leaves from the cups and set them on their own plate. He lifted both his teacup and saucer to drink. Quinn did the same.

"How do you know the saucer should come with the cup?" asked Lucas.

"You're British. I assume you know what you're doing."

"British people are inherently lazy in the knowledge of tradition. Never assume."

"What's the point of knowing something if I'm going to stand out from what everyone else is doing?"

"Because certain people will notice. And these are the kind of people you want to respect you, other respectable people."

"Have you always been like this?"

"No. Once upon a time I was just as dull as you are." Lucas's smile deepened. "But now I live." He inhaled the steam of his tea and took a sip.

Quinn also sipped, then coughed. The tea was stronger than he'd expected. It coated his throat with a thick, smooth residue that felt like cough syrup, though it didn't soothe the ache.

"Why did you cough?"

"It's strong."

"What made it strong? Do you think I steeped it too long? Used too many leaves? Was the water too hot?"

Quinn thought of Larisa setting a timer for the tea she'd once made him in her apartment. *Did she sit where I'm sitting now? Had she wanted to know about tea?*

Larisa.

"Tomorrow you should be able to provide answers to these questions."

Quinn gathered himself, feeling like the conversation was coming to an end and he was about to be abandoned. *Think. How are you going to do this? What will make him trust you?*

Lucas took a bite of bruschetta and chewed. He hadn't shaved that day, but the dark line of stubble didn't disguise the fine mechanisms of his jaw or the line of his chin. A much stronger profile than Quinn's, which he thought looked like he'd been stretched, then squared off with a dull knife. When Larisa had sat here pretending to care about tea, because she would've pretended and done it convincingly, had she admired that jaw? Had they already been lovers?

Yes, he thought. *He wouldn't have brought her here before they were truly together.*

Don't let him leave you, thought Quinn. "I'd rather spend my time with you."

Lucas swallowed his bite. "Why would you want that?"

"You were important to Larisa." Quinn watched Lucas's expression sour at the word *were*, which gave him great satisfaction. *Possessive bastard.*

"A submissive does not negotiate. He trusts that the desires of his master are best for him."

Quinn bowed his head to cede the point even as he thought, *But we don't even remotely trust each other, do we?* When he looked up, Lucas was reading a message on his phone. Quinn forced himself not to look too closely, though he felt the hunger of its offering. A message from a business connection? He wondered if he stole the phone, the CIA could use whatever was on it to put Lucas in jail.

"My decorator has arrived. I must away. Please don't leave this room until you are dressed." Lucas motioned toward the closet. "Return the tray to the kitchen. Please compliment Francie on the bruschetta."

Quinn hadn't eaten any bruschetta.

"You should say something more than, 'It was pleasantly edible.'" Lucas stood. "Tonight, we're having a film viewing. You're welcome to join. My friends are naturally curious about you. But I believe your time would be best spent in the library."

"Because I already know so much about film?"

"You can think that if you like." Lucas stood, pulled down the bottom of his vest and gave Quinn one last measuring look before he walked out, heels clipping against the tile like the ticking of a clock counting down as the sound faded.

Alone, Quinn took another sip of his tea. He ate an entire cucumber sandwich and waited to see if he felt too full. He tried the bruschetta and almost dropped the uneaten remainder in surprise. If he'd been asked moments before, he would've confidently said he'd eaten bruschetta many times. But those experiences were a dull mimicry of the astounding explosion of flavors in his mouth. He could identify each ingredient from the smooth caress of the cheese to the crunch of the bread that had been toasted just enough to keep from becoming soggy. When he went to the kitchen—after he found the kitchen—he told Francie how well she'd balanced the flavors and textures. And then, because it seemed such a waste to hide his enthusiasm, he told her it was the best thing he'd ever eaten. This was certainly not a Lucas-approved compliment, but she seemed pleased.

The kitchen was a marvel in and of itself. It was exactly the kind of magical place that might produce such food as to win Quinn over to the idea that eating could be a delight instead of a chore. There was a stone oven built into the wall and strings of figs and apples, dried chilies, and braids of onions and garlic hanging from the exposed wood beams of the ceiling. In the cold room, a surprisingly large, wine-washed hind leg of a pig. On the window ledge over the sink, a row of herbs overgrowing their pots. He agreed to an espresso with a sugar cube and sat in the breakfast nook filling his lungs with the steamy breath of the room. The lose-limbed activity of Francie and Carla and the heat, that felt like a womb closing him in, soothed his frayed nerves.

He stayed only until he'd sucked down the dregs of his drink, setting its little cup back on its little saucer. Caffeine hummed through his system like an alien entity, a buzz he'd normally have found alarming, but now saw as the necessary push he needed to send himself into the proverbial lion's den. The sooner he found something the CIA could use, the sooner he could leave.

Leaving the kitchen was like stepping from a pleasantly warm summer day into the ice box of artificial climate control. He shivered even though he was wearing two shirts and the sweater Larisa had bought for him to wear in New York. Francie had given him directions to the library, but he took his time getting there, looking more closely at the rooms he'd seen during Lucas's whirlwind tour of the villa. He still couldn't find any cameras or any signs that the house belonged to someone who needed a strong security presence.

The villa's library was on the second floor of the palazzo. Shelves lined the walls of the main square with a balcony railing along their walkway looking down on the fountain and the fruit trees. One room off the square had been set up for reading, with a variety of couches and armchairs and an archway alcove that led to a larger room with more chairs and a piano. Another room off the square was set up as an office with a computer and desk, receiving chairs, a dark wood banquet with a bar, and beside it, a wall-length oil painting depicting the murder of the biblical strong man Samson at the hands of his unfaithful lover Delilah.

Quinn knew nothing about oil paintings, but he thought this one looked strangely elongated, the bodies slightly disfigured, the way a JPEG became distorted if it was stretched to fit a new shape. But what did he know? He moved up to the desk and found a collection of photographs in frames, which seemed to him a surprisingly prosaic thing for Lucas to have in his home. They marked the desk as his personal working space, which was also surprising. The door had stood open for Quinn to enter without feeling like a trespasser. There were files stacked on a corner of the desk. A computer sat before the chair without a lock screen. Before he could stop himself, Quinn was reading an email from someone named Vane Block about a problem importing aging barrels to a winery in Orvieto.

Can it be this easy? Quinn's hand drummed the back of the chair, glancing all around for a covert spy or a hidden lens. The hand almost reached out to click back to the main inbox, but he stopped himself. Anything he did on a computer would leave a record, and what he found might not prove worth the risk.

He shifted his gaze back to the photos, a reasonable activity to be caught doing, while he tried to think. There were some tilted toward the receiving side of the desk, the ones meant to impress visitors—Lucas with various politicians, a pair of Chinese actresses, and Paul McCartney at a charitable event. Then there were two frames on the back side of the desk, beside the computer. They were both of Larisa. In one she wore an evening gown. The camera had caught her in mid-spin, the skirt of her dress flaring out as she bent forward in a burst of laughter. She looked so very young. Quinn had never seen her as deliriously happy as in that frozen moment.

In the other photo, Larisa and Lucas sat together in the booth of a restaurant, a half-eaten, NYC-style pizza on the table. He had his arm around her. She'd tucked her cheek against his neck. Quinn took his phone from his pocket and snapped a picture of the pictures. For a moment, he considered sending it to her with some obnoxious caption like, *Look where I am.* But that wasn't really the way he wanted to say hello for the day. He didn't really know what to say. Everything in his head began with an apology.

But if he was really sorry, wouldn't he already be on his way home? So he wasn't exactly sorry. He just wished he'd come up with a better plan to make her safe.

To make himself feel better about his bad plan, Quinn covertly snapped a photo of the email on the computer screen. It seemed innocuous, but who knew what might be useful? He'd just begun his search. He went back out to the balcony of bookcases and began to half-heartedly look for books that would tell him about tea. It didn't take long to find them. On a table in the corner, next to a lone chair that looked out the windows to the villa's front drive, a stack of books and a glass beside a bottle of chilled, sparkling water awaited him.

How does he know what I like? thought Quinn as he cracked open the water. When he sat down, the chair encompassed him, almost too soft. Did Lucas think this was the best chair for him? Or was this a test like "The Princess and the Pea?" If Quinn was really a man of value, he'd move himself to one of the chairs in the study.

But then he looked out the window and thought it was a nice view. And the clouds looked like they were gathering the energy for rain, which he thought would be a nice thing to watch. It rained so rarely in LA.

So he sat and attempted to read a giant book on the history of cultivation and consumption of tea leaves. But while his eyes followed the words, his mind wandered. Larisa in this house. Larisa being told what to read and where to sit and what to wear. Larisa in love before she'd learned how dangerous love could be.

The rain came, a gray drizzle that was more compelling than diagrams of plants and colonialism, as told by a colonizer, and the vague unease of what Lucas might do to him the next day if Quinn failed to be adequately knowledgeable.

Voices sounded down below in animated, rapid-fire Italian. Quinn pulled himself up from the mold of his chair and edged over to the balcony, just close enough to see down below. A cluster of people orbited around Lucas. They moved along the edge of the palazzo, pointing at fixtures, shaking their heads over the trees, waving arms through the air while others nodded in agreement.

"They're getting ready for the New Year's ball."

Quinn started back to find Hannah had snuck up on him and was standing at the railing a few feet to his right. She wore leggings and a chunky sweater, her hair up in a messy bun on top of her head like she was any other American girl on vacation.

"It's quite a thing apparently. I'm not going. Filipe's taking me to a rave out on gypsy land. Oh sorry, not gypsy, at the *Roma* encampment. What are you staring at?"

"You're not actually dating Lucas."

She laughed, but not loudly enough for the group below to hear. "Absolutely not. I mean he's charming, but I don't do micromanagers."

"You should tell Larisa."

Hannah rolled her eyes. "Larisa never believed we were dating. She just doesn't want me anywhere near him. Whatever. I gave the family the most exciting Christmas we've ever had, and I earned myself an all-expenses paid Italian vacation."

"She's worried."

"She always is with me. I'm sure she's told you I have poor judgement and should be locked in the house like Emily Dickenson until my father finds some quiet milquetoast for me to marry."

"All she told me was you were nicer than you seemed." Quinn let that hang in the air, watching Hannah's bravado falter.

"You should be careful," she said finally. "The eye of Lucas is not kind. And you've certainly caught his eye."

"He's just jealous. It isn't enough."

She frowned, and Quinn realized he'd said too much. Now she was looking at him like she knew why he'd come. Fear plummeted through his gut. Quinn lunged forward but was too late to stop her as she called out, "Lucas!"

Below, the group stilled. Several people looked up in surprise.

Quinn dropped the hand he'd been reaching out to cover Hannah's mouth. He flushed red, heart pounding.

Beside him, Hannah had returned to her air of buoyant triumph. "Lucas!" she called. "You should teach Quinn to dance."

Lucas squinted up at them.

Quinn struggled to breathe, certain the truth was written on his face. *I'm here to find a way to send you to jail.* Somehow, he managed to nod as he said words he'd never expected to utter, "I want to learn to dance."

From the distance of floor to balcony it was impossible to read the nuances of Lucas's expression, to see if there was any suspicion in the moments between Quinn's declaration and Lucas saying, "Brilliant! First thing after breakfast tomorrow."

Lucas and his group moved on to another room. Hannah waited until their voices had faded before she said, "He's not going to let you in if you just do whatever he wants. He doesn't let anyone in. His friends say there hasn't been anyone since Larisa."

"That's not why I'm here."

"Well, it should be." She lowered her voice. "If you expect to beat him, you have to throw him off. You won't do that by playing by his rules."

"You've misunderstood."

"Well then, forgive me for assuming you're better than a guy who abandons the woman he loves just because she kept some secrets to try to make his life easier."

The reminder of the Christmas catastrophe brought a fresh flush of heat to Quinn's face. "I was going to be a father."

Hannah started to walk away. "Not that you want free advice, but you seem like a guy who doesn't have a lot of experience, so I'll tell you something Dr. Larisa once told me. Animals bond through physical touch. It releases some kind of chemical or whatever. So even when we don't want it, or we're trying to resist something, our bodies can betray us."

Chapter 6

Keeping Busy

"You're awake," said Quinn.

"Depends how you define awake." Larisa rolled over to look at her clock and found her eyes too sticky to read it. Somewhere down by her feet, Sabrina hissed an irritated warning. *Since when do you sleep with me?*

"I'm not really alone much. And I don't want him to know."

"Yeah, me too."

A pause as Quinn digested this information. Larisa, slowly becoming more awake, realized how it sounded. If she explained Ana to Quinn, he'd worry. She didn't want him to worry.

"Big holiday recovery day with the girls yesterday," she said. "I think they can tell something's wrong."

"Of course you wouldn't just tell them the truth."

"I told you and look what happened. You left me."

"I don't know what's more disturbing, that you still think lying to me is the better option, or that me leaving is somehow not partially your fault. Parish has nothing to do with Lucas."

"Except you wouldn't know if he hadn't told you."

Silence. Larisa realized she'd just proven Quinn's point. She took a breath. "You're right, I'm a professional liar. I do it without thinking, and I do it anytime I feel like someone I care about is threatened."

"But lying doesn't solve anything. It just postpones the inevitable."

"It's actually served me pretty well until I met you."

Larisa fishtailed in her bedding to try to move to sitting. In the process, she nudged Sabrina who gave her another growl.

"Is that Sabrina?"

"Yes."

"She's sleeping with you?"

"She misses you, and apparently I'm a poor substitute."

"I miss her back."

Larisa glared at her cat. "He misses you too."

"Sid can come watch her if you're super busy."

"I'm more than capable of taking care of the cat."

A judging silence filled the line.

"So, how are things with Lucas?"

"He's teaching me about tea."

A bittersweet warmth spread through Larisa's chest. "Eucalyptus and lavender."

"Yep. And I guess I'm going to learn to dance so I'm not embarrassing on New Year's."

"You're staying through the week?"

"Is there something for me to come back for?"

"So what's your plan? You're going to stay until I manage to trust people? Promise never to keep things from you again?"

"That'd be a start."

"Then you're going to be there a fucking long time. You know he does historical dancing for New Year's? You'll have to wear heeled shoes and let people touch you."

"I'll figure it out."

"And you're going to dance with him?"

"Probably."

Larisa felt the now familiar upswelling that came with oncoming tears. It came so quickly that it took a moment to be able to speak. "You have no idea what you're dealing with."

"Then why don't you tell me."

From the outside of Larisa's bedroom door there came a scratching sound, then Ana cooing softly, "Larisa, are you sneaking around?"

She lowered her voice. "I can do better. I promise. If you come back, we can figure this out together."

"We're past that," said Quinn just as softly. "I'll talk to you later."

As she listened to the line disconnect, tears rolled silently down her cheeks. She sat still, pulling Quinn's voice through her mind over and over, trying to hear the things he hadn't said. How was he feeling? What had Lucas said to him? Did Quinn really feel safe, or was he just saying things because he was angry?

The doorknob jiggled in its cradle. "Larisa," called Ana.

She wiped at her eyes, went to the bathroom to splash water on her face so it would be less obvious she'd been crying, then she unlocked the door.

"Who were you talking to?" asked Ana.

"My mother. She thinks I'm bad at relationships."

"All mothers think that." Ana used her new manicure to scratch her arm. The skin was already red from previous scratching. A particularly bad bug bite or the first sign of withdrawal. "What are we doing today?"

"Getting ready for Kahleah's party."

"Where we're going to kill the guy?"

"No, we're not going to do that to her. The killing will take place on New Year's."

"Hmm, good idea. Lots of accidents."

"You've killed other people?" Larisa carefully moved past Ana toward the kitchen to feed Sabrina.

"A girl doesn't tell." Ana giggled. "But I can say you're the best I've worked with." She gave Larisa a crooked smile and a thumbs up.

There wasn't any food left in the apartment, so Larisa took Ana to the diner down the street for breakfast. They sat in the corner booth and Larisa watched Ana pack away a stack of pancakes, eggs, and bacon.

"How long have you been in LA?"

"Five years or so."

"So you came here when you were sixteen?"

"Something like that."

"With your parents?"

"Why so many questions this morning? You're not mad at me?"

"Why would I be mad at you?"

"Reasons."

"You know, I used to help girls like you. One of them died."

For a moment, Ana's expression darkened, and Larisa thought perhaps she'd gotten through. Now they might have a real conversation. But then Ana giggled.

"Girls like me? There are no girls like me. I'm one genuine article!"

"Did Lucas say that?"

Ana stuffed her last bite of pancake in her mouth. "Where do we go next?"

Larisa hated taking Ana to her parents' house, but her most important task of the day was to pick up the crystal set and take it to Kahleah's house. She was also going to browse through her mother's collection of formal centerpieces to see if anything would work for Kahleah's table.

As they drove, Ana sat turned sideways, her face pressed to the window.

"You don't get around much?" asked Larisa.

"Sure I do. Always. It's beautiful."

Larisa didn't find anything particularly impressive about the transition between Santa Monica and WeHo, but she'd lived in the city her entire life. Not once had she stopped to think how it might impress someone coming from somewhere else.

"If you like this, wait 'till you see my parents' house."

If there was a way for Ana to redeem herself of her evil purpose, it might have been her enthusiasm for everything she saw as soon as they pulled up the circular drive. She exclaimed over the landscaping, the pressed seashell shapes in the cement, the mural of the cosmos that decorated the floor of the atrium. On and on, details so familiar to Larisa she never saw them now were drawn out and appreciated so loudly that Sarah came out to meet them and check on the noise.

"We're just picking up the back up crystal," said Larisa as she held herself back from, *Don't tell Mom.* An unnecessary instruction since her parents would meet Ana at the gala. Larisa had no hope of coming without her.

The Kahn basement was like a well ordered pawn shop, with decorations for every conceivable occasion, gifts unwanted that could not be given away, collections of art that no longer fit with the house aesthetics. While Larisa looked for the crystal, Ana babbled to herself about how fancy everything was. Her fingers moved restlessly through boxes, stroked the heads of statues. Then Larisa heard her say that Lucas would it.

"Lucas likes to collect things like this," said Larisa. She remembered that the figurine Ana was holding had been purchased on a trip with Lucas and later gifted to Larisa's parents. She'd seen the figurine hundreds of times at Suzette's events and never once thought of Lucas.

I did so well blocking him out of my life, she thought. But now that the memory had come, it dragged others up with it. After she found what she needed for Kahleah's party, Larisa took Ana up to her childhood bedroom. While Ana explored, Larisa dug through her desk, then her closet, then the storage containers under the bed until she found her college photo albums. One album was entirely dedicated to pictures with Lucas.

Here they were hiking in South America. Here they were dancing in Austria on a New Year's Eve that felt lifetimes removed from the one she was facing the next night. Every picture was a memory marker that pulled her mind back to scents, tastes, and heat. Lucas always watching her, seeing her so well. And she'd been stunned by it. All her life she'd felt watched, but she had never felt truly seen until Lucas.

Quinn suffered from a similar malady of recognition. He desperately wanted to be recognized for his professional skills.

And he wanted to be recognized personally, the way actors crave the star power that comes with recognition, the way it gives them meaning. So Larisa knew at least part of Lucas's strategy would be to charm Quinn, maybe drive him away from Larisa by being someone with the power of sight, to reveal things about Quinn that no one else saw, and, at the same time, point out how Larisa would never match up. She ran her fingers along the plastic shield of the album pages, feeling the lump of the thing she'd hidden behind her images from the Orvieto winery owned by Lucas's friend Winter Duryea.

I'm not there yet, she thought as she snapped the album closed. Still, she put the album and its hidden secrets in her purse and took it with her when she left the house.

"What's that?" asked Ana.

"Old photos." Larisa passed her the album. "Buckle up."

Ana ignored her. "Oh, he's so young."

"Buckle up, or we're not leaving."

"That's fine. I can't go to your friend's house anyway."

Larisa kept her face carefully neutral. "Why not?"

"Can't be seen in association." Ana turned a page. "He's amazing, isn't he?"

Something twisted in Larisa's gut. "He's not. He just pretends to be, so it's harder for you to get away from him when he betrays you."

"If he betrayed you, you deserved it. Or maybe he just got tired of you." Ana jabbed a finger at a picture of Larisa's younger self on the patio at Umbras. "You look so tense. I bet you don't know how to be happy."

"So I'm taking you back to the apartment?"

"Just drop me off on Sunset." Ana put on her seatbelt like it was a chore. "I have stuff to do."

Larisa should've been rejoicing. She was finally going to be alone. She could call the CIA, set everything up, maybe even get Hagan killed, all without having to worry about Ana spying.

Instead, she felt a niggling little panic worming around in the back of her brain.

"I don't like the idea of just dropping you off on the street."

"I'll be fine."

"You're looking to score?"

"What if I am? You going to try and talk me out of it?"

"I'd say we should call Sid and see if he'll change his mind about showing you around."

"He said he doesn't do that shit anymore."

Larisa had almost reached the bottom of the canyon drive. Just one more turn and she'd be at Sunset. "I bet Kahleah's fine with you coming tonight. We can dress you up so you're not noticeable."

The car in front of them braked causing Larisa to also brake. Ana punched the button on her belt and yanked open the door. "Be good tonight so I don't have to call Lucas, okay? You're doing a great job."

Then Larisa was watching Ana's jutting shoulders sway through the exaggerated movement of her hips as she strode down the sidewalk and around the corner.

"So you're bringing this girl to your mom's gala?" asked Kahleah.

"I know it's a terrible idea."

"Actually, I think it's great. But it doesn't seem like you."

"Because people will talk?"

"Because you're not known for your soft heart."

Larisa made a face. Before she could answer, Cade, Kahleah's cheating husband, breezed in. "Hey, babe. Hey, Risa." He kissed Kahleah without making eye contact. "Everything set?"

"I'm set if you are," said Kahleah.

"Ready, ready already."

They stood in silence as Cade jogged up the stairs to get

dressed. "My newfound soft heart would like to murder him," muttered Larisa.

"You shouldn't say that," said Kahleah.

"He deserves it."

"We just got new security installed. The whole house is wired. You don't want that on the record in case, you know . . ."

Larisa laughed despite herself, then realized this created a problem for her evening plans. "Where can I talk where nothing will see or hear me?"

They walked out to the backyard. Kahleah counted steps from the front door out to the lawn. "Here," she said. "This is where I take my calls when I'm home."

"Who's listening otherwise?"

"Cade's security company."

"Creepy." Larisa couldn't help but glance at her friend and remember the old days. Kahleah with her flashy nails and big, natural hair when it wasn't in braids of some bright color. Somewhere down the line the girl who'd taken pride in being called the Black Malibu Barbie had purchased her first set of pearl earrings and cardigan sweater set and become someone else.

"What are you wanting to hide?" asked Kahleah.

"Nothing particular."

"I thought softhearted Larisa told her friends things."

"If I told you, it would make you nervous."

"Just saying that makes me nervous."

"I just want to try something."

"Is Quinn coming?"

"Why would you think that?"

"Because you've been joined at the hip since October?" Kahleah laughed. "What's with you? Was the fight really that bad?"

"I'm just tired," said Larisa, which was true. In these vacant moments when time refused to pass and the next task was too far away, she felt herself drifting into a languor, as though the stillness also stilled her mind. It was becoming difficult to think if she wasn't thinking about things that needed to be done. Now her work for the dinner party was complete and there was nothing to do for New Year's until the next day. Larisa felt herself sinking.

"I miss your boots," she said.

"What?"

"Those platform boots you loved in college, the pink, transparent plastic."

"Oh, those. They're in my closet still. I put up this curtain thing, so Cade doesn't have to see some of my old stuff."

"Should I tell him that even Michelle Obama sometimes wears tall boots?"

Kahleah clutched at her arm. "Don't you dare give him any ideas about DC."

"Would he really?"

"I think he would."

"Well then, you'd have to divorce him."

Larisa hooked her arm through Kahleah's, and they walked back up to the house.

The modest dining room had been transformed into something elegant and understated. Larisa thought it was a little boring, but she also knew it was exactly what the night needed. Collections of tealight candles were clustered at stations down the center of the table. And on her instructions, the regular bulbs in the chandelier had been switched out for soft light bulbs. The catering staff was setting the table. Larisa had given them their instructions, but she let Kahleah answer their questions and supervise.

An hour later, everything was ready. The silver was spotless. The place settings perfectly spaced, the smell of rich food drifting in from the kitchen. Larisa drummed her nails on the table. Waiting, waiting, waiting. The lethargy had grown from a feeling to a real force of nature. She kept glancing into the living room thinking she might lay down on the couch for a nap. But there wasn't enough time. She was beginning to worry about why she was so tired, if it was a sign of something else. And if she napped, she might not wake up as her best self. Tonight, she needed to be her best self.

"Why did you have me invite Senator Hagan?" asked Kahleah.

"He's gotten himself in trouble." *Too much honesty,* thought Larisa. Quinn really had no idea what her life was like. If he really thought honesty was the thing that would mend their relationship, he was wrong. Nothing good ever came from complete honesty. She'd just overstepped a line, and now she was all tensed up waiting for the obvious questions: *How do you know?* and *Why are you involved?*

Instead, Kahleah said, "Anything I can use?"

"Depends how smart he is."

"Don't let Cade catch you when you go outside. If he finds out I knew you were going to stage an ambush—"

"Worst case, he ends up dead by midnight, and Cade's supporters can decide who might fill his seat."

"Larisa!"

"Right, no murder talk."

Fuck, I'm turning into Ana.

When the guests began to arrive, Larisa hung back in the dining room so Kahleah and Cade could stand alone in the atrium greeting their guests. She checked her phone and found Quinn had sent her a picture, the view out of the library windows looking down on the Umbras garden. She smiled to herself as memories washed over her. Scenes she hadn't thought of in years unearthed and breathed to life. Lucas chasing her through the labyrinth. A picnic on the lawn, eating a stinky cheese that attracted all the garden cats. Ana was wrong, Larisa had been happy, if only for a little while.

She texted a response, then glanced up and saw John Hagan standing at the opposite end of the table, staring at her. He was one of those men who had perfected the tan-curated, LA look. His face was a little tightly stretched but still glowed with a skin care regime that probably rivaled Larisa's mother. He was a man who lived well.

"You," he said.

"Me." She flashed him her Valley Girl smile and waved her fingers at him. "Most people who look at me like that are men who got in trouble with my father. But somehow, I'm thinking this is different. Why is that?"

"He sent you." Spasms of microemotions flicked across Hagan's face. "Here? You're here?" He started to back out of the room. This wasn't what Larisa had expected. They knew each other after all, the way LA people knew each other. There wasn't any need for panic. But now she'd have to take action, or she'd lose him.

Larisa lurched around the table and grabbed his arm. She jabbed the pointer finger of her free hand into the spare tire above his hip like it was a gun. She did it as part of her flirtation, but he flinched like he believed she really had a gun. Part of feeling like she wanted to be asleep, was the strange feeling of reality not quite being real. When some action broke free from the brain fog, it apparently did not go through the usual checks and balances of *Is this a good thing to do?* Not once in her entire life had Larisa considered pretending to pull a gun on someone, not even as a joke, and yet here she was doing it as though it was second nature. She even lowered her voice to a mobster's gravitas as she said, "Let's go for a walk."

Maybe she could do this because nothing felt real. It was all just a game. Some kind of mirror of regular life colored in a washed-out sepia glow of suspended reality. Some far corner of her mind knew this was how she was processing the shitshow her life had become—how else did one cope with an ultimatum to kill a politician or else? The "or else" had been left hanging undecided in that swamp of her mind, festering and replicating through every minute of Ana's overly cheerful company until it colonized every part of her with its threat.

So it felt reasonable to scare this man by jabbing her finger into his side. She walked him out of the dining room, through the den, and out the patio doors. She didn't stop until they were at the edge of the lawn by the fake hedge that hid the electric fence.

"Alright. Let's make this fast and clean, shall we?"

Hagan shuddered.

"Relax, I'm not going to murder you at my friend's house."

Hagan did not relax.

"Why does he want you dead?"

"What?"

"Answer me." She jabbed him again, then stepped around so she could watch his face.

Hagan stared at her like her question was insensible, or he'd become insensible to sense. Then he blinked and seemed to come back to himself. "I backed Agent Smith."

"Explain more, please."

"She set up an operation here five, six years ago. Began siphoning off his North American business."

"Why now?"

"She took a big account. He called a quorum to have her put down. There was pushback."

"You pushed back? Who else?"

"I don't know. Other North American interests. She's faster, cheaper, more attentive. We didn't think he'd care so much. He's running three proxy wars in Africa and a genocide in Asia." Hagan swabbed his forehead with the back of his hand. "The CIA agent who made the deal is already dead. I think his boss is too."

"Which agent?" asked Larisa, feeling she probably knew the answer, if only because in her life, the universe was too small.

"Klune."

Well shit, thought Larisa. *There's no way Osna will want to talk if his partner's dead.*

She tried to think, told herself to feel later. "Why was the CIA involved?"

He gave her a look. "They were the big account Smith stole."

Fuck. Larisa tilted her head up and stared at the sky. What had Osna and Klune said in November about Lucas coming to LA for a possible assassination? She'd dismissed it as manipulation at the time. Now it looked so very different. They knew he'd be coming to LA because they'd done something to piss him off. Or at least one of them had.

"You ever get that feeling like your life's conspiring behind your back, John?"

"Doesn't everyone?"

"Not like this."

Fuck. Fuck. Fuck.

"I can protect you," said Hagan. "Whatever he offered you, my people will cover. You don't have to do what he says."

"You're not very smart, are you? If I don't kill you, he'll send someone else. Your only play here is for Lucas to think you're dead."

Hope kindled in Hagan's eyes. "You have a plan?"

"I had a kind-of plan that might not work if Klune's out of the picture. Do you have experience in faking murders?"

"No."

"So then . . ."

"Do you have a CIA person you talk to about this?"

"I just told you, they're dead."

"Right." She pulled out her phone and dialed AWAG. (Asshole With a Gun, otherwise known as Agent Osna, her archnemesis.)

He answered on the first ring. "I'm on vacation, so if—"

"I need you to murder someone."

"If this is a prank—"

"I've had contact with Lucas. He wants me to kill Senator John Hagan, or he'll kill some people I care about." The words vibrated through her ears like an overloud phone alarm, but tinny, as though sounding from far away.

"Where are you?" asked Osna.

"Doesn't matter. Set it up for tomorrow. It'll happen when he leaves my mother's gala."

"When did Lucas make contact? I don't have a record—"

"Delete all the recordings of this call. Don't bother me with your incompetence." Larisa hung up, forced a grin on to her face as she faced Hagan. "One fake-murder, coming up. But you have to make it look good. Tonight, drink excessively. Say very inappropriate things. Mention that you're fighting with your wife."

"How did you know we're—"

"You came alone. You're not wearing your ring. Or did Cade promise you sex workers for dessert? Oh, by the way, since I'm doing this for you, you should support his campaign."

"He's running on a clean energy ticket."

"That's great. You're for clean energy now too. Any questions?"

Hagan shook his head.

"I'll add you to the guest list for tomorrow. Until then, make sure people notice how much you hate your life." She motioned for them to start walking back up the lawn to the patio.

"Do you think I'll have to stay dead long?"

"Probably forever. It's unlikely Lucas is going to jail anytime soon." This was her on-the-record position, but in her head, she thought it might all be over in a week, maybe less. Osna would be impressed with her information. He'd know how to use it.

He lost his partner. He'll be even more of an asshole than usual.

"I think they'll just take him out," said Hagan.

"Take him out," repeated Larisa. She'd heard the phrase plenty of times in movies, but never in reference to a living person, a man she'd slept with, a man she'd—

"They have a source with him, who's trying to locate this cache of nerve gas they think is going to Syria. I think she's also trying to identify his account numbers or the accountant. But after that, it should be over fast. I bet a couple months. Long enough for my wife to forgive me."

"For funding terrorism?"

"For a weekend in Vegas."

They'd reached the house and were back in view of Kahleah's

new surveillance system. She lowered her voice. "I want to meet Agent Smith."

"Why?"

"I have information that would interest her."

"Why would you help us?"

Larisa looked at him with the full glare of her disdain. "I'm not helping *us*. I'm helping me."

"I knew you were on the right side. After I saw you on the island, I wasn't sure. But then you never told him I was up there snooping, so . . ."

"What are you talking about?"

"The island? Way back when. Lucas invited us to look at his inventory, and I snuck around trying to find the stuff he wasn't telling us about. I found you up in the roof pool."

Larisa squinted. Now that he described it, she did have a vague memory of that. It seemed absurd to think he'd assumed she might tattle on him to Lucas. But then, back in the day, she might have. She hadn't known enough to see it as significant.

"You know a lot of people would love to know where that island is," said Hagan.

Chapter 7

Quinn's New Year's

reakfast was served every morning at nine o'clock in the music room. Before that, no one in the house was allowed to speak. Whenever Lucas woke up, whether that was five o'clock or eight thirty, he went to the music room and selected a piece to play over the villa's sound system. There were speakers in every room of the house. On his second morning in Italy, Quinn was drawn from sleep by the heralding trumpet of Mahler's Fifth Symphony, then shaken to full wakefulness a moment later when the full orchestra burst through his room. His new friend, Chef Francie, chided him when he attempted to tell her good morning and explained the rules of music and silence, then breakfast, which was also conducted without speech.

The music room was smaller than the study where Quinn had spent the previous afternoon. The room contained three stereo systems, a table and chairs, and nothing else. The walls had been sculpted and textured for acoustics. There were no windows, and every door became part of the wall when closed. Even if Quinn had wanted to have a conversation over breakfast, sitting in the middle of that room was like being in a cave of sound. He couldn't have made himself heard over Mahler.

So they sat opposite each other. Lucas ate a full breakfast of eggs, sausage, and beans, and Quinn drank his little espresso with a square white island of sugar in the middle. Just like the bruschetta the previous day, the coffee was a marvel of flavor that awakened his mouth before the caffeine had a chance to reach his brain. He tasted it black, then added the sugar. A quick glance across the table found Lucas watching Quinn's face as he sipped. If there was a message to be read in that inscrutable expression of judgement it was that only children and Luddites ruined their espresso with sugar.

But then Lucas closed his eyes and drifted into the music. It was Quinn's first opportunity to look at him directly without being observed doing it. Not that he was delusional enough to think Lucas didn't know he was looking, but it felt safer than looking at him when his eyes were open. Those eyes, which governed that questing expression, the scientific gaze centered on test-subject Quinn, were the darkest blue and never kind.

With his eyes closed, swaying slightly in his seat, Lucas gave the impression of a normal person. The growth on his face had thickened into a black shade along his jaw, which contrasted nicely with his skin. Somewhere in his DNA lineage there were people from the Mediterranean, or maybe even Italians, though Quinn would have been embarrassed to be caught making a guess at racial heritage when what he could have been seeing was an expert tan.

The beard growth under Lucas's chin and at his neck was flecked with gray more thickly than his hair, where it looked almost painted in at his temples. There was a small round scar on the right side of his forehead and the slits of earring punctures in both earlobes.

That morning, Lucas was channeling a beatnik, 1960's look with a black turtleneck and a brown sweater. He'd even finished the look with cat-eye glasses and black wings of eyeliner, a pastiche of historic gender performance. And, for whatever reason, Quinn couldn't stop staring. Lucas looked so soft, so approachable. So lovely in the morning compared to the villain who'd clenched his hands around Quinn's throat in the night.

He didn't really hurt me, thought Quinn. *He was making a point. We both knew he wouldn't go too far.* And now that some time had passed, Quinn found himself thinking back to the event and feeling differently than when it'd happened. Not that he would admit it, but part of him had enjoyed it. Or, perhaps not enjoyed, but felt a certain kind of rush realizing Lucas could have really hurt him and Quinn wouldn't have been able to stop him.

Quinn thought that Hannah had been wrong in her advice the day before. This wasn't a man who needed to be defied. This was a man who needed to be loved just like anyone else. He just wanted an exceptional love.

I'm not even good at faking regular love, thought Quinn.

The Fifth Symphony faded through its last bars. Lucas opened his eyes and caught Quinn looking. For a moment, they studied each other, and it felt like something shared instead of something Quinn was subjected to.

The moment passed. Lucas drew up his eyebrows like an expectant teacher. "Nomos," he said.

"Situation expectations for appropriate behavior," answered Quinn.

"And if a man excels in the eyes of his peers that excellence is called what?"

"Did we talk about that yesterday?"

"You didn't read anything about Greek classical tradition while I left you to your own devices?"

"I read about tea." Quinn pushed down frustration.

"Excellence in ancient Greece was defined by the ability to kill people, feats of physical strength. Thus, the Greek word for excellence is *arete*, originating from the god of war, Ares."

"I don't kill things."

"Obviously we've moved on from that. In the classical era, *arete* evolved to mean 'man of the world.' You have excellence when you're good at what you do. And that brings you honor. This is the difference between the *Iliad* and the *Odyssey*. I assume you know the basics of those stories?"

"One involves Brad Pitt."

"Are you trying to be irritating?"

"It depends on whether or not it's working."

Lucas sighed. "Which version of *arete* is Brad Pitt?"

"The first one, with the god of war."

"Correct. Which makes Odysseus the new man. He solves problems with his head. He's cunning. He lies."

"I feel like we've moved on from seeing that as a kind of excellence."

"Exactly. That brings us to the Romans. They thought both of these forms of *arete* were selfish and dishonorable, and that's why the Greek civilization failed. Everyone was in it for their own glory. But Rome was a collective. They brought law and order out of Greek individualized chaos."

"Is there going to be a test?"

"I'm gifting you this knowledge so you can be a better person."

"You think I'm a bad person?" Quinn peered out at Lucas from beneath his eyelashes. It was an obvious move, but the caffeine was kicking in and the long silence of breakfast had made him feel he needed to make up for lost time. He wanted to get Lucas talking, but not about historical philosophy, or whatever this was.

"I liked Pitt in that movie," said Quinn. "Men don't get to show off their legs that often. But that movie, everyone was half naked, and tan, and sweaty." Chef's kiss.

Across the table Lucas appeared unmoved.

"Didn't you think the lighting was well done?" In using this line, Quinn was not quite mocking a line one of Lucas's friends had used the night before after their film society screening of some ridiculously boring black-and-white film from the forties.

If Lucas caught the reference, he didn't show it.

"We're late for your dancing lesson."

End of conversation.

Quinn had no choice but to stand and follow Lucas out of the room. Dancing, he thought with dread, was a test he was sure to fail.

The villa had its own ballroom, a replica of a famous Renaissance-era ballroom in a Medici palace. It was a long room with mirrors on one side and a stage on one end for musicians. There would be live musicians playing the music for Lucas's New Year's ball. And yes, it was a Renaissance ball, which meant that the dancing Quinn had unwittingly signed up to learn wasn't something useful like how to twerk without looking like an idiot, or even waltzing, which might have been useful for the events Larisa's mother threw.

"Since we've just eaten," said Lucas, "Or rather I've just eaten, we'll begin with the pavane, then move on to the more energetic galliard."

"The what now?" Quinn choked.

"You cannot become a good dancer in two days. But if you try hard enough, you might fool some people into not noticing." Lucas took off his sweater and draped it over the back of a chair set up against the wall. Without it, Lucas was a long column of black, proportionately muscled in a way that seemed to enhance his elegance rather than distract from it. He held his hand out into a space where Quinn supposed his partner was supposed to go, then, as Quinn's mouth fell slightly ajar, Lucas glided down the length of the room. One step, pause, a second step, pause, three steps in succession, repeat. Then he did the same pattern walking backward, paused, turned to his left so he was facing the mirrors instead of the long end of the room, and knelt as his arm circled him, guiding an invisible partner around his head.

He stood. "Do you have it?"

"I think so?"

I'm so fucked.

Lucas pulled out his phone, tapped twice, then swiped. One of the slowest, most depressing, oldest-sounding pieces of music Quinn had ever heard filled the room. "Let's see it," said Lucas.

Quinn held out his arm, trying to arrange his fingers like they knew something about ballet. *When was ballet invented?* he wondered. Perhaps it wasn't Renaissance style to have ballet hands. *Fuck*. He'd already messed up the steps.

"Alright. Let's just think about this," said Lucas. "You have a body."

"I'm aware."

"Are you though?" Lucas came up and tapped his knuckle against the top of Quinn's spine. "Stand up straight."

"I am straight."

"Straighter. There. Now try again."

Straighter was much harder. Quinn felt he couldn't see his feet, and it suddenly seemed very important to be able to see his feet and the completely smooth, obstacle-free floor so he wouldn't trip. Also, standing so straight made it harder to hold up his arm. It began shaking. But he made it to the backward steps with enough awareness to think that Lucas was probably checking out his ass in the very tight skinny pants Larisa had bought for him.

Does he want me like that? wondered Quinn. And then, in whatever obscure connection his brain had made without conscious thought, he remembered being on the set of *The Key* and telling Dansby that it didn't matter what the Russian general wanted on his own. Dansby's job was to make him want only Dansby, even if he'd never wanted anything like him before.

But Dansby was a walking, talking, sometimes thinking, seduction machine. He exuded the aura of being up for anything with anyone, and that had translated on to the screen. If Dansby's polar opposite existed, it was Quinn.

"Turn out your feet," said Lucas. "You're graceful. You're a bird."

"It would be easier with a partner," hinted Quinn.

"It's not supposed to be easy," said Lucas. But after a moment, he came up alongside Quinn and walked through the steps beside him. Quinn began to drift toward Lucas, passing it off as unbalance. Their fingertips brushed.

"Is there a handhold or something?" Quinn glanced at Lucas, certain that his machinations were obvious, but Lucas was looking down at his hand where Quinn's fingertips had found his.

After a pause, he said, "You hold your hand out. The woman,

or whoever's doing the woman's side, comes in on top. Sometimes they rest, sometimes they interlock, like so."

Lucas's hand was cold, but it still sent a spark of energy humming down Quinn's much too straight spine.

"Easy enough," said Quinn. Then, just to see what would happen, he added, "You have really soft hands."

"A better compliment would be, 'I should take better care of my hands. What's your secret?'"

Quinn deflated. So much for seduction.

They covered the length of the ballroom forward, then backward. Then they turned a quarter of a circle, then another until they faced the mirrors. Quinn knelt and held his hand up to guide Lucas around him. Lucas seemed to be avoiding eye contact. More likely he was just keeping his posture.

"And now you stand, and we separate. I go to this edge, you to that one. The pattern repeats until we come around and rejoin."

"Cool," said Quinn. "I like it. What's next?"

Lucas gave him a long look, as though telling him that this success meant nothing, that Quinn had proven nothing. Then, with a deft swipe across the screen of his phone, the music changed to something much livelier. Lucas began to hop and leap on the balls of his feet.

No smile, not a hint of joy, but all the movement of it, as though Lucas had turned the gestures of celebration into a mathematical equation.

"Can we break that into segments?" asked Quinn. "One frame at a time maybe?"

As Lucas pogoed back to him, a triumphant grin broke across his face. "It doesn't slow down." He continued to move, bouncing up and down, to the side, then back, not even winded.

It's slower than Riverdance, thought Quinn, who'd never once been tempted to stand up and move his body like those people. He flexed and pointed his foot as he watched Lucas repeat the same series of steps. *Do it and he'll be impressed.*

Three hours later, everything below Quinn's knees hurt so

much he wanted to saw them off, but he'd finally been able to keep pace with Lucas around the ballroom. His posture was terrible, his form dubious, but he could do the steps.

That night, just after he'd locked the door to his bedroom, Lucas came in. The only warning Quinn had of the intrusion was the sound of the lock turning from the hallway.

"Why don't you knock?" asked Quinn, flustered.

"This is my home." Lucas glided into the room, looking around as though he'd half-expected Quinn to be hiding something. Quinn was technically hiding something—himself. He wanted to be alone, to not feel like he was being watched, every tick of his face analyzed for hidden meaning.

"I've come to measure you."

Quinn opened his mouth, but no words came out. He was still dressed, had planned to spend the night dressed, instead of wearing the billowy nightshirt Lucas had given him.

"Your costume for the ball." Lucas pulled a rolled-up tape measure from his pocket.

"Can't it wait until tomorrow?"

"No."

I don't want you to touch me, thought Quinn. But it didn't appear Lucas would back down, so he pulled off his sweater and came forward two steps, making Lucas come forward two more to close the distance between them.

As Lucas circled him, Quinn tried to stand taller. Every hour since he'd arrived, Lucas had been finding faults with his body, and this was the worst of it. Now he was expected to allow Lucas to dress him, which was Larisa's job. She loved his body. *When I go home, and she does my wardrobe, will I think of him?*

The answer was undoubtedly yes. The soft pressure of Lucas's fingers as he held the tape in place across Quinn's shoulders, then down the length of his torso, felt like pinpricks of fire leftover from that afternoon being driven into him.

You should use this, he thought. But he couldn't see how, not with any subtly. And doing something obvious, like turning suddenly and planting a kiss on Lucas's cold judging lips, was just not something Quinn was prepared to do until he knew it would pay off.

"What do you feel?" asked Lucas.

"Don't you have to keep track of the numbers?"

"I'll remember."

The words hung in the air, surprisingly sensual, overwrought with inuendo that Quinn couldn't parse.

"What do you feel?" he asked again.

"I'm tired, and I want to be alone."

"Why?"

"I just am."

"Why?" Lucas circled around to Quinn's front, looped the tape around his hips, and held it there like he thought Quinn would run away.

Such blue, blue eyes, thought Quinn.

"I find you exhausting."

For a moment, Lucas's eyes narrowed, then light broke across his face as he laughed. Other people might have apologized or offered to give Quinn space. Lucas said, "You'll grow accustomed to it."

On New Year's Eve, Quinn made his entrance to the ballroom at Lucas's side wearing a gold and white doublet with a matching one-shoulder cape that was fancier than Colin Firth's costume in *Shakespeare in Love.* He entered on Lucas's arm as his guest of honor, or a lover. Quinn was too nervous trying to stand up straight to wonder what people thought he was doing at Lucas's side. Every step felt like a test, every person who came up to greet them, an opportunity to fall short of Lucas's expectations.

But then Quinn realized that Lucas wasn't introducing him. He was just a halfway invisible appendage attached to Lucas's arm. People glanced at him with passing interest, then focused on Lucas, some of them fawning over him in their praise. When Lucas seated himself on a gilded chair set on a dais in a corner of the room to preside over the ball, there was no corresponding seat for Quinn. He was left standing alone and uncertain at the edge of the room, suddenly cold without the warmth of a shared spotlight.

Don't be so pathetic, he told himself as he looked around. Here and there, he recognized some of the Florentine Film Society members he'd met earlier in the week. And then, floating through the crowd to save him, was Red Dress from his first night in Italy, whose real name was Winter Duryea. She invited him to dance. And held his hand like she knew what he was feeling and that it was going to be okay.

But out on the dance floor, Quinn withered under the knowledge that Lucas was certainly watching him, critiquing his performance. Lucas wore his signature crimson velvet with stark black trim, which stood out from the crowd and caught Quinn's peripheral vision so that with every flash of stark color he found himself losing track of his footing. *Is this how my actors feel?* wondered Quinn.

Hours passed before Lucas came out onto the dance floor. They passed each other as they moved through the formations. At every opportunity, Quinn made eye contact. He didn't know how to fake adoration, but he could imitate desire, and if he was going to suffer through a Renaissance ball, he was going to make it count.

When Lucas stopped dancing, Quinn stopped also, but he stayed with Winter, allowing her to introduce him to her friends, a group of people apparently all in the wine business; she owned a vineyard in Orvieto. By then, most of the guests were several drinks toward intoxication, and it was easy for Quinn to track Lucas around the room, noticing who approached him and who he approached.

It was hard to imagine there were terrorist masterminds or

drug lords or commandants looking to stage a coup in their native countries among the guests, but Quinn told himself that this was an amateur assumption. Modern criminals didn't wear their terrible deeds on their faces; Lucas was an obvious example. He laughed often, sometimes so loudly it carried across the ballroom. None of his guests complained about dressing up in period costumes to celebrate New Year's. They all appeared to love him. The food was small and perfect. The lighting just bright enough that everyone looked their best. It was the most enchanting, most perfectly orchestrated scene Quinn had ever seen in real life.

So it happened that Quinn began to enjoy himself. And he began to imagine taking initiative. Perhaps this was why, when Lucas made eye contact with him during the last pavane of the year, Quinn cut in on Lucas's partner. His feet hurt, but he drew himself up to his straightest of straight posture, turned out his toes in his cramped buckled shoes, and took Lucas's hand as they made their way down the length of the room. One step, pause, a second step, pause, three steps in succession. Lucas glanced at him. Quinn drew his mouth up in a naughty almost-smile. He was either saucy, or he looked like a toddler who'd gotten away with something and was waiting for his father to punish him. Either way, Quinn thought, it'd been a good move because when they separated to follow their respective columns along the edge of the dance floor, Lucas watched Quinn until they turned and came up to reunite and start the pattern over.

After the dance, everyone went outside to watch the fireworks shoot up into the sky over Florence. Having Lucas's eyes on him during the pavane had left him a little breathless with a heady combination of adrenaline and nerves. He hadn't quite expected it to work. And now that it had, he wasn't sure what expectations he'd awoken. He wanted to flirt and nothing else, a PG rating for his real-life spy thriller. As they stood together, Quinn watched the fireworks and Lucas watched him, his expression as stern and unreadable as ever.

The commotion of the guests in their revelry felt like a

blanket draped around them, hiding them from sight. Quinn drew his eyes from the sky and matched Lucas's gaze. "Yes?"

"You did well tonight," said Lucas.

Thank you felt like too much, so Quinn just ducked his head in acknowledgment, a rocket soaring through his chest the same as the rockets in the sky, its explosion leaving small residual bursts of heat popping all over his ribs. He forgot to text Larisa and wish her a happy New Year.

No one invaded Quinn's room that night. He slept as he had before, locking the door with his key even though it was clearly ineffective, and tucking himself up into the bow of the bay window behind the chair. He dreamed of his father telling him being a dad was more than any man could handle. The echoes of firework explosions blended with the unceasing cries of an infant, and his father saying to ignore it.

Quinn was drawn from sleep midmorning by music that sounded like a 1970's top-forty, bubblegum duo singing in Italian. Another day with Lucas.

Larisa's New Year's

"This is very exciting," said Ana as she stuck to Larisa's side like a nervous baby deer. "I've never been to a party like this."

"They'll start serving the food in about fifteen minutes," said Larisa. "Make sure you get a crab cake before they're gone."

"Imitation crab," sighed Suzette from Larisa's other side. They were standing together, father, mother, daughter, Ana, in the Kahn estate atrium, receiving guests as they arrived. Miraculously, her parents hadn't asked who Ana was or where she'd come from. And, as soon as Larisa's friends arrived, Ana would be out of sight as well as out of mind.

It'll all work, thought Larisa. It was almost a prayer. She'd never fake-murdered someone before, but the stress alone felt like enough to ruin her, and all she had to do tonight was make sure the reporters covering the event took pictures of Hagan drunk.

Krissy and her husband, Dev, came through the door and greeted Larisa's parents with a disturbing amount of schmoozing, which shut off like a light when Krissy reached Larisa. "Did you see that Rosa's on bed rest? She's not coming."

"When Kahleah gets here, we'll take a group selfie for her."

"Or I can take it," said Ana.

"Oh hey, Ana. Dev, this is Larisa's friend of a friend, Ana from Russia."

There was a beat of suspended awkwardness as Dev looked

Ana up and down. It was obvious to everyone that his brain said *stripper* before he managed to stick out his hand to shake.

Jaden and Adrian came through the door next. Behind them, talking like old friends, was John Hagan and Kahleah's cheating husband, Cade. For a moment, Larisa froze. It wasn't panic, or surprise, or anything she could name. Her body and mind all just screeched to a halt as people continued to move around her. *This is really happening.*

If Ana finds out, she'll tell Lucas. What will he do to Quinn?

"Good evening, Senator Hagan, Mrs. Hagan," said Suzette. "So pleased you could join us."

Hagan had brought his wife, Pam, who looked so much like a political wife she almost seemed a nonentity. But then, Larisa unfroze, and her first thought as she managed to shake Pam's hand and introduce herself was, *I'm going to fake-murder your husband tonight. Will you be sad about it, or not?* Then the woman passed on into the house, and Larisa promptly replaced her name and face with a picture of Jackie O.

Hagan didn't make eye contact with Larisa like his wife had. Probably for the better.

"What did you do to him last night?" Kahleah nodded to where Cade had rejoined Hagan and resumed their conversation. "He had a sit-in with Cade after everyone left, then this morning he called and asked to pick us up tonight. They've been talking like that for an hour."

Larisa shrugged. "Clean energy is the future."

Kahleah gave her a sour face. "That's it? You're not going to say anything else?"

You're better off not knowing, thought Larisa. She pushed down the feeling of a giant wave rushing to crash over her and said, "I appreciate your help."

"Are you in trouble?"

Larisa took a moment longer than usual to be surprised that Kahleah hadn't accepted the brush off and moved on. Larisa's thinly disguised excuses had always worked before. She depended on her friends to not be too curious, to care only when it was easy. But now she was remembering what she'd thought the night before, that Kahleah had changed—was changing— was in the process of some metamorphosis, and this new version of Kahleah didn't like being brushed off. Before Larisa could answer, her father turned his attention to them.

"What trouble?" he asked.

"Nothing, Dad."

"What you both need is a vacation. One of those girls' trips you used to take." He looked at Kahleah, almost pleading. "Distract her."

Suzette paused her greetings long enough to sing, "They could go to Italy," before meeting her next guest.

"Distract you from what?" asked Kahleah.

But the conversation had already gone too far down the road of acknowledging their problems, a thing that wasn't allowed to happen the night of a Kahn party. Gunter retracted, gave Larisa an apologetic face like he was sorry for possibly breaking her façade of normalcy. Kahleah was still waiting for an answer, but Ana was getting restless.

"Cake crabs?" she asked with begging eyes.

"OMG there are crab cakes?" Krissy seized Ana's hand. "Lead the way, baby."

Larisa allowed herself to melt out of the receiving line and follow her friends into the house. Kahleah fell into step beside her. "Where's Quinn?"

"Not here, apparently," said Larisa. A poor choice of words that only deepened Kahleah's glare.

"Whatever. You don't want to talk. I don't have to force you." She moved ahead of Larisa and cut her off to go through the door into the ballroom first. Three steps later, Larisa lost her in the crowd. When she turned to go back and use the back hallway to get around to the buffet, she bumped into the person coming up behind her.

"Jackie," said Larisa in surprise. Not Jackie. Jackie had been dead a long time.

"Pam."

"Right. Pam. I'm sorry. Can I help you find something?"

"You wanted to speak with me."

Larisa frowned. She was tired, astronomically depressed, and cohabitating with a junior spy, coke fiend, but the rigors of medical school had given her special reserve skills when her body was on the fritz. Even in the midst of a brain fog she didn't tend to forget things. She especially wouldn't have forgotten a plan to talk to Pam, because she had no reason, interest, or time to talk to Pam.

"Is there someplace private we can talk? Preferably outside?"

"Sure." Larisa led the way out to her parents' patio. The last time she'd been here, she'd been with Quinn. They'd still been uncomfortable together. Like two gloves where one had been turned inside out. But he'd been so sweet, so determined to make it work. Was that still true? Since Christmas she'd been focused on the danger he was in. Now she wondered if maybe he was happy away from her. If it was a relief not to always be trying to pull back the layers of lies she'd wrapped around herself like sheet metal. She wondered if he'd ever look at her the way he had on Christmas morning, as though she was his own miniature sun.

Pam set two smart phones on the patio table. Larisa did the same with her phone because it seemed polite, if not a little strange. But then politicians were paranoid. And this conversation was most likely going to be about her husband so . . .

"I'd like to check you for concealed devices."

"Ooooh-kay." Larisa held her arms out, glancing at the house to see if anyone was watching from the windows. Pam's hands were surprisingly expert as she pressed the bodice of Larisa's dress against her skin, then peered down the tunnel of her cleavage.

Satisfied, Pam led the way across the lawn. "You have a proposal for me?"

"Ah, maybe? I'm not sure. It's been a really long week. Lots of drinking. Could you . . .?"

"Last night, you told John you were willing to provide me with information to help with my problem."

"Oh."

Oh.

Oh!

"Us." Larisa laughed. "Wow. How does that . . .? Were you before he was . . .?"

Pam nodded.

"I find that really disturbing, but somehow not surprising."

"We probably don't have a lot of time."

"You're really Agent Smith?"

"I thought you knew that. Otherwise you wouldn't have asked him to set this up?"

"He said 'us' like he was all in with terrorists, so I figured he could make it happen. I didn't think—Are you really fighting about a trip he took to Vegas?"

"No."

Larisa nodded. This was all making more sense. Sort of.

"Why were you sent to kill my husband?"

"I'm an old friend of Lucas's." Larisa put her hand to her mouth. "That came out wrong. Sorry, I'm in shock. We dated when I was in college."

The light of interest dissolved from Pam's expression. "I'm not interested in old stories of his orgies. I need actionable information."

"I have what you need."

"If that were true, he wouldn't have let you go."

"He trusts me."

Pam laughed. "I'm not as gullible as I look, girl."

"It's true."

"If that's true, you support his work and allowed millions of people to die."

Seriously, so tired of this. Doesn't anyone care about self-preservation?

"I'm not a hero," snapped Larisa. "The stuff I know, if I'd told anyone, he would've known it was me."

"What's changed?"

"You can help me figure out how to use what I have without it being obvious it came from me. I keep my life. Lucas goes away."

"He'll be dead in a month if the gas isn't found. The CIA won't allow him to sell it."

"So they'll kill the person who knows where it is, smart."

Pam shrugged. "I told them it never should have been made. But they like to have their big dick assurances."

"Lucas stole the gas from us?"

"Who else?"

"I'm remembering why I always stay away from politicians."

"What is it you think you know?"

"His accounting firm. The approximate location of his secret island."

The interest returned to Pam's expression. "Alright. I'd like to go back and do some research to check your story."

"You can ask John. He saw me on that island. I caught him snooping."

"He didn't mention it." Pam paused as though recalibrating her expectations. "Anyway, I'd still like some time."

"Three days. I have people with Lucas right now. I need to get them out."

"A week."

Before Larisa could argue further, Pam turned and walked back to the patio to collect her phones. No pleasantries, not even a wave, which was breaking like ten rules for political wives at the same time. Larisa smiled. *Well, that was something.*

For the first time in her life, Larisa wished she was a smoker. This was the perfect moment to light up, to stare thoughtfully into the shadows of the trees and shrubbery that lined the backyard, to contemplate the nature of existence. Also, she thought nicotine would be a good feeling in her blood, something that might jerk her awake, make everything snap into place with shocking clarity. As it was, she felt like she was drifting underwater, her senses muddled, unable to fully process what was happening.

You need to talk to someone before you explode.

Larisa dismissed that thought. There wasn't time to hold a committee. She needed to go make sure the CIA didn't mess up Hagan's fake-murder. She started back to the patio. Up ahead of her, Pam's progress into the house had been paused as the sisters rushed out of the house.

"There you are!" cried Krissy.

"We're going to selfie for Rosa!" said Jaden.

"It's too dark out here."

"Nope. Quinn taught me how to do this trick so the camera gets enough light." Jaden pointed to the string of patio lights overhead. "Get together gals. You too, Ana."

They crunched together with Jaden in the center holding her phone up. "'We love you, Rosa' on three. One . . . two . . . three!"

Larisa didn't have the energy to shout, "We love you, Rosa!" with everyone else, but they didn't notice. She stood by as they all looked in awe at the picture Jaden had taken using Quinn's secret technique. When had he taught her? The birthday in November probably. Forever ago. Quinn was so steadfastly antisocial it was surprising to realize he'd made a connection with any of her friends. In her mind, he was still the thing she hid behind her back while she held her hand out to keep the sisters from getting too close.

Because she'd wanted him to feel comfortable.

Because everything had felt so fragile. She hadn't wanted to give him too much.

Look how that turned out.

"So, Quinn," said Krissy. "He's MIA."

"Yes."

"What's wrong with him?"

"It's okay if you tell us he turned out to be an asshole," said Jaden. "We're still shipping you and Lucas."

Larisa flinched so badly that everyone saw it. And in their blank expressions, especially in the look Krissy was giving her like, *How could you throw away a man like that?* the rage came.

"Lucas was the asshole," said Larisa. The words rang across the backyard, making invisible concussions in the air. "He was lying to me almost the whole time we were together. And now he's gone after Quinn because he can't stand the idea I could be happy with someone else."

In the back of her head, a voice screamed, *Don't tell them! Don't tell them. Things will never be the same.*

"Gone after how?" asked Jaden.

Larisa pushed back tears. She didn't have time for this. She needed to find Hagan and make sure he was ready for his close-up. She needed to make sure Ana was alright. She needed—

A sob escaped her throat as she heard Quinn laughing at her on the night of Jaden's wedding because he hadn't understood why she'd bother with friends if she wasn't going to trust them the way friends were supposed to. At the time, she'd wanted to argue that they kept her from being lonely. But that wasn't true. She'd felt alone most of her life. And now, more than ever, she was so very alone.

Maybe it didn't have to be that way.

"I'll tell you. Just don't interrupt until I'm done because it's kind of long and its way out there, and I'm so sleep-deprived that if I still worked at the hospital, it'd be illegal for me to go into work."

"Tell it then," said Kahleah. She was smiling what looked like a real smile for the first time in months. Larisa searched each of their faces, these friends of hers who she'd quiet given herself to, and yet here they were. The only ones ready to honor what might be Larisa de France-Kahn's first moment of truth telling. Her more jaded self thought they were only there for the juicy gossip, to collect something they could sell. But in all the years they'd known each other, they'd never betrayed her that way.

It felt like they were girls again, and it seemed right to give this, her darkest secret, to them here, in her parents' yard where they had been single together without schedules or commitments, when their whole lives had been before them, and it had felt like a beautiful promise they could reach out and grasp.

Chapter 9

A Garden Maze

In celebration of the new year, the sun finally broke through the clouds. Lucas allowed the house to sleep until ten, then a Japanese pop song began to pour through the speakers, equal parts sun-shiningly delightful and grating. Quinn was finishing his morning toilet routine when Lucas came into the bedroom holding a picnic basket.

"What are you doing in there?" Lucas called through the door.

Quinn ignored him.

"We're going to be late."

Quinn flung open the door, toothbrush in his mouth, toothpaste foam leaking past his lips. "What?"

"Faster."

There's no winning with this man, thought Quinn as he spit and rinsed.

"Clothes," said Lucas even though Quinn was already dressed.

"Yes, these are my clothes."

With an impatient huff, Lucas set down the picnic basket and went to the stately wooden armoire along the wall opposite the bed. He opened it and took out a hanger with an outfit that looked like it had walked off the set of a Henry James film.

"Put it on."

"Am I allowed to say no?"

Lucas gave him that look, a cold calculation that made Quinn feel so small he snatched the hanger and went back into the bathroom.

Only a few minutes later, Quinn was dressed in a three-piece leisure suit and boat shoes and had followed Lucas out the exterior bathroom door, across the little patio, and down into the villa's garden. Under the sunshine, the landscape that Quinn had been seeing out the windows appeared transformed from murky gray into vibrant color, alive with the activity of birds and insects, and, to his surprise, a cat that lived in the hollow base of a statue.

"What do you know about gardens?" asked Lucas.

"Plants live in them."

"Try again."

"British people like them."

Lucas abruptly stopped walking. The picnic basket was again set down. Lucas took Quinn by the shoulders and moved him a few feet to the left so he looked out over what appeared to be the same view as where he'd been standing before Lucas had moved him.

Don't touch me, thought Quinn. But he didn't allow himself any sign of irritation. After all, they'd touched while dancing the night before and it'd been fine. But now Quinn wasn't ready for the invasion. Today, the threat that seemed to come with certain flavors of Lucas's touch reminded Quinn of that first night when he'd put his hands around Quinn's throat.

You're supposed to be proving you're submissive.

"Look down this line." Lucas illustrated a line through the air with his arm. "This is a themed garden. It's oriented on an east-west axis. There are four sections. Each one represents a garden tradition, Japanese, English, French, Persian." As Lucas pointed, Quinn could tell that there were segments cut out of the space where the plants, and their patterns, seemed to change. But he couldn't have said which area was which, and none of them seemed to belong to the maze, which materialized out of the far end of the axis, seemingly separate from anything Lucas indicated.

"Where do you want to start?"

"English?" Quinn hoped this was the right answer to the question he didn't fully understand.

Lucas led them down into the plants. To Quinn's surprise, there was a path there that'd been hidden by a rise of ground. Its wind-weathered cobblestones wound around bushes and grasses and the stray winter flower. Lucas narrated an unending list of names, both English and Latin, but Quinn barely heard them. He held his hand out and let the leaves brush along his palm; he cupped his fingers around fern fronds. Some were rough. Some were lined with little hooks that caught his skin. Some were so soft touching them left them a little less vibrant.

"Are you listening?"

"Yes."

"What did I just say?"

"Picnics are not supposed to be stressful," muttered Quinn.

"You find knowledge stressful?"

I find you stressful.

"This isn't a picnic," said Lucas. "Come."

He led them off the path, wading up to his knees in foliage that bristled with irritation as he passed. Quinn thought he knew how they felt, ruffled, but not important enough they were allowed to protest.

Gradually, the plants around them changed, became less organized. Trees shaded them, then broke away, and Quinn found they'd come around the side of the yard and down to a plateau that housed the entrance to the maze. Here, a patio had been built with a railing on the hillside, and on it a table with umbrella and chairs. Lucas set the basket on one of the chairs and began to unpack a table linen, small knives that looked like butter knives but malformed, and the most artful cutting board Quinn had ever seen.

"Sit."

Quinn sat, watching as Lucas set out small jars of condiments, then cut and spread cheeses and meats along the board. *Oh,* he thought, *we did this in New York.* Less than an hour after he'd met

Lucas, after Larisa had beaten him with his own belt and they'd had sex for the first time with him knowing she was the Queen. She'd tended to him. She'd fed him. A knot of dread tightened in Quinn's belly.

"You recognize this?" asked Lucas.

"I'm not hungry."

"This has nothing to do with hunger."

It has everything to do with it, thought Quinn.

They were talking about two different types of hunger. Or perhaps they were the same, but their textures cast them in different shades. All Quinn could think about was how this moment and that moment would now be tied together. He would think of Larisa in New York, that heady whirlwind of collision and revelation that had changed his life, their life together, and now this moment with Lucas would be part of it. Quinn found himself staring at Lucas's hands as he arranged the board, wondering if those long fingers were going to find their way into his mouth. And what he would do to stop him without violating his role.

It's like he knows how important that moment was for us, and he's trying to taint it.

Lucas wasn't a god. He had no way of knowing.

And yet.

Quinn turned sideways in his chair and focused his gaze on the entrance to the maze, which was marked with a bower of wisteria just on the edge of blooming. The friendliest entrance to a maze he'd ever seen. For obvious reasons, Quinn didn't like mazes. He hadn't entered anything like a maze since a very bad experience with laser tag for Sid's birthday. He didn't understand why people found it entertaining to be trapped and lost and wandering in a situation outside of their control. And yet, here he was, in a less visible kind of maze with a less clear objective.

"Talk to me," said Lucas.

"About what?"

"Anything."

Anything. Half of Quinn's mind was in New York with Larisa. He could still feel her, how gently she'd held him, like something precious. He didn't want to leave it, so he pulled himself out of the memory just enough to go back to what he'd been thinking that morning when he'd been brushing and re-brushing his teeth. "I suppose I keep thinking about what it would've been like to be a father."

"Fatherhood is a vast unknowable chasm," said Lucas. "Especially for you."

Why for me? thought Quinn. Then he knew—Lucas was referencing Quinn's own father abandoning him as a toddler, which meant Quinn was imagining being a father without any practical experience of having one.

"I want other things."

"But you're still angry Larisa didn't trust you."

Angry was too flat to describe how he felt.

Larisa. Quinn reached over to the board, selected a meat, a cheese, and a daub of mustard that looked similar to what she'd fed him in New York. He placed it carefully in his mouth the way she had, making sure the mustard didn't smear, gazing at him with an intense concentration as though she was memorizing every microsecond of his reaction as the food touched his tongue, as he chewed, as the flavors came together.

I love you, he thought.

"I think she had good reasons for doing what she did. I just don't like them."

"She didn't respect you."

Quinn pushed down the instinct to argue; it felt like Lucas was leading him somewhere. "What about you?" he asked. "Has she lied to you?"

A slow, almost sinister smile, as though Lucas thought it quaint that Quinn would ask.

"She's never had cause."

Quinn's first thought: *I'm so fragile she thinks I need to be managed.*

Quinn's second thought: *Lucas has no idea.*

The second thought should've been comforting. Instead, Quinn just felt tired. He'd come here to prove to her he wasn't fragile, that he could take charge of a bad situation and solve the problem. And yet, here he was thinking he would've done almost anything to see her bright hair catching the sun as she descended the hill toward him.

"What else are you thinking?" asked Lucas, relentless, gazing at Quinn with a different kind of intensity, one of hard edges and unfeeling calculation.

What am I doing here? thought Quinn. And then, because he knew some expression reflecting his thoughts had crossed his face, he just said it. "I don't know what I'm doing here."

Quinn felt the silence growing and turned to see Lucas smiling at him with an unnerving light in his eyes. "That's the first true thing you've said in a week."

"You think I've been lying?"

"I think you're lost." Lucas leaned forward, a perfectly stacked bite of some cured meat, cheese, and a wafer in his hand. "And this is the perfect place to be found." The hand moved forward, an offering.

Quinn opened his mouth and accepted it.

Later, when he was alone, he didn't call or text Larisa. When she called him, he watched the call ring through to voicemail.

Chapter 10

Showdown at the Green Goddess

Kahleah: Did you see the news? It happened.

Krissy: I almost believe it. Those pictures.

Kahleah: Me too. I feel responsible. Risa, do you think someone will come asking about that dinner you came to?

Larisa: It's been ruled accidental death from intoxication.

Krissy: Did we just commit a crime?

Jaden: We're helping prevent one. Larisa would totally have killed that slimy politician to save Quinn.

Krissy: I'm worried about Quinn.

Rosa: Morning all. Or is it afternoon. Could someone please tell me WTF happened?

Ana's scratching was getting worse. She hovered behind Larisa's shoulder, watching her try to write the article for the blog post on that famous BDSM novel Larisa's publicist had asked her to do. All Ana did was scratch herself.

"I can take you to a clinic," said Larisa.

"For what?"

"The withdrawal."

"I'm not an addict." Ana flopped back on the couch. "When will you be done? I want to do something fun."

"Hagan is dead," said Larisa as casually as possible. "Doesn't that mean you're going to leave me alone now?"

"I don't have my new assignment yet. Nowhere to go until then."

Leaving aside how very unbothered Ana seemed that a man was dead, Larisa felt her concern tick up a level. "That's how this works? You don't have a home to go to, days off? A regular life?"

"Overrated." Ana jumped up and prowled over to Sabrina's tower, then began to make hissing noises at the cat. Sabrina, of course, hissed back, her claws coming out to swat at Ana when she got too close.

"Der'mo!" Ana yanked her hand back. "I hate your cat."

"She hates you just as much. There are other people in LA who Lucas wants dead?"

"Just Agent Smith. But he said I don't have to worry about that one. It's being taken care of."

Larisa shivered. "You're so good with death."

"So are you." Ana gave her a pointed look Larisa couldn't interpret. "That's why Lucas is so good. He sees things in people they don't see in themselves."

"What did he see in you?"

Ana gave her a secretive smile. "A woman doesn't tell." And then it looked like she did want to tell, but Larisa's phone vibrated with a new message. She snatched it up before Ana could get a good look at it. Her heart sank.

AWAG: Need to meet. Today. Nonnegotiable.

"What is it?" asked Ana, creeping forward like she might steal Larisa's phone.

After a night of confessing, Larisa found she didn't have the energy to do any more lying, at least not under Ana's suspicious watch. "It's the CIA. They want to meet."

"Lucas said you were doing that."

"Of course I am. I have to look cooperative, or they'd arrest me."

Ana gazed at her with half-lidded eyes, then a grin broke over her face. "That's why he trusts you with this big thing. You're the best. When do we go?"

"You want to go?"

"I will spy for you from a distance."

Great, thought Larisa. Osna was already an asshole. Every meeting with him was stressful, and now she'd have to survive him while being watched by Ana.

Dread pooled in her gut. She needed help. A distraction. An army. A new message buzzed in.

> Rosa: Jaden just gave me the update. OMG,
> Larisa. You're such a badass. What's the next
> step?

And just like that, the most improbable idea came to Larisa. She replied to all. And when the sisters agreed, she messaged Osna.

> Larisa: The Green Goddess. Beverly
> Hills. 2pm.

Agent Osna was already seated at a patio table for two when Larisa arrived, the sisters flanking her like an aged-up version of Regina King's posse in *Mean Girls*, hair done, lips plumped, heels, bags, and smoothies from the Green Goddess juice counter. Jaden had even brought along her dog. When he saw them, Agent Osna started up, then fell back into his seat as they surrounded the little table, chair legs screeching over the pavement as they were dragged over from adjacent tables to create a semicircle of intimidation around the agent. They hadn't planned it that way, it just made sense, an old tactic from the days of bad boyfriend takedowns, and that one time when they'd banded together to convince Rosa's father to let her come to Palm Springs with them for spring break even though it was sinful. Larisa sat directly across from Osna, Krissy and Jaden to her right, and Kahleah to her left.

"Shall we start with introductions?" asked Larisa.

"Nu huh." Kahleah made her trademark hissing sound through her teeth. "Look at him. He already knows us."

"But I'm not satisfied that we know him," said Jaden. "Can I see your badge?"

Moving so slowly it looked like he expected to be shot, Agent Osna took out his badge and passed it across the table. He flinched when Jaden snapped a picture of it with her phone.

"What's going on here?" he asked Larisa.

"I told them everything."

"Well, that was stupid."

"One minute, and he's already questioning your mental capacity, Risa," said Krissy. "He doesn't respect you."

Larisa pinned Osna with her gaze. "It occurred to me that Lucas's recent behavior made me look guilty of something I haven't done," said Larisa. "So I brought witnesses."

Osna laughed. "You think these girls are going to save you? Do you have any idea how easy it would be to have you all locked up in a jail no one has ever heard of?"

"I was thinking more of a tropical island you've never heard of." Larisa couldn't help but smile. For years she'd been dreaming of making Osna sweat like this.

"What island?" he asked.

Larisa shrugged. "Let's keep this simple for now. Is Senator Hagan safe?"

"Obviously."

"Nothing obvious about those pictures in the paper," said

Jaden. "How did you make it look so real? Is it all digital, or do you use a body double?"

Osna stared at her. "State secrets." He retrained his gaze on Larisa. "I did something for you. Now it's your turn. I want something good."

"What's your plan with Lucas?"

"Classified."

"Hagan said nerve gas is missing. Is it true you'll kill Lucas to prevent him selling even if you can't find it?"

Osna put his hand over his mouth to cover the softly uttered, "Fucking Hagan."

"See that?" asked Jaden. "Managers do that in baseball when they don't want the cameras to see what they're saying."

"Are we being watched right now?" asked Krissy, almost dissolving into giggles because she knew they'd left Ana stationed at the corner by the parking garage pacing up and down pretending to have an argument on her phone.

"Of course we are," said Kahleah. "He's got a partner running reconnaissance. They always come in pairs."

Larisa watched Osna's gaze darken. He was probably thinking about his partner, the newly dead one who'd gotten in over his head trying to save money by defecting to a new arms dealer. Larisa felt just the tiniest tinge of sympathy for him. It passed quickly.

"I want you to have LAPD arrest me for Hagan's murder," said Larisa.

"Can we say Senator Hagan, Risa?" said Kahleah. "It's more respectful."

"I want to be arrested for *Senator* Hagan's murder," said Larisa. "If I'm not, Lucas will suspect it was fake. From jail, I'll need to be rescued. He'll pull some strings, get me out. I become your spy."

"Risa, I thought our plan was to not get arrested?" whispered Krissy.

"You're too late," said Osna. "We already have a spy who doesn't have to waste time building back his trust."

Larisa held eye contact. Not for all the world was she going to show this man what she felt about his new spy. So, even though she knew it was Quinn, she said, "He's finally found a new woman?"

"Something like that."

"Who is it?"

Osna tilted back in his chair, curled his lips around the straw of his drink. "You should have played ball in November. You're basically irrelevant now."

"If she's so irrelevant, why are you showing up having emergency meetings like this?" asked Kahleah. "She said stage a murder, you staged a murder no questions asked."

"Hagan was dirty. We've wanted him for years but couldn't prove it."

"Wait! Did you actually kill him?" asked Jaden.

"Who is your spy?" repeated Larisa.

"Your cousin, Hannah. She's been with him two weeks and has already given us more than you ever did. Personnel at the house, schedules, contact names. She hasn't even had to fuck him."

Before Larisa knew what she was doing, she was on her feet, smoothie in hand. She threw it at him. Green slush exploded over his face.

"You fucking bitch!"

"How long does she have to find the gas?"

"Need to know." He smeared green across the cheap polyester sleeve of his suit.

"I need to know."

"However long until it goes on market."

"How do you know when it goes on market?"

"We don't."

"Stop lying to me!"

Osna squinted at his sleeve, then, after a pause, stuck out his tongue and licked it, made a face, then turned his attention back to Larisa as she stood over him, shoulders heaving, wishing she had something else to throw. "She has a month, then tactical takes him out," he said. "We'll start over with whoever takes over his business and hope for better results." Larisa thought she detected something like a dangerous bottom line of defeat in Osna's voice. As though he'd already given up and was looking for someone to blame for the inevitable failure.

"I know nothing about what ya'll do, but I call bullshit," said Jaden.

"Agreed," said Kahleah. "You don't kill the guy who knows where the shit—I mean crap—is."

Now Osna was smiling one of those self-righteous smirks he put on when he felt powerful. "If your cousin ends up being collateral damage, at least you'll have the comfort of knowing you protected yourself."

If Larisa stayed any longer, she was going to escalate the violence in a way that would definitely make her reputation worse. She motioned to the sisters. It was time to leave. "You'll be hearing from me," she said to Osna.

They walked toward the parking garage. Ana was nowhere in sight.

"This is good, right?" asked Jaden.

"Nothing about Ana is good," said Larisa.

"We can do a lap around the block," said Krissy.

Larisa shook her head. "She's probably gone."

"That means it worked." Kahleah rubbed Larisa's arm. "You're free."

The only problem was that Larisa didn't feel free. She felt buzzed. She'd done battle with Osna and come out of it feeling justified instead of demolished. It felt like the strangest high she'd ever had, a cross between pre-sex sexual tension and what she imagined it would've felt like if she'd ever managed to be the daughter her mother had wanted.

Riding the train of this high, she had Kahleah stop by a

sketchy mobile phone shop that looked like a gas station to purchase a prepaid phone. Then, in her strangely empty apartment that smelled faintly of Ana, in the technicolor glow of her little Christmas tree, her Lucas photo album open on her lap, Shubert sonatas on her stereo, Larisa called Pam.

"I had a meeting today."

"I know."

How would she know?

They're working together.

Or something.

This gave Larisa pause. She didn't want anything to do with Osna. But she also had decided this was her next step, and if she hesitated too long on the edge of it, she'd lose her courage. Full steam ahead vengeance.

"I saved your husband's life.

"I spoke to him this morning. He's grateful. As am I."

Larisa didn't want to spend time dwelling on how she'd saved Hagan's life or how she was now going to have to trust the lives of two people she loved to his wife, who seemed more qualified at expressing requisite niceties than feeling truly grateful.

"So you should be able to tell me who put in the order to have Lucas killed."

"If you're feeling sentimental, I can give you a list of the things he's done."

I am . . .

. . . not.

She flipped back to the photo Ana had admired of Lucas on the beach. Life had been so simple then.

"My cousin has been recruited to help the CIA. She's with him in Florence now."

And Quinn.

"I'm sorry to hear that." Pam released an audible breath into the phone receiver. "If you're worried our plans endanger her, you can send me a photo and I'll have my people—"

"Let's move on." Larisa began to pull photos out of the

album sleeves. "I have two locations for you. One is in Umbria, Italy. The other is about three hours south of Japan, by boat." Larisa ran her hand over the coordinates she'd written on the back of one picture. "Where was the gas coming from?"

"New Mexico. Your secret island is more likely."

"If I give this to you, do you promise to make it look good? Lost tourists or something. No guns blazing like you're acting on privileged information. It can't come back to me."

"You have my word."

"He'll spot the tourists. It might spook him into moving out into the open. You'll have to have your people set up to watch from out of sight."

"Exactly what I was thinking."

"And you'll destroy the gas when you find it."

"I will."

This is a bad idea.

No reason to think she's more trustworthy than Osna.

Larisa read out the coordinates.

For several long moments, silence stretched over the line. Larisa's hands trembled as she tucked all but one of the photos back into their sleeves. The last one, a photo of Lucas and his favorite baker's son, Rifat, standing in a kitchen covered in flour, she set up under the Christmas tree. Maybe she was sentimental, or at the very least nostalgic. *Nothing wrong with remembering a happy time,* she thought.

"I will tell you as soon as I know something," said Pam.

Larisa breathlessly hung up the phone. The high intensified. Finally, she'd done it. Ten seconds passed, thirty, a minute. *I should check in with Quinn.*

Larisa: I told the girls everything today.

Larisa: Are you free to talk?

Larisa took a breath and found she couldn't top out. The

feeling of unfulfilled breath sent panic through her nervous system. *It'll be okay. He's okay.*

Nothing moved on her phone screen.

A new thought, so horrible the room began to spin. *Lucas knows the murder was faked.*

Chapter 11

Crawl to Me

Monday was an exhausting marathon of Lucas's undivided attention, small meals, aggression disguised as interest, and insults disguised as tests. Tuesday was more of the same so that, by the time they settled in for an afternoon reading session in the library, instead of dreading the unending silence that would be filled with Lucas's questing observations, it was a relief to accept the stack of books Lucas handed him and retreat to a chair alone. Or mostly alone. There was no escaping the feeling that even as Lucas appeared to be captured by his own reading, he seemed aware of Quinn's every shift, twitch, and wandering thought.

He was supposed to be reading about the history of tea leaves, but he couldn't concentrate. Yesterday, during reading time, he'd tried to explain to Lucas that he'd never been a strong reader, but Lucas had written that off as an excuse. Today, Quinn brought out skills he'd honed in junior high detention, pretending to read while his mind went for a walk.

An agitated, fast-paced walk.

I didn't come here to study tea.

I need to go home.

But going home now just meant surrendering to Lucas's permanent place in their life. It meant Larisa being under surveillance by the CIA. It meant curating their public relationship so Lucas would think it was flawed even though he would always see through them and make his own decisions.

He darted a glance across the room to Lucas sitting sideways on the sofa with a book propped up on his thighs, the picture of a Byronic hero in a modern romance novel.

"What?" asked Lucas.

"Nothing."

"Unacceptable."

"I was thinking I wish you were an actor."

"Strange thought." Lucas turned the page.

"Not in my line of work." Quinn debated, then decided to say, "Your body is provocative."

"You say that because you think yours isn't."

There's no reaching him.

But now Lucas was pinching his finger in the book to hold his place and turning to face Quinn, his free hand a pillow under his head. *Those eyes.*

"Get down on your knees," said Lucas.

Heat flushed Quinn's cheeks. The command in Lucas's voice brought him halfway to obedience before he could even think about it. The book fell. Lucas's eyes glinted.

"Now crawl to me. No, not like that. Slowly. You're not hiding now, you're showing."

Quinn was on his hands and knees, frozen in the middle of the open square of rug between them. *Don't hide, show.* It felt incorrect, even silly. He'd given actors similar direction, and yet now it felt impossible to apply it to himself. How could he be hiding if he was here, choosing to sit under Lucas's withering gaze? But the voice had commanded him and so, though it felt wrong, Quinn started forward again. This time, he moved more slowly, accentuated the movement of his spine from shoulders to hips, tried to feel each vertebrae break free of the stiff upright posture Lucas had pounded into him during dancing lessons.

I'll never be enough, he thought. *Nothing will please him.*

And then, as he came up to the sofa and stared down at the floor with the crown of his head pointed up toward Lucas, he thought, *What if he enjoys being displeased?*

"What do you feel?" Lucas's hand reached out and brushed lightly at the back of Quinn's neck, then the rounded knob of his right shoulder. "Don't you know your body?"

My body is Larisa's, thought Quinn. Only with her had he felt beautiful.

"Turn and go back," said Lucas.

Quinn kept his gaze down as he turned. Why? Was he afraid of the desire he might find there? Or that he'd find only cold calculation?

"I'm looking at your ass," said Lucas. "I'm thinking of all the things I might do to it."

Quinn stopped. He hadn't reached his chair yet, but he couldn't breathe because he was listening so closely for movement behind him. *Take me and let's get it over with,* he thought. Which was exactly why Lucas wasn't leaving the couch. The slow burn of building desire meant more than a sudden plunge into gratification. He could feel that Lucas knew—somehow he knew—that Quinn was more afraid of what would happen with a slow build up than a brief flame.

A brief flame could be dismissed, pushed aside. It didn't fundamentally change the nature of what it touched.

But this. Dancing on New Year's. Sunday afternoon in the garden when Quinn had allowed Lucas's fingers into his mouth, alchemy. And now, the unspent heat in his groin, transmutation.

"Enough," said Lucas. "You don't have it in you. I suppose we can blame your parents."

Quinn hauled himself back into his seat, quickly pulling the sheltering book onto his lap. "Blame them for what?"

"For you. For this abhorrent severance between you and your body. I can't fathom Larisa ever got anything out of beating you."

"I suppose you'll have to ask her." Quinn pressed his palm against the flat page of the book, watched his sweat wrinkle the paper. He opened his mouth to argue.

"If you're going to say you like being this way, don't. You like it because you don't know any different. You've had to hide yourself your entire life, haven't you? Imagine the pressure of supporting your mother after she was abandoned. Did you try to replace him for her? Was she easy to love?"

"You don't know what you're talking about."

"Then tell me. What do you feel?"

"I'm going to my room."

"I haven't given you permission to leave."

Quinn glared at the book. "I'd like to leave."

"Avoiding me isn't going to help." Lucas stood, crossed the room, and planted himself in front of Quinn. "You're never going to be a great artist until you face yourself. Stand."

Quinn stood. Lucas set his hands on Quinn's arms and gave them a little shake, then shook them harder so that Quinn's shoulders moved. "Feel it?"

"What?" Quinn whispered.

"This is part of you. All of it is yours. There's nothing wrong with it." One hand dropped down to Quinn's hip. "What are you so afraid of?"

"I'm not afraid."

Lucas's hand moved over, cupped Quinn's erect penis. "And now?"

Quinn lifted his head and met Lucas's eyes. "Should I be afraid of you?"

"Yes." Lucas's head bent down, his lips nipped the side of Quinn's neck. "Fear is the beginning of knowledge. You can't be afraid of what you don't know."

It sounded profound, but Quinn only heard about half of it as his body rallied to life, focusing all his attention on that roving mouth.

"You only want me because of her," he said, trying to draw back. The chair was in his way.

"That's more than you deserve."

Quinn slid sideways, past the chair and out of reach. "If only you could manage to stop being insulting for ten minutes in a row, I might find you charming."

"You make it easy to be insulting," said Lucas, almost grinning, as though this was all a game, and he liked it all the better because Quinn was pushing back. "I want you to suck me off."

"No."

"You're not allowed to say no."

Quinn gave him a long look. "The way Larisa talked about you, I thought you were this great bondage teacher. She left some things out."

For a moment, a slight tremor rippled across Lucas's expression, telling Quinn his words had landed. When Lucas spoke again, his voice had become rigid.

"Why don't you just admit you're not a submissive?"

"I can't be submissive to someone I don't trust."

"Trust is for children," spat Lucas. "Do you want to be a child? Shall we put up safety bumpers?"

"According to you, I never had the chance to be a child. So yeah, maybe some cushioned barriers would be nice."

"I'm not going to pad your vanity."

"Your mistake for assuming I have any." Quinn turned on his heel, eyes on the door.

"Don't walk away from me you piece of shit, waste of space. I get to decide when this conversation is over."

A spark of energy fizzled down Quinn's spine. *Yes,* he thought, *fight me. See if you win.*

Lucas walked around and positioned himself between Quinn and the door. "You're so fucking defensive. My God." Lucas raked a hand through his hair as though to smooth the frustration out of it. When his hand dropped down to his side, he seemed calmer.

"Winter and some of her friends are coming for dinner tonight."

Quinn stood still, waiting for the connection.

"I have something I'd like you to wear."

Quinn was still waiting. The silence expanded before he realized Lucas wasn't planning to say anything else. Everything that'd just been said had been erased, and now they were having a new conversation.

"You want to dress me for dinner?"

"Yes." An almost smile.

"Why?"

"Because I just thought of this satin slip I have in the back of the closet. And if you wear that the entire night and still not feel anything, I don't know that there's hope for you."

"What's taking so long?" Lucas called from Quinn's bedroom.

Quinn stood in the bathroom staring at his reflection. The 'satin slip' had turned out to be a semitransparent, skintight sheath he'd rolled down his body. His first thought was that it'd been designed for a female body because of the deep cut of the neck and back, but then he realized his lack of breasts and the squareness of his hips didn't change much about how it fit. He looked like he had curves, and his shoulders seemed to have widened several inches into a long line of commanding bone structure.

Also, his skin was showing through the sequined, red fabric.

Also, Lucas hadn't allowed him to wear any underwear. The dark shadow of his ball sack was far too visible.

"How many people are coming tonight?"

"I'm opening the door," said Lucas.

Quinn preempted him, and strode out, resisting the need to use his hands to cover himself. "I'm not wearing heels."

"This is a barefoot dinner," said Lucas as he motioned for Quinn to do a turn. The fabric swished across Quinn's bare shaft, the perfect amount of pressure. *I can't walk in this,* he thought.

"What do you think?"

"Red's your color, not mine."

"You don't have a color," said Lucas.

"Is this your dress?"

"What would you think if I said yes?"

"I'd be impressed."

Lucas stepped back to take in the full effect. "It's Larisa's. Or it would've been if she hadn't left. A birthday gift."

Oh.

What was that expression on Lucas's face? Regret? Or was Quinn just imagining it?

The lie came easily. "I haven't called her yet."

"I assumed as much," said Lucas.

"I should, shouldn't I?"

"You think she's missed you?"

A question that felt like a trap, so Quinn walked toward the door. Lucas liked dinner to start at seven and it was already ten minutes past, which meant the guests had already arrived. "We're late."

"Wait a moment."

Lucas took Quinn's hand and turned him so they were facing each other, holding it a moment longer than necessary as though testing the softness of his skin. *Don't you dare tell me I'm not moisturizing,* thought Quinn.

"Do you know what I want for you tonight?"

You want me to play Larisa, thought Quinn, even though it was an absurd thought.

"I want you to be free. Just open up, spread your damaged wings, fly."

"I'd just like to get through this without an accidental emission."

"That's what I'm talking about. You're so limited. All your brain patterns, your expectations, they're all about safety." Lucas reached into his pocket and pulled out a small, delicately painted tin snuff box.

No.

"Open your mouth," said Lucas.

Quinn backed up against the wall, reached for the door that was too far away.

"Submit," said Lucas.

"I'm not ready."

"You'll never be ready unless you're pushed."

A finger stroke along his bottom lip left a powdery residue. Quinn's tongue snaked out to wipe it clean and in that opening, a tiny, round invader slipped in and dissolved on his tongue. He lurched for the bathroom to spit and wash out his mouth, but Lucas held him in place.

"You'll thank me for this."

Chapter 12

A Whale in Molasses

It had been thirteen hours since she'd betrayed Lucas to Pam, but it felt like a week. Larisa hadn't slept. She'd called Pam to tell her not to act on the information, but Pam hadn't answered. Her phone had been turned off. Even more maddening, Quinn hadn't answered her calls. By dawn, there were ten of them. And approximately as many text messages, which, as she read them in the light of day, sounded remarkably calm compared to her lived experience.

> Larisa: It's strange to think of you at Umbras.
> Seeing the picture you sent, I'm thinking
> about things I haven't thought about in years.
>
> Larisa: I want you to come home. Can't you
> just come home, right now? Whatever you're
> doing, it's not as important as us.
>
> Larisa: Did I tell you I told the girls the thing?
> They did really well. I bet you're not surprised.
> I wish I could tell you I feel good about it. But
> it was so scary. I'm sitting here just waiting for
> it to come back and bite me. Trusting people
> has never gone well for me.

Larisa: Maybe I feel that way because of L. It's hard to remember what I thought before him. There have always been people who wanted to get close to me because of who I am. But college wasn't terrible. The sisters were a little like that, but they're human in regular ways. L is something else. I didn't see it coming. Not when he sold his version of our story to the magazine, not when he told me what he really did for a living.

Larisa: Did you know we actually met here in the US? I always tell people I met him while I was doing that summer in Italy. But he was the reason I went to Italy. Fall of junior year, I took a themed romance train from LA to NYC with some girls I barely knew. He was on the train working in the BDSM car. I'd never wanted anything more than I wanted him. And let's face it, I get what I want.

Larisa: It's now morning your time and you haven't read any of these messages. Is your phone off?

Larisa: Are you sleeping with him?

Larisa: I think you're not ready to talk about what you're feeling. Or else something terrible has happened. Please just let me know you're okay.

Larisa: I can't tell what's real in my mind anymore. Everything feels equally plausible and implausible.

Larisa: When this is over, I'm not going to want to talk. Can we just agree to lie in bed and stare at each other for a week before we start the hard stuff?

Larisa: I'm out of my mind. Nothing for us has ever been easy.

Larisa: The first time I saw you, Parish had her
head in your lap, and you were rearranging
her hair so she looked like she was posed for
a centerspread. I thought, That man knows
what he wants.

Larisa: If I can't figure out how to be honest,
I'm not sure I'm the person you want.

Larisa: I did something else last night. I want
to take it back, but I can't.

Larisa: I feel like a whale trapped in molasses
being stalked by a dead dinosaur.

Her phone began to ring. She was so tired, when she read Quinn's name, it didn't immediately register that it was a real call.

"Hello?"

"Morning." His voice sounded sleep clogged, as though he'd just woken up even though it was the middle of the afternoon in Florence.

"You just getting up?"

"Uh, yeah. Not up yet. There was a party last night."

"Party?" Larisa tried to think, then she knew. "The story-telling party." Despite herself, a smile snuck onto her lips. "Did you tell any stories, Quinn?"

"I. Don't. Know."

Any other person, she would've thought he was toying with her, but Quinn sounded genuinely unsure, even disoriented.

"You okay?" She'd never spoken a more inadequate question. She wanted to be there, to take him in her arms, and let their bodies do what words couldn't.

"Yeah . . . sorry, I was going to call later. But I woke up and saw all the notifications. I guess it's been more than twenty-four hours."

"I'm sure you're busy."

"Sounds like you are too. Good job telling the sisters."

"Thanks."

"I think they're worthy of you." He was waking up now, a warmth coming into his voice that made her eyes burn.

"What if I'm not worthy of them?" *Or you?*

"That's sleep deprivation talking."

"Yeah, I should try to sleep before Teale comes over."

"Your discussion thing is coming up, isn't it?"

"To be honest, I have no idea. I just kind of drift." Which was not true, but once again she felt certain she couldn't tell him the truth. *I gave Pam the information to take Lucas down.* "You two talk about the news at all?"

"Like Italian news?"

"News from here."

"Lucas was worried about something political yesterday, but we didn't talk about it. He's not sharing much."

"You don't have to worry about that anymore. I've taken care of it."

Silence as Quinn digested this news. Finally, he said, "How do you know?"

The truth was she didn't know. But she also couldn't bear to think that she'd finally given over her closely held secrets, and it wasn't going to count.

"I'm not ready to leave," said Quinn.

"But you will, right? Before you get in too deep?"

"It isn't the same for me as it was for you. My eyes are open."

Larisa nodded, told herself this was enough, even though she knew there was no level of self-awareness that could protect anyone from prolonged exposure to Lucas.

"I love you," she said.

"Yeah, okay."

"Quinn—sorry don't go—I just need to say something." She sucked in a breath, fighting down a rush of dread that this might be the last time they spoke. "I know you feel like me lying to you is the way I'm compensating for your limitations, to protect you from yourself. That's totally valid. My therapist would probably have a field day with all this. But I want you to know that I do it to everyone." She struggled to laugh. "You're not actually that special. Limitations aren't a weakness. They're a secret power. You know what I love about you? You've perfected the fine art of never going too far. I just . . . I want you to know that, even though I'm sure you already do."

"I'll talk to you tomorrow, Larisa."

Larisa dragged herself to bed and lay in a twilight of half-sleeping/half-waking, her mind aimless with exhaustion that sleep wouldn't cure.

I've betrayed him and it might not matter.

Quinn didn't say he loved me.

He's fallen. It's already too late.

Eventually, she must have fallen asleep because the next thing she knew, she'd flopped to the other side of the bed where the pillow no longer smelled of Quinn. The pillow yowled, then her murky view of the ceiling was obscured by Sabrina's pouty face. A howling meow.

"You're not starving."

Sabrina turned and showed Larisa her butt, slapping an indignant floof of a tail into Larisa's open mouth.

"Seriously, cat."

Sabrina began to make biscuits on Larisa's stomach, claws included, a way to comfort both Larisa and herself as a chorus of happily barking dogs rose from the courtyard.

"Would you stop that?" Larisa pushed her cat off the bed, then regretted it as though Quinn was just about to walk through the bedroom door and catch her being less than angelic to the kitten he'd gifted her when they'd been more enemies than friends.

It'd been such a gentle gesture from such a severe man. She

wondered if it'd been one of the first moments she began to see who he was underneath.

A difficult hip maneuver and a yanking on her shoulders got Larisa repositioned so she was on her side and could see the bedside table where her burner phone sat still and silent. Not a peep from Pam.

"You like him better than me." She reached to scratch Sabrina's chin and the cat dodged out of reach, giving her a dirty look, and releasing another strangled meow.

Larisa dug her phone out of the sheets and checked messages. Rosa's baby hadn't come even though the doctor was sure it would be early. Krissy's son had chipped a tooth playing basketball. Jaden's mother-in-law was coming for a visit. Kahleah had been quiet, which Larisa thought was usually a sign of something really being wrong, but she didn't have the energy to switch over and compose a private message.

Someone else will notice Kahleah has gone quiet.

Sabrina once again mounted Larisa's chest and began to dig her claws into the flimsy fabric of Larisa's camisole.

"Alright, alright."

Larisa dragged herself to the kitchen. It took three attempts before she was able to pull the tab on the wet food can. Sabrina was entirely ungrateful for the amount of effort. Tea for Larisa, a blend of revitalizing leaves she'd picked up at a shop in Portland at a farmers market years before. They were probably stale, but she didn't want caffeine, which would give her all the jitters of unspent activity without any true energy.

The simplest breakfast would be yogurt, but the fridge was empty. Sarah, her parents' house manager, usually sent meals over along with weekly groceries, but she was on vacation along with the Kahn family chef. Eggs and toast was doable but would require Larisa to stand at her stove. Too much work. She microwaved the egg and skipped the toast.

Doorbell.

Teale was early. She looked down at her lacy cami and

matching shorts, imagined the state of her unwashed hair, decided none of it mattered, then went to the door, for some reason breaking her cardinal rule of checking the security window before opening it.

Instead of her friendly, ambitious, multicolored hair publicist, Larisa's mother stood on the front step. Her assistant stood beside her with two lattes in hand. Behind them, two neighbors Larisa vaguely recognized paused to let their dogs sniff each other, yapping with the kind of delight that felt like an insult to anyone who delight had abandoned.

"WTF, Mom?"

"Good morning to you too." Suzette took the drinks from her assistant. "Thank you, darling. I'll manage from here." Suzette slid past Larisa into the apartment.

"Did we have plans I forgot about?"

"I believe you have a meeting with your publicist?"

Larisa opened her mouth, then closed it. Teale worked at the same PR firm as Larisa's former publicist, Rockie, who still worked for Suzette.

"You have Rockie spying on me?"

"Nothing so sinister." Suzette breezed into the kitchen, sniffed the air, and followed her nose to Larisa's tea. "Have you become a witch?"

"No."

"Is that from a homeopath?"

"It's just tea, Mom."

"Yes, but what does it do for you?"

Larisa stole the tea out from under her mother's nose and sank down on an island stool.

"So you don't want this?" Suzette held up the latte. The guilt layered over the question made it impossible to argue. Larisa pulled the spare latte next to her tea.

"We don't need your supervision."

"You're probably wrong about that. But I'm here on official business."

"What official business?"

"To reopen the conversation about Milan Fashion Week."

"Oh my God. Are you serious?"

"We can wait until Teale arrives."

"I don't need Teale. The answer's still no. Nothing has changed."

"You're apparently single. Or you will be when that *New Yorker* piece goes live."

Too late now, thought Larisa. Remembering her panic in New York, which had led her to sabotage an interview meant to be a glowing lovebirds piece by convincing Quinn to act like they hated each other, made Larisa feel even more tired. So much work, and she still ended up in the exact place she'd been trying to avoid.

Well, not exactly. She'd never envisioned a possible timeline where Quinn was the one stolen off to Italy with Lucas.

I need to talk to Dr. Bade, but I can't talk to Dr. Bade.

"Mom, I need you to hear me on this."

"I am hearing you. I just don't think you appreciate the situation."

"What situation is that?"

Suzette waved her latte through the air. "You're tainted."

Tainted. The word rang in the air like a judge's verdict, a kind of scarlet letter stain.

"I went to the salon yesterday and two people came up to me to ask how you were doing. One of them recommended a treatment facility in Lake Tahoe."

"I'm not on drugs."

"I know that. But that's the thing, from the outside, you look out of control. That incident with the dog walker this fall. The fire at Christmas—"

"No one knows about that."

"But it happened. Why are all these things happening to you?"

Lucas, thought Larisa, but she knew even he couldn't be blamed for all of it.

The doorbell rang. Larisa didn't want to get up, so she yelled, "It's open."

Teale arrived with more lattes. "Oh," she said when she saw Suzette. "I didn't realize . . ." She saw Larisa already in possession of two hot drinks.

"She's leaving," said Larisa.

"I guess I'm leaving." Suzette heaved a dramatic sigh. "You were such a sweet child. Do you remember that? So beautiful, so poised. I thought I was the luckiest mother."

"Yeah, well." Larisa pinched her fingers against her eyes so the pain would hold back her tears. She hadn't ever felt like her mother had been proud of her, but knowing there had been a time, and now it had passed, was worse.

"Good luck on Thursday," called Suzette as she showed herself out. "I hope you don't have any of those Internet perverts bother you like they do on the socials."

The front door closed. Teale's sweet marijuana scent wafted forward to mix with the streams of coffee and tea as she sat at the island opposite Larisa.

"You okay?"

"Sure."

Teale hesitated.

"I'm fine." Larisa reached for the drink Teale had brought her and took a sip she didn't want.

"So, *The Rumpus* is very excited about tomorrow. I've read through what you sent me, and I'd like to go through it with you to pull out the salient points that'll be easier for people to understand." Teale was opening her portfolio, frowning down at the papers inside.

"What is love?" Larisa asked her small collection of beverages.

"Oh, I like that. Great opening line." Teale found her pen and scrawled a big cursive note. "Does this mean you saw the new meme that's been going around? The one your mother mentioned."

"I haven't been online." Larisa reached for her phone, suddenly wondering what she'd been so busy with that she hadn't been keeping up with socials. Her first stop was Facebook, where, at the top of the feed, was a picture collage titled, *Italian Vacay Photo Dump Two*, from Hannah.

And there, as though it'd been cut from a slightly crooked postcard, was the back façade of the Villa de'Umbras.

"Larisa?"

Larisa's gaze jerked from her phone, realizing Teale had been talking and she hadn't heard a word. *Big smile*, she thought. Try not to reveal how much of a mess her insides were. "Teale, you know what? I trust you. Whatever needs to happen, just do it, and tomorrow night I'll follow your directions, okay?"

Without waiting for an answer, she made a triangle of her three cups, pressed it between her hands, and carried it to the front door, which she opened with her elbow because it was one of those long-handled knobs. Outside, she sat down on the ground, an instant magnet for the dogs still racing around while their humans chatted.

The humans looked like ordinary people, happy in their own ways, unhappy in their own ways. Neither of them appeared to be carrying around any giant burdens of prematurely abandoned true love, or something that looked like it, talked like it, but had turned out to be something else.

Love was never the problem, thought Larisa even as a voice in her head answered, *Love bridges all.* Which sounded like it was from the Bible, but Larisa hadn't ever been indoctrinated in that particular language, so it was probably a line from a movie. *Amazing how many movies end up teaching women to stay in bad relationships,* thought Larisa as she vengefully popped the plastic lids off the coffee cups.

Was it really so bad?

Yes.

No.

Yes.

The dogs came running. She moved the coffees far enough apart they had space to not get in each other's business. As they drank, she sipped her tea, trying to inhale its revitalizing fumes.

Chapter 13

A Revealing Cooking Lesson

What happened in dreams, stayed in dreams.

This was the only way Quinn could process what had happened at dinner, wearing a dress made for Larisa, while high on some drug, his body vibrating as though every blood vessel had become a squirming thing in his skin. Some of it he'd enjoyed, but even the good parts were colored in the gauze of a nightmare where all he could do was helplessly watch himself from a distance.

Winter and her wine connoisseur friends had been there, all wearing outfits that left little to the imagination. This was a party they always had, a smaller New Year's ritual than the ball, where they lounged around the library massaging themselves on the variety of fabrics and textures and hard corners of the furniture while they took turns recounting the erotic highlights of the past twelve months.

Had Quinn shared a story? He couldn't remember. He had floated, he had survived, then it had ended.

Never again, he'd promised himself. And since then, aside from the shock to his system and a prolonged come down from whatever pill Lucas had fed him, things had been not great, but okay by comparison.

It was Thursday, which meant Quinn had been in Italy over a week and not seen a trace of criminal conspiracy.

The past few days they'd settled into a routine that seemed

designed to sandpaper Quinn's ego raw. When Lucas wasn't grilling him on obscure pockets of philosophical thought, he was pointing out Quinn's ignorance, being frustrated by his lack of curiosity about food, history, clothes, the pattern of the garden, and assigning him reading. Quinn had passed his tea ceremony test, but failed to be remotely impressive identifying various, apparently famous, pieces of classical music.

Today promised more of the same plus the extra stress of a social event in the evening, an artist's lecture. Some local university professor had conducted a botanical study that involved some of the plants in the garden and wanted to test out his findings on a soft audience. The idea of Lucas and his friends being a soft audience made Quinn briefly wonder about the apparent cutthroat culture of the Italian botanical world, but then he forgot because it didn't matter. Nothing mattered except finding a way into Lucas's secrets so he could leave.

How many did he need? One or two big ones, he'd thought. Though now, maybe none. He wondered if Larisa had finally told the CIA what they'd wanted to know, or if she'd found another way. When had she done it? At least forty-eight hours later, and he couldn't tell that anything had changed. Certainly, commandos with guns hadn't broken through the doors to arrest Lucas. Anything short of seeing Lucas arrested didn't feel like it would be enough.

Every night, before bed he thought of his CIA set consultant who'd said over and over criminals operated almost completely in the open. There were so many layers of handlers and security, they touched almost nothing criminal themselves. The only viable court cases in the past century had involved money and on the spot seizures of contraband.

Since he'd now been all over the house and grounds and seen nothing that looked remotely like a secret cache of weapons, Quinn had decided to focus on money. At some point down the line, Lucas could be tied to transactions of illegal arms. It was just a question of figuring out who managed it for him. Then the

CIA could set up a trace, look at the right accounts, and build a case.

After breakfast, Lucas went up to his office for meetings and Quinn went to sit in his chair with a fresh stack of books that he rotated to lay open on his lap in case Lucas came out to check on him. Mostly, he lost time staring out the window, thinking of everything and nothing, straining his ears to listen.

What he heard had been ordinary. The kinds of things one expected a lobbyist to say to his on-site staffers in Washington the first day congress was back in session. The bills on the docket, holiday season gift deliveries so extravagant they made Quinn's head ache.

Outside, it was raining again. He took a picture of the gray scene through the window and sent it to Sid, but not Larisa because he hoped she was sleeping, and he knew a phone notification would wake her.

Quinn: How is she?

Sid: Sabrina or Larisa?

Sid: Haven't seen either.

He could hear Sid's rebuke through the silent phone. Why would he want Sid to keep track of the woman who'd been lying to him?

Quinn: Just say hi.

Sid: When are you coming back?

Quinn scrolled through his emails from the studio. Everything was still quiet for the holidays. But it wouldn't be long before he'd be missed. *The Key*'s London premiere was in three weeks. FilmStreams would make a decision on hiring him for *Poseidon*. All of it felt like another world, another life that belonged to a different man.

In the palazzo below, a door opened, then closed. The sound of it echoed down the cold stone walls of the first floor and came up to him just before a young woman walked into the square and approached a man who'd already come in without Quinn realizing it. The man had a round, soft body with a face hidden behind thick black hair and an even thicker beard. He wore a graphic T-shirt under a fitted black jacket in the European fashion, but when he spoke his English was American.

"Have a good vacation?" he asked with a knowing smirk.

"Rifat, you're still with us." The woman's English had an accent, maybe German. She wore Converse All Stars and short socks with a skintight black leather corset dress that came up and made a collar around her throat like a cheap BDSM costume someone might wear for Halloween.

"Whatever you've heard, it isn't true," said Rifat. "Most of it isn't true."

"I heard you took the boat out, drank too much, almost crashed."

Rifat laughed. "Did *you* do anything memorable?"

"Managed this problem." She jerked her chin upward toward Lucas's office door. "He needs to calm down. What's happening in LA could be good for him."

What's happening in LA? Quinn's ears burned.

"You have an agenda I should know about before we go in?" asked Rifat.

They started walking toward the stairs. Quinn pulled himself back into his chair and opened the book on Renaissance architecture he'd spent the past hour reading and rereading page one hundred, "The Art of the Villa Garden."

"It's not my job to make him reasonable," she said.

"But there's more on than the—" Rifat stopped midsentence. Quinn thought he must have seen Quinn sitting in the corner. They were almost in front of Lucas's office door. Close enough it seemed okay for Quinn to look up as though he'd just noticed them.

"He's running a little behind," he said. "Unless you're here to see me?" He looked at the woman hopefully. She laughed, much more embarrassed than a woman dressed like that should be.

"I'm here for Lucas." She looked to Rifat. "You?"

"Same."

"You better be quick," she said. "He'll be distracted once he knows I'm here."

"I'll wait, you be quick," said Rifat.

"I can't rush his process. Especially not today. I've been a very bad girl." When she saw Quinn wasn't the least embarrassed by her suggestion, she blushed.

"My mistress also doesn't like to rush," he said. "But sometimes she uses a Lexan, which obviously moves things along." He smiled. The woman blinked at him.

"You don't take the Lexan for him?" Quinn put on a sad face. "You're missing out." He gave her a closer look. "Or is it that you don't trust him? I get that."

Rifat laughed uncomfortably as the woman opened her mouth, then closed it, speechless. This was the moment Lucas swung open the door to his office and caught her blanched with embarrassment, Rifat laughing, and Quinn probably looking quite satisfied with himself as he withdrew back to his chair.

"Have a good time," he said without looking back to see if Lucas was watching him or his people.

And they were definitely his people—employees not friends. As soon as the office door closed again, Quinn stood and walked quietly to the door to listen. But there was nothing. He knew from all his hours sitting in his chair that Lucas's desk chair creaked when he leaned back in it and the wheels made a sound on the bare floor. He knew that even when speaking softly, there were things that could be heard, bodily movements, the occasional clear word rising from the hush. But there was nothing. Which meant they weren't only completely silent and standing still, but also that they were definitely not doing bondage.

So what were they doing?

He waited a few minutes more, ears straining, but there was nothing to hear. Were they using some kind of muffling device? A cone of silence? What would happen if he opened the office door? What would Lucas think if he just popped in to say how much he loved the wildness of Renaissance gardens? Quinn raised his hand to knock, then dropped it down to the doorknob. He'd just interrupt them.

Then a stray thought derailed him. Romanesque gardens were wild. The Renaissance wanted order and curated tranquility through repetition.

No, it was the English who let their gardens run wild.

Quinn felt his mind unraveling. He retreated from the door, walked quickly out of the library, down one long hallway, then another, around to the back of the villa, and down the stairs. He passed a room where every foot of the walls was covered by oil paintings, then another open space filled with gym equipment. He turned the corner and almost ran into Hannah as she came from the other direction.

"What are you doing over here?" she asked after she'd recovered from the surprise.

"Walking. What are you doing here?"

"You should walk outside."

"It's cold outside."

For a moment, Hannah looked ready to argue. But then she did a double take. "You look spooked."

"I just met Lucas's submissive."

"Jealous?"

But she's not his submissive. She's not anything like she's pretending to be.

I should have gotten her name. The name of her fake employer. Something.

Quinn cupped his hand over his mouth to try to slow down his breathing. A cold breeze was on his spine, like his shirt had been cut open and exposed his back to the air.

"Don't feel bad," said Hannah. "They circulate. He has like three or four come take care of his needs."

"How often?"

"Couple times a week? I tried to get into his office once during a session, but the bedroom's right off the office. It was too risky." She glanced at him as though aware she'd just made a clear admission of spying and wasn't sure what he'd think of it.

"And what about the guy, Rifat?"

"Rifat?"

"The big, hairy American."

Hannah looked uncertain. "That sounds like the baker's son. But he's from Iran. His family immigrated when he was a baby or something. One of the cooks told me."

Quinn knew they were talking about the same person, and maybe Hannah was hung up on subconscious racial bias, but the guy he'd met walked and talked like an American. Quinn couldn't shake the chill on his back, the wrongness of those two people. An Iranian baker's son who sounded like he was from Nebraska. A woman pretending to be a professional submissive who didn't know anything about Lexan canes. They'd been familiar with each other. They had mutual friends who gossiped about what they did on vacation.

They're part of the layers between him and his work.

"You look like you need to get out," said Hannah. "I'm taking a cooking class today. Come with me."

"I don't know how to cook."

"That's why it's a class, silly." She reached for his arm. Quinn jerked away. He didn't want to be touched by anyone except Larisa.

Larisa.

Larisa.

Larisa.

On the phone, she'd sounded like she was having a time of it, alone even though she was letting her friends in.

"We can go for cannoli afterward."

"I don't know what that is."

"You ate one after dinner last night."

What Quinn remembered from dinner was the way Lucas had watched him eat as though every mouthful was a test. He remembered the way his head swirled from the wine.

"I don't want to go out." *I need to stay and watch when those people leave. I need to think of questions to ask.*

"I'm offering because it's the specialty of a certain bakery, the name of which I'm sure we can find out if we walk by the kitchen on our way."

A bakery front operation, thought Quinn, certain that Larisa didn't know anything about it. Even if she'd given the CIA her information, they might not have enough. The bakery could be the key.

Quinn was elbow-deep in flour, worrying he was missing something important at the villa, when Hannah decided they were going to be friends.

"So, you and my cousin."

"Let's not."

"Come on. Forgive me already. I did it for a good cause." He attempted to imitate the chef's precise finger positions as he rolled potato dough for gnocchi. "Did you call her like I asked?"

"I can't blow my cover like that."

Strange thing to say. Quinn turned it over in his mind as he worked his dough. He couldn't think of any secret that would be ruined by Hannah managing to pick up the phone and call her cousin. It seemed the thing a decent person would do.

"Do you think Lucas brought you here as revenge or bait?" asked Hannah.

To Quinn's right, one half of a French couple had managed to make his gnocchi look exactly like the chef's. Quinn's looked like oversized larvae.

"I think its revenge," she said. "Lucas doesn't let anything go."

"Larisa didn't do anything to him."

"She left him." Hannah blinked at him like this was an obvious correlation. But when he didn't respond, she said, "You think bait? That means you're letting yourself be used to lure Larisa back to him."

"He's too smart to think that'd work."

"Maybe not permanently. But it would mean something if she came for you." Hannah mashed one of her gnocchi between her fingers. "And it would mean something if she didn't come."

Quinn swallowed down bile, the first true rush of gastric distress he'd had since he arrived. Of course Hannah would give voice to the question he was trying not to think about, like it was some easy thing with an easy answer.

I'm here so she doesn't have to be, he wanted to say. But that brought them too close to his mission. He certainly wasn't going to admit that he wanted Larisa with him, to guide him, hold him, make it feel like he'd done the right thing, tell him his way of seeing the world and doing his work had value even if Lucas thought otherwise.

I feel like I've left half my body behind. A thought he could've shared, but Hannah didn't deserve to know how lost he felt.

"I don't need saving." Quinn squinted at his gnocchi. Not perfect, but certainly better than Hannah's. "And she wouldn't come even if I did. I'm the one who left her, remember?"

"That's right. Christmas." As though it'd happened months ago. "You'd be a happier person if you forgave me."

"I'll forgive you when you go home and make things right with her."

"I can't go home until I get what I need." Hannah lowered her voice. "There's a cache of—"

Panic sizzled down Quinn's arms. "For fuck's sake, stop talking."

The chef glanced at them, then looked down at their gnocchi. He gave Quinn a thumbs up. The group moved on to the second stage of the meal, battering and frying eggplant for eggplant parmesan.

That's what she meant by cover. Quinn's breath caught in his chest. *She's working for the CIA. Because of course she is.*

Hannah didn't speak for the rest of the class, and she didn't speak while they ate the fruits of their labor. Quinn could feel her stewing like the world's most dangerous irate teenager. For whatever reason, she believed she'd been baptized with a mission to undermine Lucas, and she was going about it like she was invincible.

"I enjoyed that," said Quinn when they walked out of the culinary school. "Thank you for inviting me."

"Oh, am I allowed to talk now?"

"You're going to tell me you're working for the CIA. They want you to find some evidence of Lucas's work, then you call in and report it to them and wait for instructions."

"How did you know that?"

"Art imitates life more often than you'd think."

"I'm doing what Larisa refused to do."

Quinn could have slapped her for the self-righteous judgement in her voice. "Ever think she had good reasons?"

"Selfish ones." Hannah shrugged. "If I die, at least it'll be for justice."

Quinn considered saying no one who loved Hannah would care about her reasons when she was dead. He certainly wouldn't say that the chances of her sacrifice making a difference were minimal. Instead, he said, "Let's go look at this bakery."

"It's across the river."

They'd taken a hired car to the school. Quinn couldn't

remember seeing any of the city pass by as he stared out the window trying to comb through the jumble of his thoughts about Rifat and the fake submissive. Now, he tried to calm himself down by paying attention so he could give Lucas a report that would prove he was capable of really seeing the way Lucas seemed to think was vital for a full life.

They walked across a bridge to the north side of the Arno River, then turned left and walked along the river several blocks. The clouds in the river's horizon were pink and orange, hiding the sunset from full view. All around them, Italians went about their lives, walking, scootering, sitting out at al fresco tables in winter coats, and gloves, and hats.

They turned a corner and walked up a street made narrow by the lines of cars parked along both sides of the curb. The street opened into a piazza with an antique carousel in the center.

"This is the Piazza della Repubblica, the oldest part of Florence. In the—"

"There's the bakery." Quinn nodded across the piazza to a sign half hidden behind the carousel.

"Lucas is right, you're kind of a brick, aren't you?"

"He's talking to you about me?"

"I just happened to be in the kitchen when he was explaining to the cook about your food limitations and all that."

All what? Quinn hadn't noticed that what he'd been eating had been remarkably different than anyone else. He'd tried more new food since he'd arrived than he'd tried in all of his life combined. *I'm not fussy,* he thought. *Is that what he thinks?* A dim rumble of anxiety rippled through his core. If Lucas thought of him as someone to manage, how was Quinn ever going to break through Lucas's walls?

The golden posts of the carousel spun by in a blur. He wondered if it was the kind of thing Larisa would enjoy. Sometime they might ride one together. He would stand beside her, holding the pole while she rode a horse that went up and down. With each rotation of the carousel, she'd rise up over him, then dip back down, and perhaps gift him a kiss before the horse carried her up again.

There's a future for us, he thought. *I'm going to make one.*

"Are you crying?" asked Hannah.

Quinn pressed on toward the bakery. There were only a few people inside. The air smelled like sugar and warm butter. The woman behind the display case looked just like Rifat, with the same rounded body type and a mass of long black hair pulled back in a braid. He glanced around without knowing what he expected to find. It appeared like a regular bakery, serving pastries and sweets he recognized from the dessert course of Lucas's dinners.

The woman took Hannah's order for two cannoli. She didn't smile or say anything besides reciting the price in heavily accented English. Not a sign of anything significant. Quinn thought he'd heard somewhere that it wasn't customary for service workers in Europe to act like their customers were their friends. So there was nothing noteworthy except that Rifat had grown up in America not Italy. And maybe his parents were bakers, but he was something else.

They sat at a table off the piazza and ate the cannoli.

"What do you think?" asked Hannah.

"How are you supposed to contact the CIA?"

"It's easy. When I take a walk, I leave a note at the shrine on the road by Umbras. Then I wait two days and come down to Santa Croce to pray. He meets me there for mass at five o'clock." She took a bite and chewed. "I'm actually going today. Want to come?"

"I'm not religious."

"Too bad. It'll save your life."

"Look, don't tell him about the bakery."

"Why not? Don't you think it's suspicious?"

"You shouldn't take the risk."

"Fine. Whatever. Can you get back to the villa on your own? Great."

"Hannah, I'm serious."

"This was fun."

She waved as she walked away. Quinn almost followed her. Part of him couldn't believe she'd been recruited by the CIA, the other part of him thought it was genius, if only the stakes were lower, and she was a little bit smarter.

She could ruin things for me.

Too late to worry about that.

He watched the carousel turn and observed the people who came in and out of the bakery. In November, in that shitty hotel room in Anaheim, Larisa had said all the evidence in the world didn't matter if you couldn't use it without knowing you'd be looking over your shoulder every day for the rest of your life.

He understood now that she'd been rattled by Lucas's appearance at the junket in New York because she'd never expected to see him again. His arrival had violated not just their agreement, but her trust in the bubble of safety she'd built with her vow of silence.

What did Quinn think he could do in three weeks? He could already feel the buildup of stress in his body wearing him down, making him less aware, less alert in his head even as his body coiled around itself like a winding spring. He needed to get home before it snapped.

I shouldn't have come, thought Quinn. *I can't do this any better than she could.*

Chapter 14

Dinner with Candles

Larisa had said his limitations were a secret power, that he knew how to stay within his limits. But Quinn couldn't help but think of her words as a backhanded compliment. No person wanted to have limits. And who wanted to be praised for their ability to not take risks or test themselves? Somewhere in the back of his mind, he knew what she'd really been saying was, *Be careful. Don't lose yourself.*

The problem was Quinn needed to prove himself to Lucas. Not quite assert dominance, nothing so overtly masculine as that, but something that was the equivalent of putting his foot down and demanding respect. That was the only way Lucas was going to leave them alone.

This thought surprised Quinn. He'd been thinking like Larisa, that an arrest, some kind of legal intervention, was the answer to removing Lucas from their lives, but Quinn no longer believed that would be enough. Even from prison, Lucas would find a way to reach them if he still believed he had a right to do so.

Quinn wasn't sure how long he'd been sitting and watching the carousel as his thoughts circled before a shadow crossed his vision in the shape of a familiar silhouette, Lucas in riding boots and a matching jacket even though there wasn't a real horse in sight.

"You found me." Quinn lifted his gaze as he licked powdered sugar off his fingers.

"They didn't feed you at the cooking class?"

"This was Hannah's idea." Quinn set his hand on his swollen belly. "I've ruined dinner."

"Dinner can wait. You're in one of the most famous squares in the entire world and all you've done is watch wooden horses spin in an endless circle." Lucas motioned for Quinn to stand. "Walk with me."

Quinn braced himself for a history lesson on the significance of the piazza. Instead, Lucas led him out to the main street where they walked crunched together on the narrow, uneven sidewalk past old buildings with modern storefronts that still looked older than most of the nice neighborhoods in LA.

"How was your session?" asked Quinn.

"Hmm?"

"With that woman, the submissive."

A wicked grin creased Lucas's hard mouth. "You want the details?"

Quinn shrugged.

"I laid her over the end of the bed with her hair up on top of her head, wrists in a brace on her waist, and red satin all around."

Quinn waited for more, the instrument used, the way the woman moaned as her climax gathered momentum. Instead, Lucas motioned ahead of them to direct Quinn's attention. "This is Piazza della Signoria. Over there, you have the Medici house of government that was also a fortified palace in its time. People were always trying to throw them out or have them assassinated." A pause, as though Lucas was contemplating how it would feel to live knowing people wanted to assassinate him.

"And this way, you have the Neptune fountain, and just to the right you can stand on the exact location where a corrupt friar, Girolamo Savonarola, was hanged. This used to be execution square, lots of blood under these stones." Lucas moved them forward to a covered archway built out from the edge of the square.

"These are the statues of the Loggia dei Lanzi. Since you're learning about architecture, you might notice these are

Corinthian capitals at the top of the columns. The statues are all remarkable in their own way, especially if you're one for mythology."

Of all the statues and their surprising variety of subtle and not so subtle violence, the one that most held Quinn's attention was three people in a white stone that looked like alabaster but was certainly something stronger. The figures were twisted together, frozen for eternity in a contortion of agony for the viewing public. The female figure, lifted above the first male, had one hand braced against him, the other hand extended out into the air, grasping for help that would never come. Below the invading man, a second male figure, bent to his knees and cowered, shielding his eyes from the female's destruction.

Of all the things that could inspire art, thought Quinn.

"What do you feel?" asked Lucas.

I would like you to meet your end as one of these statues. Trapped forever, able to see, but never touch.

It felt like a story idea a younger version of himself would've written down and tried to develop.

"You don't have to make something up." Lucas sounded tired. "At this point, I know even the pinnacle of human beauty fails to move you. Not that you care, but this is a marble by Giovanni de Bologna titled, *The Abduction of a Sabine Woman.* It was inspired by a Roman creation story about Romulus and his belief that if Rome was going to become a great civilization, it needed women to increase the population. So his men went to a neighboring village and put babies in all the women so they'd no longer be suitable to the local men."

"Something to celebrate." Quinn felt a whisper of dread in his gut. Was Lucas trying to send a message that he knew Quinn was spying on him?

"You can at least appreciate the strategy."

"I appreciate living in a less ruthless world."

"We could do with a little more of it." Quinn heard the twinge of a threat in Lucas's voice, or perhaps it was just a hint toward the violence that always lurked there, a coiled snake Quinn had yet to see lash out. He hoped he didn't stick around long enough to see just how much Lucas enjoyed imitating historic conquests.

They walked back down the river and strolled the sidewalk the way he and Hannah had come. After a few paces, Lucas linked his arm through Quinn's and they walked as the Italians walked, arm and arm for an evening passeggiata. Quinn managed not to flinch at the familiar touch and told himself he was safe here in public. They were just walking.

Don't self-sabotage.

"You mentioned Laxen caning to my friend."

"As a joke."

"I'm surprised Larisa would take a Laxen to you. With no cushion on those bones, she'd rip the skin right off."

"She doesn't. I was just trying to rile her up."

"So you've done research of your own."

"In the beginning, I read a lot. I was trying to convince my girlfriend it could be a good thing for us."

"Parish."

Quinn hated the way Lucas said her name, like she was a small thing, as inconsequential to Lucas as he assumed she was to Quinn.

"And now you know Rifat is my baker's son."

"Hannah told me."

"We had some accounts to settle today."

Quinn wondered why Lucas was bothering to explain Rifat's visit. The weight of Lucas's arm around his seemed to be growing, the press of Quinn's arm into Lucas's side more insistent. Or it all could just as easily have been his imagination.

"I admit I'm surprised," said Lucas. "Of all the things that would spark your interest."

"Lots of things spark my interest." Quinn said this with enough sarcasm he expected Lucas to laugh, but Lucas seemed to miss the offering. This was a serious conversation. Quinn realized he didn't know if they were talking about the bakery or BDSM.

"What else? Name something that isn't related to your work. One thing that you've taken upon yourself to study and indulge in."

Quinn watched the river flow by. He thought of Larisa, who believed in him so fully and yet felt like she had to protect him. He'd been angry she'd kept the baby a secret from him. And yet now, somehow, it also felt like the most beautiful kindness. In a world full of cruelty, Larisa was the person who stood in the gap and risked everything to try to make things easier for other people.

"You can't do it, can you?" said Lucas. "So, what was it about bondage?"

It wasn't bondage, thought Quinn. *It was Larisa. I wanted Larisa, and that was a way to reach her.*

"I used to write," said Quinn finally.

"Those stories in your notebook."

"I would get so involved I'd be late for work. I wouldn't do my homework."

"This is an extension of your interest in film." Lucas sounded disappointed. "And it comes with the same root problem. How can you tell a great story if your world is so small?"

"Well, it's not small anymore, is it? I know what it's like to walk arm in arm with the man who . . ."

Man who what? In Quinn's peripheral vision, he saw Lucas's lips doing that twitching thing, a smile that also felt like an insult marring his stunning, self-possessed beauty as he glowed in the late-afternoon sun. *He's killed people,* Quinn reminded himself, as though to hold this thought up as armor against what else he was noticing.

"Who what?" asked Lucas.

"Who knows so much about everything he'll always outclass me," said Quinn.

"A more interesting answer would've been, 'A man who walks arm in arm with his girlfriend's lover.' And perhaps you're thinking how far you'll go with this little dance we're doing. You've begun to think about how you might push me into that oncoming car or poison my breakfast."

"I won't do that until I have the answer to my question."

"What question is that?"

"You know." Quinn's eyes tracked a Fiat coming toward them, and for a moment considered if pushing Lucas out in front of it might solve most of his problems. "It's also your question, isn't it? Who am I to her?"

"Ah, that question." Lucas laughed softly. "It's a moot point. You'll never be to her what I am."

Quinn's throat tightened with the old dread. He felt the pressure of all those long November evenings with Larisa trying to figure out how they were going to be together, what his role in her life could be. He'd longed for her to condemn him for being mediocre, for not doing more with himself, for not being interesting the way she was.

A true submissive would've admitted his shame, asked to be punished for his failing to live up to the glory of his predecessor. Was that what Lucas expected? Quinn had no idea, but he wasn't in the mood to play that game. He was tired of accepting this man's judgement like his opinion was the only one that mattered.

"You're right, I can't replace you. Larisa will never be afraid of me like she is of you."

Lucas withdrew his arm from Quinn's. He strode ahead several paces, back hunched as though braced against Quinn's gaze. Quinn watched the hard line of those shoulders rise and fall with exaggerated force. Then they went still; he turned and faced Quinn.

"If she fears me, she knows it's for a good reason. She'll finally be shocked into realizing what a waste of life and God-given talent you are."

Quinn stopped still in surprise. The venom in Lucas's voice spoke of a man who lived one step away from unleashing rage, but there was something else. It overrode Quinn's sense of self-preservation. Lucas had paid him a compliment. "You think I have talent."

"That's not what I said."

"It's exactly what you said."

For a moment Lucas looked confused, then irritated. "You have no idea how much you bother me."

Now Quinn was grinning. "If you'd like to complain, I'm happy to—"

Lucas closed the distance between them and planted a kiss on Quinn's lips. A darting step forward, then a retreat so fast it almost didn't register until after, as Lucas stood before him frowning. The kiss had seemed to shock him as much as it did Quinn.

Quinn's lips felt like they'd been lit on fire. He raised a tentative hand to touch them. "I'm very confused right now."

"I agree. Don't expect that to happen again." Lucas turned and began to continue down the sidewalk, then he stopped and turned back again. "We're going to have dinner tonight."

"Differently than the other nights we've had dinner?"

"Just the two of us. I'm cooking."

A car was summoned. It took them to a pasta shop where Lucas apparently knew the owner, then on to the Mercato Centrale for produce and dried apricots, and finally to Lucas's macellaio di fiducia (fancy Italian butcher) before they wound up the long street out of the city and into the hills to the villa. By the time they arrived, the house was empty. The staff had been given the night off. The botanist's lecture moved to the following week.

In the kitchen, Lucas planted Quinn on a stool on the receiving side of the central island and donned an apron. A throaty jazz singer crooned broken-hearted standards from invisible speakers. Quinn watched as Lucas set up his prep station like a master chef, then set water to boil. He began with his spices. Sprigs of this and that cut from the plants lining the window. Something else from a jar, ground up under a pestle.

"You can talk while I work," said Lucas.

"About all the things I'm insufficiently interested in?" asked Quinn. He meant it as a joke, but it came out sounding bitter, a cover for his jumpy nerves and the heat of that riverside kiss that still hadn't entirely died away.

It was just a kiss, he thought.

But it felt like everything had changed. He was no longer in a house filled with people who might save him from Lucas's attention with an unexpected interruption. They were alone. Before, they'd been playing the roles of sparring adversaries. Now, it felt vitally important for Quinn to hold on to the resentment he'd been nourishing in response to Lucas's critiques so he wouldn't forget the demanding, judgmental Lucas he knew, who was somehow the same man standing on the other side of the island tapping a spoon to his chin.

"How does it feel to have your new film out in the world?"

For the first time since they'd met, an entirely ordinary question, one that felt like an invitation instead of a trap. And for the first time since they'd met, an answer came easily. "It's horrible," said Quinn. "And wonderful. Both at the same time, every day."

Lucas turned to check the water. He waved his spoon in the air to indicate that Quinn should continue.

And continue he did. As Larisa had astutely pointed out that fall, when Quinn found himself with a captive audience, and the freedom to talk about his work, all his social anxiety faded, his awkwardness smoothed into passion. He talked about how irritating reporters were asking the same questions over and over, how everyone wanted to know about Dansby and Quinn kept having to lie about how great it was to work with him because the kid didn't deserve to be roasted. He talked about Steve Helston giving him unsolicited advice about backing off the location shoot for *Poseidon,* but Quinn didn't feel he could back off because he had no interest in making a green screen movie and spending half his year in front of a computer trying to match shadows and lighting.

And maybe he used his hands to illustrate what he was saying.

And maybe his voice changed pitch in his animation. And he realized that in all the chaos of the past few months, there hadn't been any time to sit with the fact that he'd released a big movie and people mostly seemed to like it.

They ate the meal Lucas had prepared at the kitchen table with short, fat candles set into rustic wooden holders.

"Any day now, I'll hear if they accepted my revised budget for *Poseidon*. And it's like, I could do it and I think it would be great. But it's such a tired franchise. An obvious money grab, right? Why not teach people to like something new? There are stories being published every day with new ideas about what characters can do and better diversity and less ugly brawn. All you'd need is a large marketing budget and a good hook."

"Ugly brawn," repeated Lucas with a quirk of his eyebrow.

"You know what I mean."

"I'd actually be interested to hear your treatise on the male form."

"Not while we're eating." Quinn's portion of the food had been small, and he'd managed to eat all the veal steak with seared baby potatoes, beets and greens, but he'd also been focused on talking and not eating. Now he realized dinner was over and the next step was coming. He suddenly felt an uncomfortable fullness in his stomach.

"Come." Lucas led Quinn up to the second floor, through the office to a curtain on the far wall. Lucas drew it aside to reveal an archway into his bedroom, a surprisingly stark, modern room with an ebony furniture set and white tile floors.

No bondage brackets, thought Quinn as Lucas led him over to the bathroom suite. There was a closet that rivalled Larisa's, and a second closet of foldout shelves made specifically for jewelry, scarves, hats, and shoes.

"You don't need to be afraid," said Lucas.

Is that true? Quinn tried to arrange his face so whatever it had looked like that made Lucas try to comfort him was gone. He stood still as Lucas came up behind him, ran a slow hand along his shoulders, then down his spine.

I'm not ready for this, thought Quinn. *I can't fake this.*

But this was what he'd been waiting for. Lucas had finally crossed whatever line he'd drawn and decided to invest himself. Quinn couldn't back out now. He shifted his weight, adjusted his feet in his shoes like a boxer preparing for a match. Not that Quinn knew anything about boxing.

"Do your feet still hurt?" asked Lucas.

"I shouldn't have done all that walking with Hannah today."

"These Italian winters are difficult." Lucas disappeared around the corner to the jacuzzi tub set up against a window that looked toward Florence. He turned on the faucets. "I take a bath every night." He poured a bath salt mixture into the water that filled their air with pungent lavender. He returned to Quinn. "Will you allow me to undress you?"

"Why don't you watch instead?" Quinn unbuttoned the top of his shirt. When he saw Lucas fix his eyes on Quinn's posed hand, he moved down to the next. He knew he wasn't sexy. He would never be that person. But he knew that if the idea of desire was already in someone's mind, all one had to do was exploit it.

He kept his eyes on Lucas's face while Lucas's eyes followed Quinn's hands as they released the front of his shirt one button at a time. He felt absolutely ridiculous turning undressing into a performance, but as long as Lucas wore that bright gleam of desire in his eyes, how Quinn felt didn't matter. He threw the shirt at Lucas's chest as he walked past him to the tub.

"Hairy little thing, aren't you?" laughed Lucas. "Larisa doesn't make you take care of that back?"

"She likes it." Which was true as far as Quinn knew. They'd never discussed any of the hair below his neck. When they'd been in bed together Larisa sometimes toyed with it, ran her fingers through it. He hadn't felt self-conscious about it until now.

Shoes off. Quinn unbuttoned his jeans. Like a pinup girl in a film from a bygone era, Quinn bent over and wiggled his ass as he pushed down the jeans. His heart roared in his ears, skin prickling as it combed the air for sudden movement, warning him that Lucas was going to come up behind him.

But Lucas stayed back, and Quinn slid into the tub without being touched or the scrutiny of full-frontal nudity.

The water was delicious. Quinn lay back and closed his eyes, not quite as relaxed as he was pretending, but still, it felt amazing. The jets at the far end of the tub lined up with his calves. He tilted his knees inward so the broad side of the muscle felt the full pulse of the water. He thought, *When we get a house, we should have a bath like this. After a session, Larisa will bring me here and do her thing with the massage oils, then she'll put me in the tub and bring me sparkling water and Advil and remind me that nothing's ever as bad as I think it is.*

Larisa.

Why didn't I tell her I loved her?

Lucas sat down on the tiled counter at the edge of the tub with his back to the wall. "I think you should write something."

"Write something?"

"Not anything like those stories about your dad leaving and your mom's work. You're past all that. Maybe the sea people story. But better."

Lucas talking about his writing sent a thrill through Quinn's chest. He found himself leaning toward Lucas, wanting more, hungry for words that felt almost like compliments. But Lucas didn't give him anything else. Almost as though he knew what Quinn wanted and withheld it on purpose.

"I don't have time to write," said Quinn.

"That sounds exactly like something a writer would say."

I'm not a writer.

But Lucas thought he could be. The promise of it felt so true, so solid in his gut. Quinn couldn't tell if he felt this way because Lucas had such high-minded ideals that when he said a person should be something, they ought to listen, or if he'd been secretly nourishing the idea for himself and not dared let it out into the open.

When Quinn's skin had pruned and his muscles turned into soft dough, he climbed out of the tub. Lucas held a bathrobe up for him and gave Quinn a hand out of the tub. *Strong hands*, thought Quinn. *Capable of anything.* Even after he had both feet solid on the floor, Quinn waited a beat longer than necessary to release Lucas's helping hand. Lucas didn't seem to notice.

"You'll want to go to bed now, but it's the worst thing for your skin to go to bed damp." Lucas went to his vanity cabinet and selected two bottles of what looked like lotion.

No. One was a lubricant.

Quinn swallowed.

From a drawer in his armoire, Lucas pulled out a satin bag. He unzipped it, checked the contents, then zipped it back up with the two bottles added.

"Tonight, you'll do a full body coat of the moisturizer. And you're going to start preparing yourself with the smallest of these plugs. Let me know when you move up."

A shiver ran down Quinn's spine. "Preparing for what?"

"If I still feel this way about you in a week, we'll move forward." Lucas began to lead the way back through the bedroom and out to the office.

"What if you don't feel this way?"

"I will be disappointed. You won't like me disappointed." Lucas paused to pluck a sweaty strand of hair from Quinn's forehead and tuck it back, his expression unreadable.

"I want to please you." Quinn prayed he sounded sincere.

"Why would you want to please me?"

It was a question without an answer. Quinn scrambled for a distraction. The lights were off in the office, but there was enough moonlight coming in to see where they were going. Quinn's eyes landed on the framed photos of Larisa on Quinn's desk.

"I want to please you because I've seen how well you love someone who pleases you."

Lucas followed Quinn's gaze. "That was taken in Vienna our first New Year's together. We danced the whole night."

"Can I ask you something?"

Lucas cocked his head, waiting.

"Why her?"

"You wish I'd never met her?"

I think she sometimes wishes she'd never met you.

"Believe it or not, I knew I'd have her from the moment we met. A beautiful girl who looked so sophisticated, had all the right values, but she'd never been taught how to think or how to listen to her desires. She was starving to be seen. I gave her everything she ever wanted and more."

"And in return she loved you better than anyone else."

Lucas shrugged. "I'm not sentimental."

Like fuck you aren't, thought Quinn. He followed Lucas out of the office and down the stairs. At the door of Quinn's bedroom, they paused. *Does he expect a kiss good night?* Quinn clutched the satin purse to his chest, pushing the rim of the bathrobe up almost to his neck.

"I hope you had a good night," said Lucas.

"I did."

"It's strange, I can't tell what you think. You're so . . . blank. I thought that was the real you, but it isn't, is it? You're just very good at hiding." He reached out his hand with fingers spread and grazed it over Quinn's face as though to pull away an unseen mask. "Someday, I'm going to tie you up so you're completely at my mercy and strip everything you think you are away. What will be left?"

"Nothing anyone would want." Quinn reached behind his back to open his door and backed into his room.

After he'd closed it, Quinn stood still and caught his breath. The shadows in the line of light under his door told him Lucas remained standing in the hallway. Quinn worried he'd follow him in. But after one agonizing moment, then another, Lucas sighed and walked away.

It occurred to Quinn he had no reason to think there weren't cameras in his room. A frightening but useful thought he wished he'd had when he'd first arrived. He went into the bathroom and closed the door. He felt up some of the paneling, looked at the lights, and decided the bathroom was probably safe. He opened the purse Lucas had given him and unpacked it. The lotion he would use as instructed because it was the most obvious thing Lucas would notice if he didn't.

But the rest—the lubricant and four butt plugs of various sizes—he was already wondering how long he could get away with pretending to use them. If Larisa had offered him this challenge it would've been exciting, a little scary, yes, but a good scary. They would've explored together. But not one part of him wanted to prepare his anus for Lucas, to put his softest self in the hands of that man.

The strong confidence of Lucas's hand helping Quinn out of the tub.

The way the candlelight had played across Lucas's face during dinner.

His voice, which allowed no space for argument even when it seemed gentle.

Quinn stared at his reflection in the mirror and told himself he wasn't falling for Lucas. But almost as soon as he managed to fix that thought in his head, a second one swallowed it. *Some parts of him are wonderful.*

A sharp shake of his head. *He doesn't respect anyone. He's not safe.*

Around and around, the warring thoughts. Quinn worked the moisturizer over his body and tried to see it as Lucas saw it. With exceptional paleness that contrasted almost comically with his dark hair, he'd never enjoyed looking at himself. One of Sid's younger sisters was still teased for her childhood error of calling Quinn the hairy ghost. He'd done his best to ignore it whenever possible. But with Lucas, his inadequacies took on a new form. Quinn's body had become a thing that had to be conditioned and prepared. It was not good enough on its own, and it couldn't be ignored.

After the moisturizer, Quinn put on his nightshirt, locked the bedroom door, and went to the bed instead of the floor by the window. He tried to look relaxed as he settled in and turned off the lamp. In the darkness, sleep eluded him. Scenes from the day scattered across his vision, fractures of conversation. Hannah and her carelessness. Lucas's kiss. The bath. Being in Lucas's bedroom.

No brackets for bondage, he thought for the hundredth time. No sounds in the office when Rifat and that woman had been with Lucas.

If Larisa had been there, she would've already figured out the mystery. She would already know everything there was to know because she didn't hold back once she set her mind on something. She wouldn't have been scared of Lucas wanting her.

But that's not true, is it?

At some point, she stopped trusting him. He did things that taught her to be afraid.

Quinn's phone vibrated. He expected a message from Larisa. If it'd been her, he might have asked where she and Lucas had played out their scenes, but then, he didn't really want to give her reason to think about that. It was hard enough for him to think of her in the submissive role, surrendering to Lucas's whims.

Sid: Talk time?

Quinn considered saying no. His mind wasn't in a space to talk to anyone. But then his phone was ringing, and his friend's voice filled his ear.

"You get my messages?"

Quinn pulled his phone up to his face to look at his notifications. Five texts from Sid. A belated Happy New Year from Dansby.

"It's been busy."

"Busy with what? You're on vacation in a foreign country."

He kissed me.

"Have you heard anything from FilmStreams?"

"Not yet. Eddie's assistant has been after me about the London schedule. You're going, right?"

"Yes?" Quinn looked at his phone calendar. "Yes," he said with more confidence. Good, *The Key*'s London premiere would give him a hard deadline. Whatever this was with Lucas, he'd need to end it by then.

"Great. You having a good time with Larisa's ex?" The tone of Sid's voice told Quinn everything he needed to know about how Sid felt about it. Mostly jealous that he'd been left behind while Quinn went off on what looked like an all-expenses paid adventure.

"It's something."

"Uh huh. What do you want me to tell Larisa if I see her?"

"I thought you weren't interested in seeing her."

"I wasn't. But she was making the rounds online today, a new meme, kinda clever, anyway. A radio show guy was using her as a punching bag. And I'm worried she'll forget to feed Sabrina."

"Will you send it to me?"

"Yeah. So, when are you coming back? Like next week or right before London or . . .?"

"Soon. I gotta figure some things out."

Holding On

The enthusiasm of her sisters didn't penetrate the dense fog that had taken up residence in her brain. She didn't know how long it'd been, only that it'd been too long and Pam should've contacted her by now with some update. It didn't matter how many times she told herself Quinn and Hannah were alright, or how many times she looked around the apartment, now empty of Ana, and tried to comfort herself with the reminder that the girl's absence meant things were going well.

All she felt was dread. Deep, impenetrable, inescapable dread.

"Would you please put your phone away?"

Teale was frostier than she'd been the day before. Larisa felt she should know why, but the answer eluded her. Not that she'd tried very hard to find it. Funny thing about waiting to hear from an arms dealer if the information you gave her ended up leading to another arms dealer's secret weapons cache was that very little else mattered. This included the live stream discussion Larisa was supposed to lead that night on the themes brought up in her first

Rumpus blog post about BDSM. Larisa barely remembered writing the blog post. She hadn't even managed to read it when it'd gone live.

She set aside her phone. "What am I talking about again?"

Teale jabbed a finger at the piece of paper covered in text that sat on the keyboard of Larisa's laptop. Instead of reaching for it, Larisa watched the feed of the laptop's camera shift and shudder as Teale adjusted the angle so the side of Sabrina's tower would be out of frame.

"This is the introduction session. You talk a little about what bondage is and what it isn't. You answer people's questions."

"They're going to call with questions?"

"No, they'll be there in the chat box. Haven't you ever done a live stream before?"

"Not one I was controlling." Larisa made a face.

"Sorry. Bad reminder." Teale paused as though she felt a placeholder was needed for polite acknowledgement. "It's only an hour. You hit the high points from the essay, then see what people want to know."

Larisa navigated to her browser and pulled up the blog post. "Wow. This is—hang on. Did you write this?"

"I tried to tell you yesterday. What you gave me wasn't the right approach. We had a deadline, so I just did it."

A defensive, auto-response pulled itself together in Larisa's mind: *My boyfriend left me for my ex. And I'm kind of in the middle of sabotaging an international criminal mastermind.*

Larisa reached for her phone to look at her history of messages with Teale. *Have I really been that out of it?*

Today was Thursday.

Next Thursday was Rosa's due date.

On Monday, Larisa had a session scheduled with her client Anastacia. Tuesday, another client, then a meeting with her own therapist, Dr. Bade. When had she scheduled that session? She only remembered thinking it was too bad Dr. Bade was still on vacation.

It'd been two days since she'd called Pam and given her the coordinates for Lucas's private island.

For lunch she'd had . . .

"Focus," said Teale. "You're on in three minutes."

"I'm sorry you had to write it." Larisa scanned through the essay. "It looks good. I mean, not how I said things, but . . ."

"You wrote it like an academic paper with sources from academic journals and scientists talking about brain chemistry and shit."

Larisa frowned. "When did I send that to you?"

"Look, it's fine. I know you're stressed."

"I'm not stressed."

Teale gave her a considering look. "Remind me why you're doing this."

"You told me it was a good idea."

"You always do what people tell you?"

Mostly, thought Larisa. She couldn't tell if Teale was complimenting or judging her. Wasn't it a good thing to make things easy for people? When she was younger, her mother had always been telling her to not make waves. Thinking of her mother gave Larisa a sour feeling, another thing her brain knew but had buried. Was she fighting with her mother?

Larisa sensed Teale's frustration building, so she came up with a different answer. "I want to be part of the conversation instead of the subject of the conversation."

"Good. If someone says something stupid in the chat, count to seven before you respond, alright?"

"I think I can do that."

"And look into the camera, not at your screen when you're talking. People will feel more connected to you that way."

Teale swiped a nervous hand through the hair that had previously been blue but was now tri-color stripes of three different shades of red. Not the most polished look for an LA publicist, but maybe that's what Larisa liked about her.

"I'm really sorry," Larisa said, and she meant it.

"It's time to go on. I'll be back here out of view to keep Sabrina away. Push that little red Stream Now button, then wait a bit before you start talking."

Larisa set the sheet of notes Teale had written against her screen so she could read while looking at the camera.

The first part was easy. She introduced herself. Maybe she used the overly bright, peppy version of Larisa who'd played for the opening of her adolescent reality show. But if so, that was okay, it translated well. She wanted to look cheerful and upbeat while talking about leather, whipping, and submissive slaves. It was harder than it should've been keeping up her peppy self. Just talking was a struggle. She wanted to check her phone, then she wanted to just take a break for a nap. Teale had written so many words.

After the introduction, she moved into the definitional part, talking as though her audience were Martians who might've gotten the wrong idea by watching Earth TV, which was an absurd analogy because bondage would never hit mainstream TV in Larisa's lifetime. This led her to the novel she'd read that everyone seemed to be talking about. She gave a summary of the book, then asked people to mention in the chat if they'd read it.

The chat that'd previously been silent, began to ping with responses from viewers. The messages came so fast Larisa didn't have time to read them.

"So, a lot of people have read it." Larisa laughed. "That's why we're here, right? We read it, and now we want more. For the next five weeks, I'm going to—"

Someone was knocking on her front door.

Ana? The mixture of reactions that flooded Larisa's brain caused her to momentarily lose track of what she was saying. Behind her, she heard Teale's panicked footsteps rushing to answer before the knocking became prolonged.

Focus, if it's Ana, you'll deal with it after this is done.

"Together, we're going to explore the world of BDSM, and how it can be part of your life even if all you ever do is read books.

If you read that book and felt something, there's no shame in that. There's nothing wrong with you. You're not any more violent than the rest of us, or any more a woman under patriarchy than any others."

The responses in the chat had slowed down enough that a divergent comment caught Larisa's eye. "User IlMagnificoXX asks: 'How did I get involved with bondage, and what role did I play?'"

Larisa pretended to think about the question as she listened to the soft whooshing of her apartment door opening and closing.

"I first tried bondage in a private session with a hired dom on a romance-themed train that's sadly defunct. It didn't actually excite me right away. I thought it was boring and showy. And it's true that there's a lot of performance in BDSM. It's a sex act that engages the mind and the imagination in ways other sex acts don't. It also takes a lot of practice. I kept doing it because I was searching for something. Eventually, I became comfortable enough, and I trusted my partner enough, that it was the only thing I wanted to do."

Larisa peeked at the chat.

"User SunshineDarling asks: 'How do I know I can trust my partner?' That's a really big question. I think it's the most important one. If you've encountered people who're focused on what they get out of playing a scene with you, or someone who's careless with your body, those are big red flags. One of the biggest things people misunderstand about bondage is that the submissive is the one with the power. They're the ones whose pleasure is most important, and a good dominant is going to put their pleasure first."

Several more comments appeared in the chat at the same time. Two of them from IlMagnificoXX. She read, "And when a submissive most wants to please a dom, they take whatever they're given. The best submissive has no limits."

Whatever Larisa was saying, it stopped. Several seconds passed as she sat still, mouth slightly open, wordless as her brain struggled to put itself back on track.

Somewhere behind her laptop, her phone vibrated with a new message. She wanted to reach for it, to hide behind the need to see who was talking to her. But she held still, she sat with the chill until it faded, and kept a smile on her face.

"Lots of good thoughts in the chat. I'd just like to emphasize that BDSM isn't about violence, it's about pleasure. If you fall for someone who makes you feel unsafe, don't tell yourself that's how it's supposed to work. It isn't.

"Next week, we're going to talk about ways you and a partner can dabble in bondage, and we're going to talk about role-playing in more detail. My post about this will be on *The Rumpus* next Monday. I think we have time for one more question. Let me look here."

IlMagnificoXX: The purest pain comes when it is taken, not given.

Larisa hit the red button to cut off the live stream. The chat froze. She read the last message over.

The apartment door opened. Teale bustled in with her hands raised for high fives. Behind her, looking embarrassed, was Sid. Larisa pulled her phone out from behind her laptop but didn't unlock the screen.

If that's what he's saying in public. What did he send to my phone?

A picture, thought Larisa. *He's sent me a picture of Quinn like he did before. But it'll be worse this time.*

She unlocked her phone screen.

Rosa: What's this about bondage on a train?

Jaden: I thought you met Lucas in Italy.

Krissy: ROSA HAVING CONTRACTIONS.

Jaden: She got hot and bothered listening to you talk about feeling things.

Kahleah: We're leaving for the hospital. Join when you can.

Nothing from Lucas.

"What's wrong?" asked Teale. "I thought that was great, except for the creepy person who's clearly an example of someone to avoid."

"That was my ex, Lucas. Hi, Sid. How have you been?"

"I didn't know you had an ex named Lucas," said Teale. "From when?"

"College. We can talk about it later. I need to get to the hospital. My friend's having her baby."

"Can we talk about your next post? I have an outline." Teale began to rummage in her bag. It was adorable, Larisa thought, how prepared and enthusiastic Teale was. Her investment made up for whatever lack of experience might have counted against her. Larisa wished she was a better client. She wished so many things.

Is it good or bad that Lucas has the time to come to my thing? It's the middle of the night there.

Was Quinn with him?

"Which hospital? I'll drive you."

Larisa looked up. She'd been staring at, but not reading, the paper Teale had given her. Now, apparently Teale had left, and Sid stood before her wearing a concerned expression.

"What's wrong with you?" he asked.

"Nothing more than the usual." Larisa hated how her voice turned up, like it was a question she needed Sid to confirm with the right answer.

"Are you eating?"

Larisa didn't want to admit she didn't remember the difference between that morning and the morning before. At some point she'd shared a bowl of popcorn with Ana, and they'd watched *The Hills* together. It felt like that had probably been last week, but it might've been Tuesday night between the Green Goddess meeting and calling Pam.

Why hasn't she called me yet?

"I ate Five Guys with Rosa on Tuesday. A cheeseburger stays in your body for like a year after you eat it. I'm fine."

"Well, I'm hungry," said Sid.

"If we're eating together, are we friends again?"

"TBD." Sid reached up and scratched his head in the place where he was going bald from scratching his head too much. "I didn't think you'd be this much of a wreck."

"You're not here to check on me because he's worried?"

"He didn't send me. I think he's enjoying his time off from you, no offence."

"He literally said that?"

Sid rolled his eyes. Not literally. "He hasn't said much actually."

"Does it feel like there are things he's not telling you?"

"Yep."

Larisa sank toward her couch, the weight of her body suddenly too much for her legs to hold up. "That's because he's trying to keep my secret." She laughed and this almost made her cry. "I'm an open book now, you see. I've fucked the whole thing up. He's going to get himself hurt trying to fix it."

Chapter 16

Desire is a Chase

Quinn couldn't sleep.

Somewhere in the villa, Lucas. He felt both too near and too far. It troubled Quinn that he couldn't settle his mind on how he felt. At some point, he'd gotten out of bed and begun to wander the halls. *If he's also awake, we'll happen into each other.*

And then what?

At night, Umbras's hallways felt like catacombs with thick, cold air so still and quiet it wouldn't have been unexpected to begin imagining the calls of the dead. *You've gained Lucas's interest, now what will you do with it?*

In college, Quinn had experimented with a poet who'd called Quinn his muse. Most of the romance had been in words and glances. The few times they'd had sex, Quinn had been the top. He liked it that way. There hadn't ever been a question of changing roles. Now there was a row of butt plugs in Quinn's room that told him exactly what was coming, and Quinn knew he didn't have it in him to fake his way through that level of intimacy with a man who acted like the apex predator of renaissance men.

Already it felt like they'd gone too far.

In the south wing, the silence was broken by a voice, bright and over cheerful. It struck Quinn through the chest and stopped his breath, his feet, his heart. He began to run toward the voice. *She's here.*

She's come for me.

But it was only a video feed. In a small den made cozy by a crackling fire in the hearth, Lucas reclined on a sofa watching Larisa on his laptop. At first, Quinn thought they were Skyping, the two of them in secret communication, exchanging notes on him. But then he realized she must have started the discussion group chats that went with her blog series. Carefully, Quinn moved into the room, afraid that if his presence was discovered, Lucas would stop the stream.

"Jet lag?" asked Lucas as he typed a message into the chat.

Quinn came fully into the room and sat down at Lucas's shoulder. "You're talking to her?"

"It's just a chat full of idiots. I'm making it more fun. What do you think?"

"About what?"

"Seeing her." Lucas reached over and thumped Quinn on the left side of his chest. "What do you feel?"

Quinn turned his eyes to the screen, feeling almost guilty, as though looking at Larisa while Lucas looked at him crossed some unwritten rule of decency. At the very least, he didn't want Lucas trespassing when he looked at Larisa.

What he saw on the screen was a woman drowning because she'd become too tired to swim. Larisa's eyes held the camera in a glossy gaze, open but not quite present, as though she was operating by muscle memory instead of active intuition. Her makeup was minimal and lacked her usual precision, her hair flat and unattended.

"How do you feel?" Lucas asked again.

"I did this," he whispered.

"Did what?"

I should be home with her, thought Quinn. *She's my home.*

With a shiver, Quinn pulled himself back into his shell and found an answer less revealing, but one he felt Lucas would accept. "I wish she'd made different choices."

"With me?"

Obviously.

"With Parish," said Quinn. "I'm not going to judge what she did with you."

"Just saying that, you're judging. You think she'd be a better person without me."

"I don't think about it like that."

I wish you'd never set eyes on her.

"Let's escalate, shall we?" Lucas typed another message into the chat.

IlMagnificoXX: The purest pain comes when it is taken, not given.

Quinn watched Larisa's face blanch, her mouth work to form words that had fled her mind. Then she recovered. Her jaw tightened as she drew herself back from the blow and decided to ignore the chat.

"Is that how it was when she was with you?" Quinn didn't want to know, but he couldn't keep from asking. His voice held low so the rage building up inside it wouldn't be as obvious. *You hurt her.*

"What?" Lucas turned on his hip so he faced Quinn instead of the laptop. "You think I ask permission when I want something?" He reached out, pulled up the bottom of Quinn's shirt and touched the skin underneath. Quinn pulled back. Lucas leaned forward, pursuing him. "Desire is a chase. We live for the challenge as much for the accomplishment of capturing it. Bringing you here is a gift I've given to Larisa. She's more alive now than she's been since that beautiful little passion play you staged this spring. The agony—" Lucas's hand came forward again, stroking the line of hair down Quinn's belly "—of losing you, the struggle of figuring out how she'll get you back, *if* she'll get you back. It's what we were made for."

Again, Quinn couldn't help but pull back, except this time he managed to smile as though his retraction was a promise. The man wanted to chase. Quinn would build a maze for him to crawl through on the darkest night.

"She won't play your game," he said.

Lucas shrugged. "Maybe not. But I'll have a consolation prize." A dark warmth filled his expression, quiet delight, anticipation, and always that shadow of malice. "You should go back to your room before I decide the time has come for you to be claimed."

For only a moment Quinn hesitated. He only hesitated because he knew this was a game he needed to play, to walk a tightrope between appearing interested, and not being encouraging. As he walked back to his room, glancing over his shoulder to make sure Lucas wasn't following him, Quinn thought of how he'd coached Dansby to play at seduction using temptation and mystery, and how very flawed that advice seemed now. He hadn't thought enough about power; how a man like the Russian general in *The Key*, or a man like Lucas, wouldn't be satisfied with flirtation. He wanted a possession.

The morning music was an opera, which was never going to be what Quinn wanted to hear as he started his day, but at breakfast Lucas listened to the music as though entranced. And when they'd finished eating, and the barricade against speaking was lifted, he said, "You have just listened to the first act of *Norma* by Vincenzo Bellini."

"The sculptor?"

"Bernini was the sculptor. But I'm impressed you know that."

Quinn shrugged. It'd been in one of the books he'd tried to read, a man who'd been able to make stone look as soft as flesh.

"*Norma* is a tragedy of great archetypal value. It's worth being studied as a foundation of the genre. You also might have noticed the exceptional aria, 'Casta Diva.' Maria Callas sang it for this recording."

"It was nice," said Quinn who hadn't noticed anything remarkable in the music. He watched Lucas's lips press together in bloodless judgement and braced for a lecture that didn't come.

"As it happens, La Scala is putting it on next month. We'll go see it."

I won't be here then, thought Quinn, and was surprised to feel a little disappointed.

"All story is comedy or tragedy."

"According to a lot of dead people," said Quinn.

"Archetypes bring a set of expectations to the audience. Will this be a story they feel safe with in the end? Or a story they should expect the worst and learn to be comfortable with it?"

"I think story is more complicated than that."

"No, it isn't." Lucas handed Quinn a tablet. "I've assembled a collection of summaries of the most famous stories of the Western literary cannon. You're going to read them and report to me why you think they are compelling. And if you feel adequately led to read any of them, I would like to know."

"We're doing literary studies now?"

"No. Now we're making you a writer."

Quinn huffed out a laugh. But then Lucas handed him a leatherbound journal, the kind studio prop masters distressed to make it look well-worn for an adventure film. This one was real leather, tanned and dyed in Florence with paper from a Florentine papermaker. He couldn't imagine marring its pristine plains with his handwriting.

"We're having guests next week. An artists' retreat. Today, you'll notice quite a lot of activity with the preparations. But you —" Lucas pointed a severe finger at Quinn "—will not let it distract you. I know this goes against all your . . . instincts . . . but if you find yourself asking 'What does that word mean?' or 'Where else has that structure been used?' or 'Where does that come from?' do yourself a favor and look it up."

"What will you be doing?"

"Meetings this morning until America closes, then some handholding of skittish investors who think the US economy is moving toward a downturn. In between, I'll be petitioning the gods to finally blow these clouds away so we can have a starlight dinner on the patio tonight. Shall we walk together?"

Quinn took Lucas's arm, and they made their way up from the music room to the second-floor balcony of the library. Rifat stood at the door to Lucas's office. When he saw them coming, he pointed at the glass-domed ceiling of the square.

"Clouds!"

"Yes, I see them, thanks very much." Lucas drew Quinn to a stop in front of the study where his bottle of water and a glass already waited for him.

"How did you make out last night with the plugs?" asked Lucas.

Quinn hesitated. In his hesitation, Lucas rested a gentle hand on his shoulder. "Nothing valuable is easy."

"I'll try again tonight," said Quinn and quickly ducked into the study before Lucas could read anything into his answer.

The chair marked for him by his water wasn't as comfortable as the one in the library by the window, so Quinn took the water and moved to his usual spot. The office door was closed but not the whole way, as though Lucas had gone through in a rush and Rifat, following him, had neglected to push it hard enough for the latch to catch.

"I already told her a mortuary report can be faked," he heard Lucas say. "Get her in there to view the body or I won't believe it."

"She tried that," said Rifat. "Security at the funeral flagged her. You want her to dig up the casket?"

"Don't be absurd."

Silence.

"It's possible she's not following orders because she's out of money," said Rifat.

"How can she be out of money?"

"That would be hard to determine. Do you want me to—"

"Send her two thousand and say that's all she's getting until she can confirm Hagan's dead."

"It would be pretty elaborate if he wasn't."

"Don't underestimate Agent Smith."

"But Larisa—"

"We're not talking about that."

Quinn's ears burned. *What about Larisa? Someone was dead, and she was involved?* He turned on the tablet and began to scroll through what Lucas had given him as he strained to hear. Tolstoy, Dostoevsky, Dickens, Tolkien, Austen, Woolf, Proust, and Grass. All white people, no Americans, which, as he thought about it, wasn't surprising.

"I'd like to make an observation," said Rifat from within the office.

Lucas grunted.

"I can't tell if you want the guy to be alive or dead."

"Go start on the drawing room. I have a meeting. And make sure the linens are scented. I don't want the standard like last time. They smelled like chemicals."

Rifat left the office. He paused just after he pulled the door closed behind him, almost as though he knew Quinn was sitting at the end of the hallway. "You look bored."

Quinn waved the tablet. "Homework."

"Double boring. Is this the reading project?"

"Yeah."

"Come with me."

Quinn hesitated so long Rifat rolled his eyes.

"I'll vouch for you."

Quinn gathered his new journal, his water, and tablet and followed Rifat around the balcony to the southern wing of the villa. "I don't think you vouching for me is going to count if I can't tell him what he wants to know."

"What he wants is for you to care and you don't, so you might as well help me."

"What's happened with Larisa?"

Rifat blinked in surprise, then quickly hooded his expression.

"Lucas has been contacting her?"

"No."

"Then what?" Quinn clenched his hands into his pockets so he wouldn't grab Rifat's shirt and try to shake an answer out of him.

"She's safe for now," said Rifat.

"What the fuck does that mean?"

"Hey, hey, chill out, man." Rifat set his hands on Quinn's shoulders, forcibly pressing down until the weight of him began to sink into Quinn's haywire nerves. "There aren't any answers I can give you right now. Trust me. The best thing you can do is stay busy."

But what are the possibilities?

Who's Hagan?

Why is she involved?

Quinn tried to breathe. The look on Rifat's face was determined. No answers would be forthcoming. "Alright, fine. I'll help you."

The drawing room was a circular room tacked on to the end of the villa with floor-to-ceiling windows around its exterior wall held up by wrought iron reminiscent of a Victorian menagerie. Another staff member was already in the process of pulling dust cloths off various antique-looking couches. Two delivery men wearing jumpsuits like what Tom Cruise and Jonathan Rhys Meyers wore in the Italian sequence of *Mission: Impossible III*, were unloading pallets of art supplies.

When they saw Rifat, they began to talk to him in aggressive Italian. A discussion ensued, then was concluded with Rifat as the apparent winner. The men threw up their hands and left. Rifat saluted their retreating backs.

"Alright. We have twelve stations, and they all need to have a good view of the center, just there." He pointed to one divan, then two others. "Those, over against the wall. That one stays." He walked over to the delivered supplies. "Where are the backdrops? Fuck." Rifat pulled out his phone and walked toward the exit. On his way past Quinn, he handed him a utility knife. "Open all that up. Don't break anything, okay?"

So Quinn went to work. Within five minutes he'd forgotten his literary assignment. The drawing room was being transformed to set the scene for the artists' retreat. It wasn't nearly as technical as dressing a soundstage, but the ideas were similar enough. As Quinn unpacked the supplies, he watched the others work around him. He got a sense of the room, the direction the light would come through the windows if the sun ever decided to appear, the way the sconces on the wall wouldn't be enough if the artists worked at night.

When Rifat returned from his phone call, Quinn had formulated a proposal he thought would impress Lucas.

"I would like to be clear that I'm not pleased with your disobedience," said Lucas five hours later as he surveyed the drawing room. "But this is better than I would've had time to organize."

"You're welcome," said Quinn, surprised by how much he enjoyed Lucas's begrudging praise. Finally, he had something good to say instead of pointing out some obscure pocket of Quinn's ignorance.

"You still have to do your work."

"Believe it or not, I've watched movie adaptations of most of those books. I read the summaries for the ones I didn't know."

"So, you're prepared to answer." Lucas pulled out his pocket watch and checked the time, which was somehow way more pointed a motion than the more modern equivalent of checking the time on a phone screen. Quinn wanted to reach out and snatch the watch from his hand, to make Lucas look at him instead.

"I think every story is made compelling by its characters and how they respond to the situation they find themselves in. I could've told you that this morning."

"You didn't go through the process of considering the form." Lucas looked irritated. "What is a story?"

"Change." Quinn thought of quoting Brian Cox's soliloquy from *Adaptation*, but decided Lucas wouldn't receive it well. He seemed angry at more than just Quinn's disobedience. He was glaring at Rifat as he taped down the extension cords for the lamps, but also nonspecifically glaring in the general direction where Rifat just happened to be working. Maybe he was glaring at Hannah, who'd come in about an hour earlier, plopped herself down on one of the divans, and occupied herself uploading photos to Facebook.

The smell of garlic and herbs was beginning to seep in from the kitchen. Quinn's stomach rumbled in anticipation. It was almost time for lunch. He didn't know what would be served, but he knew he'd enjoy it. For this alone, he might have forgiven Lucas any number of flaws.

"Change," repeated Lucas.

"For there to be a story, something has to change. Forces come together. A question is posed. What will this person do?"

"And it must be consistent with their character, otherwise the narrative becomes implausible, and it undermines the reader's faith in the story."

Quinn glanced at Lucas. Something was definitely bothering him. "You sound like a betrayed reader."

"I often find modern storytelling lackluster. It's best not to give it my expectations." Lucas continued to survey the room without looking at it. "I'm going out of town."

"Now?"

"In a few hours." A pause, Lucas's mouth moving over words he was trying on and discarding.

"Do you want me to come with you?" asked Quinn.

"No, it's . . ." Lucas shook his head, then reached out his hand

and stroked a finger along the inside of Quinn's wrist as though storing him up for the absence. "You'll write while I'm away. No excuses."

Lucas's hand had retreated into his own space, but Quinn could still feel the line of heat he'd left on Quinn's skin. His awareness of it radiated outward, traveling up his arm, awakening the tips of his fingers.

"No excuses," he said.

"And you'll show me when I return."

Quinn nodded. He didn't know what else to say. Words weren't the problem as much as his voice, his ability to control the tremor he was sure lurked there, ready to undermine him. He wanted to say, *I might miss you.* But it would come off too full of emotion, and he worried Lucas would like that. To him, any reaction was an invitation.

Chapter 17

Real Spy Shit

After Larisa told Sid why Quinn was in Italy, Sid went out into the courtyard of her apartment complex and began shouting like he was arguing with an invisible person. On one level, it was cathartic to watch him explode. He allowed himself a reaction truer than Larisa would ever be able to claim for herself.

Seeing him, she felt her brain fog begin to lift. Yes, what she felt was real. It was real, and it was justified. There was nothing normal about what was happening. If she wanted, Larisa could storm around the courtyard shouting as well. Tempting, but it wasn't really her style. And she was too far inside her head to be able to release without first identifying exactly what she felt. So, Sid would do the feeling for her. She'd do the thinking.

They picked up ice cream and drove to the hospital to sit with Rosa's family, which included not just her parents and in-laws, but the aunties and cousins and their children (except for the one who was watching Rosa's other kids at home) who were all, as far as Larisa knew, devoutly religious, mostly variations of the Catholic theme. Not that Larisa had anything against Catholics. She just always felt like she was going to open her mouth and have sin pour out when she was around them. Plus, she hadn't seen any of Rosa's extended family since before the disaster of the previous spring.

"We didn't bring enough ice cream," said Sid.

Larisa side-eyed the one side of the waiting room overflowing with Rosa's blood family as she walked to the other side of the waiting room and handed Krissy a two-scoop cup of mint chip with a lid.

"Perfect," crooned Krissy. "Your show was good. I liked it."

"Me too," said Jaden. "But not as sexy as I thought."

"It wasn't supposed to be sexy." Larisa accidently made eye contact with Rosa's Aunt Carmen and felt, or imagined, a decidedly frosty silent message.

"Where's Kahleah and the men?" asked Larisa.

Krissy pointed down the way where her husband stood with Cade, Adrian, and Dev. "Kahleah isn't here."

"She said, and I quote, 'I'm not sitting in one of those damned hospital chairs for the next six hours.'"

Some dim thought tickled the back of Larisa's brain, a link to some earlier thought or impression. Without entirely knowing why, she sent a message to Kahleah off the group chat.

Larisa: You okay?

And then, because she felt Kahleah didn't respond well to direct status update questions.

Larisa: Your ice cream's melting.

"So, we're all very curious about this train you mentioned," said Krissy.

"You always told us you met Lucas in Italy, at a sex house party," said Jaden.

"Yeah, I just thought that was a better story," said Larisa, not looking up from her phone, hoping the girls would drop it. *Too much honesty,* she thought.

"Yeah, but it was still in college, right?" asked Jaden. "So where were we while you were riding this romance train?"

"I went with other people. Look, can we not talk about this right now?"

Larisa dared to glance up from her phone and saw both Jaden and Krissy staring at her. Across the way a whole row of faces was also watching her, their expressions more stony than surprised. As she watched, one leaned over and whispered in another's ear.

"Should we go say hi?" asked Sid.

Larisa took a breath. "They can stare if they want."

"Risa, I thought we were doing honesty now." Krissy was pouting in a way that made Larisa want to tell her even less, but the truth of the statement remained. Larisa had committed to being more open. She just hadn't thought it would be about this, an old secret that no longer mattered.

"You remember Kaylee from the house?"

"There were like five Kaylees," said Krissy.

"Well, I went with her for her sister's birthday, October of junior year. They invited me."

"So . . . that sorta explains it. But why the big secret? I don't remember hearing anything about Lucas until summer." Jaden looked to Krissy for confirmation.

"Even if I'd told you, you wouldn't remember," said Larisa, "You were obsessed with Shane then."

"Shane?" asked Krissy at the same moment Jaden's eyes flew open. "I don't remember Shane either.

"He was my fiancé for like five months," said Jaden. "We don't talk about him."

"Oh right. He was that douche who cheated on you with Larisa, and you walked in on them doing the—"

"He asked me at homecoming. That first fall weekend." Jaden was talking slowly, putting pieces together. "And this train thing?"

"The week after." Larisa drew herself up, squared her gaze to meet Jaden's.

"You never liked him."

"I knew he wasn't good for you."

"Not your call to make."

"I tried not to. It just happened. He proved I was right."

"Hang on. Are we saying what I think we're saying?"

"I think I'm gonna go."

Krissy looked ready to protest, but footsteps were running down the hall. Tate skidded to a squeaking halt on the sterile linoleum. He glanced to his right at the family, then to his left at the sisters. He started toward them, then thought better of it and started back toward the family. He stopped again, and shouted, "It's a girl!"

Rosa's mother rushed to him. Krissy rushed him with Jaden on her heels. Larisa stayed in her seat. When everyone's attention seemed focused on Tate, she nodded toward the door, and Sid nodded his agreement.

"That gummy feeling in your gut?" she asked. "Feels like betrayal but not quite as sharp? I've got a playlist for that."

When they got into the car, Sid gave a low whistle of appreciation. "Your life, fuck."

"Amazing I'm not on anything, isn't it?"

"God damn miraculous." He cuffed her gently on the side of the shoulder. "You're okay, though."

They drove around the city for the rest of the night, long after Larisa grew tired of finding songs that fit the mood. In the silence, they exchanged words that felt too large to speak, and maybe they didn't entirely understand each other, but they were coming from something that looked like the same place.

Finally, Sid said, "What happens if I just go over there and bring him home?"

"I don't think he'd want that."

"He's no hero. I mean, this whole thing doesn't make sense. You've seen his decision-making skills. In high stress, he never makes the right choice."

"You mean a choice to save himself."

"Yeah, I guess that's what I mean."

"I'm doing everything I can to fix it."

"What am I supposed to do?"

"You could drive me, I guess. I'm not doing great with

driving." She watched him consider this, knowing it wasn't what he'd had in mind. "I could use your help."

"Yeah, sure. Send me your schedule."

Just like that, Larisa wasn't alone anymore.

The sisters' group chat filled with pictures of everyone but Larisa holding the baby. She and Quinn didn't talk on the phone. The first day, he texted to say he was busy. The second day, she said she was too tired. Which was true. If they got into another fight about her inability to be reliably honest, she wasn't sure she'd be able to survive. So he sent pictures of Umbras. She sent back pictures of Sabrina. He said: *I think Lucas and I have come to an understanding.* And Larisa chose not to think about what that meant.

Sid returned to the apartment on Monday and Tuesday and drove Larisa to consultations with her troubled actress client, Anastacia, and the small business owner, Claire, who worried about her husband keeping secrets. And then, even though she said she could drive herself, Sid took her to meet Dr. Bade for drinks, which solved the mystery event Larisa had entered in her phone. Meeting for drinks made more sense than having a consultation with her therapist while she was still technically on vacation.

"You have a driver now?"

"He's just a friend," said Larisa. To Dr. Bade's probing look, she added, "I'm not sure it's great if I'm alone right now. I've been losing time."

"Disassociating?"

"Or just drifting, maybe."

"I was going to ask how your holidays went, but . . ." Dr. Bade sipped her drink and adjusted her posture ever so slightly as though shifting from social mode to work mode. "What started it?"

I betrayed him.

But Larisa didn't know how to explain Lucas without a lot of backstory, which would also involve admitting that she'd held back a good part of her emotional and romantic history for five years of therapy.

"Quinn and I are having a rough time. All the media attention, and his film coming out, and…" Larisa waved her hand through the air to summarize all the things she couldn't say.

"You've never had a problem like this before." As though worried that had come out the wrong way, Dr. Bade redirected. "I mean, you usually manage your celebrity without having it bother you. What do you think's different now?"

Larisa thought that Dr. Bade thinking she handled media attention well was also Larisa's fault. Sometime, when they were having a real session, it'd probably be good to apply her newfound resolution for honesty to her therapist. But this was not that day.

"It's hard for me to attach," said Larisa as she took a breath. "I think I've been surprised by how much Quinn's gotten through my defenses."

"You invested a lot in him."

Larisa stared down into her drink. *Or something like love. Attachment. Nostalgia.*

"Even though it only lasted a few months, you shouldn't underestimate the power of your dreams for a life with him," said Dr. Bade.

The conversation was beginning to feel like a funeral for her relationship with Quinn. Larisa didn't like the burn at the back of her throat, the forewarning of tears. *He's going to be fine. We're going to get through this. He'll forgive me for Parish. He'll come home. Lucas won't hurt him as long as it seems like I'm cooperating.*

And then, as though this thought had summoned her, Ana appeared, standing at the end of the table holding out a Sharpie and napkin. "Hello."

Larisa's mouth dropped open. *How does she keep finding me?*

"Sorry to interrupt. But I'm such a fan. Will you sign this?"

As Ana handed the napkin over, she flipped the edge up with her thumb so Larisa could see the faint writing on the inside.

Meet me out back.

Larisa scribbled her signature and flashed Ana a smile. She watched the girl walk out the door.

"How does it feel when someone does that?" asked Dr. Bade.

"Surreal," said Larisa. *This is why I'm losing time,* she thought. *My life has become a waking nightmare.*

"I'd like to say something gently, just for you to consider. It feels like you're hiding."

"Aren't we always hiding a little bit?" Larisa offered a sly smile she didn't feel, as though her therapist was just another reporter waiting to be charmed.

"Yes, but we shouldn't hide from ourselves."

Almost tears, the burning warning, the heat on her face. Larisa needed to make an exit. She didn't even care if it looked suspicious. It'd been a mistake to agree to meet Dr. Bade. There was too much she couldn't say, too many things she needed to figure out.

"I don't think I'm up for this today," said Larisa. "I'm sorry."

"You're sure? Well, let's get a real session on the books so we don't leave this unattended."

I'm attending to it, thought Larisa so sharply it felt as though she'd spoken.

But an appointment was made, and Larisa left more money than necessary for the tab so she wouldn't have to wait.

As she walked out, she texted the sisters. Even if they were all busy hating her behind her back for what she did to Jaden, the honesty had cost her too much to not use it.

> Larisa: I just had a covert message passed to me by bar napkin. The spy shit just went to the next level.

I'm not hiding as much as usual, Dr. B, thought Larisa.

As she turned the corner, she snapped a quick photo of Ana

before she was noticed. The girl seemed even skinnier than before, with deep purple moons under her eyes.

"Hey."

"Hey."

"How are you?"

Ana shrugged and scratched at her elbow. "We have a problem."

"Are you talking to the CIA?" asked Ana.

"You know I am."

"Oh yeah, right. I mean like for real talking to them."

"If you're asking that, something must be wrong. What is it?"

"There's been suspicious activity. Lucas isn't happy."

"Why don't you come into the bar, I'll buy you dinner. We can talk."

"Don't play innocent."

"Ana. I want to help."

Ana blinked. "Did he ask about the island?"

"He who?" asked Larisa.

"The CIA agent obviously."

"We talked about Christmas. He thinks Lucas is using me to pass information to American buyers. He even asked about Senator Hagan, who was apparently one of those buyers."

Either Ana knew this already or she didn't care because she shrugged like it didn't matter. "Lucas doesn't think you killed him." She sounded almost apologetic.

"Where have you been staying since you left my place?"

"Don't try any of that. Did you kill him or not?"

"I didn't," said Larisa with a strategic pause that lasted long enough for Ana to stop itching and listen closely. "I facilitated it. If Lucas thinks I'm going to burn my life down just because he says jump, you can tell him—"

"He has a new thing for you."

"I'm not doing anything else."

"You will if you want your friend Quinn to continue having a nice time at Umbras." Ana looked earnest, the purple bruises under her eyes seeming to grow as she opened her expression into something almost pleading. "This is the last thing. Very simple. You need to unlock a door and let someone into a hotel."

"Why can't you do that?"

"I'm busy with a CIA that knows more than it should."

"I didn't tell them anything."

"I believe you," said Ana. She chewed her lip. "Just be ready when I tell you. You're going to LV."

"LV?"

"Las Vegas. Isn't that what you call it? LA and LV? The sister cities?"

Ana suddenly seemed so much younger than her true age. Larisa wanted to take her arm and pull her out to Sid's BMW and ferry her away from whatever choices had brought her to this life. But then she thought, *If I was doing her job, I'd try and look as young and vulnerable as I could. I'd play every weakness I could find.*

"It's a test," said Sid when Larisa climbed into the car. "He doesn't think you killed Hagan. Maybe he's setting you up to fail."

"Yeah, maybe. There's something else though. They feel like the CIA knows things."

"Your cousin found something they could use?"

"Maybe." Larisa still couldn't believe Hannah was at Umbras trying to find information for the CIA. *If she gets hurt it'll be my fault,* she thought. Just like Quinn was her fault, and Jaden being heartbroken junior year. And so many other things. Larisa could've proven in a court of law that being around her was a sure way to ruin your life. But she didn't have time to think about that.

Larisa pulled her burner phone out of her purse and dialed.

"Is that what I think—"

"Quiet."

The line opened to silence.

"I want an update," said Larisa. "Face-to-face."

"Not possible," said Pam.

"Make it possible."

"I'm out of the country doing the thing I said I'd do."

"And?"

"It's where you said. No obvious security. A pair of tourists made it all the way to the beach. Met the owner. He made them dinner. Sent them back to Japan so drunk they couldn't remember anything except that it'd been a lovely time. I watched the whole thing by infrared."

"It's set off alarms."

"He's always been skittish," said Pam.

Lucas is strategic, not skittish.

He knows. But there was nothing Larisa could do about that now. "What next?" she asked.

"Waiting game. Unless you want to poke the bear."

"Please don't." Larisa paused, still not sure she believed Pam hadn't leaked information to the CIA. *Why would she trust them?* "Do you have any operations in Vegas?"

"I'll be in touch."

The line went dead.

"I don't like any of this," said Sid.

"You think I do?"

"Let's think about Italy. Doesn't your mom have something going on there soon?"

"I'm not going to Italy," said Larisa.

"Not even for Quinn?"

Larisa opened her mouth, then closed it.

"You know what Quinn thinks?" asked Sid. "He thinks you can't say no to that guy. He's got you like brainwashed or something. That's why you're afraid."

"If Quinn wanted to see me, I'd go."

"He's not going to ask you to do something you obviously don't want to do."

So we wait and see who makes the next move first, thought Larisa.

"You know what's funny?" she asked. "In the movies, the right choice is always obvious. You watch, and you almost always know what's going to happen. Right choices end up with happy endings."

"You're making the right choices," said Sid.

"But they don't feel right. I've abandoned my government. I've faked someone's murder. And instead of being glad that someone's still alive, all I can think is, what happens to Quinn when Lucas finds out I lied? What happens to my cousin?" *What if he already knows?*

"They made their own choices," said Sid.

Brainwashed, thought Larisa. *An interesting idea. It implied a lack of choice, an absence of culpability.*

Larisa stared out the window wishing for all the world she believed that was true.

Chapter 18

Crafting A Character

When the music played as usual the next morning, Quinn thought Lucas had returned. The anticipation he felt over seeing Lucas at breakfast confused Quinn, especially since he'd had his first truly peaceful night's sleep that night, most likely because he knew no one in the villa would sneak into his room.

This is what he does to people, thought Quinn as he walked to the music room. *He shows them one side of himself that's terrible, and that makes his softer side look benevolent. You don't ever know how to feel, and he watches you twist yourself up over it.*

Lucas wasn't in the music room waiting to judge Quinn's appearance. The table had been set for one. The music was apparently preprogrammed as part of his continuing education. Even when Lucas rushed out of town for an emergency trip, he remembered to plan the music.

Given his freedom, Quinn decided not to stay in the music room. He loaded his breakfast dishes in a precarious little stack and carried it to the kitchen where Francie and Carla were frying zucchini flowers. They paused their work to watch him carry his dishes to the breakfast nook. Francie gave a little golf clap as he successfully laid everything out again.

"Do you know where he's gone?" asked Quinn.

Carla rolled her eyes as though this was such a typical question, and Francie shrugged as though she didn't understand him.

Fine, keep your secrets. Quinn had decided he wouldn't use Lucas's staff against him. Whatever secrets they knew were a hazard of working for him, and they didn't deserve to be punished for having a good job.

Quinn wasn't in the mood to think about Lucas's secrets that morning anyway. Remembering that yesterday he'd worried Lucas might have gone to LA, he texted Larisa.

Quinn: Lucas has left on a mysterious errand.

Quinn: Any reason he'd come see you?

Larisa: I hope not.

For a long moment he studied her response, trying to read behind it. *She would tell me if something was really wrong,* he thought. But he couldn't tell if this was something he believed or just wishful thinking. With a deep breath, he resolved not to worry about it. Lucas's absence felt like an opportunity, and he was going to use it.

The night before, he'd sat in this nook drinking grappa with Rifat. Rather, Rifat had done the drinking while Quinn had sipped a single shot of the burning liquor and prayed he didn't melt from the inside. Originally, Quinn had come to the nook to think about writing, and Rifat had interrupted his solitude with the age-old challenge, "Are you really going to do what he says even while he's gone?"

Yes. Quinn had wanted to write, but not just for Lucas. Something had been awakened. Even in the midst of what was on the outside, a high-stress situation, he felt his mind reorganizing itself, falling into patterns long ago abandoned for more practical necessities. But Rifat's question had carried a dare with it, so there had been no writing that night. Just drunk Rifat talking about a girl he'd left behind on a tropical island who'd been too young for him, but he still dreamed of her. And Quinn realizing it'd been a long time since he'd sat and watched someone get wasted, and what a normal thing to be doing with a man who certainly knew where Lucas had gone and what he was doing. But Quinn hadn't asked. And Rifat hadn't once hinted that he wanted to unburden himself.

In the light of morning, it felt like a wasted opportunity. He was running out of time. Hollywood had finally come back to work, and Quinn had a pile of emails waiting for him on his phone, each one of them representing a countdown to the hard deadline of *The Key's* London premiere.

I'm no longer worried about making this trip matter, Quinn wrote in his new journal beside the stray thought he'd had about Lucas manipulating people's emotions by softening toward them when they least expected it. Several question marks followed the thought since the observation felt incomplete.

He stared out the window and tried to soak up the peace of the morning. The window looked out on the terrace before it sloped down into the gardens. Another cloudy day that looked like rain, all the green cast in a sheen of mist, indistinct and dreamy. He texted Larisa a picture. She immediately wrote back.

Larisa: 🤍🤍🤍🤍🤍🤍

Larisa: Maybe you shouldn't send me
pictures. I'm trying not to think about things.
Pictures don't help.

In another world it would've been something they shared. Perhaps if Lucas had been a better man. But then, Quinn realized if Lucas had been a better man, Larisa would never have left him. Not in all the cosmos was there a timeline where the three of them existed together in peace.

In a garden labyrinth that never sees the sun, a statue gazes down on a young woman as she passes through the maze. The statue has watched many such women. They come because they have no options left. They dare the fates to grant them one impossible wish.

Quinn's phone vibrated. Sid had sent pictures of the dorm rooms where his youngest sister wanted to go to college.

Sid: There were roach skeletons.

Sid: They think people want to go there to be part of the spirit team and spend money on branded clothes.

Quinn: I'm writing. Leave me alone.

Sid: Writing...............?????

Quinn put his phone on silent and turned it upside down. In his journal, Quinn wrote:

Theme:

It's a terrible thing to love. Even when it comes easy, it goes hard sometimes.

You want to be better than yourself. And it makes you worse.

He thought of how Larisa had looked during her live stream and worried she'd isolated herself even though she said she'd been working on honesty with the sisters. *If you're involved with Lucas and the dead person he was talking about, would you tell me?*

No.

On the outside, their relationship looked unstable and covered in red flags, he wrote. *But it isn't that. If they could be alone together, they'd be fine. But that's not their fate.*

After a moment of consideration, Quinn turned the journal sideways and wrote: *Who is 'they'? The woman and . . . ?*

She understands he has to prove himself, he wrote.

They both hate that this is how it has to be, but they don't hold it against each other. Their trust is absolute.

Except it wasn't. Hadn't trust been the problem? She hadn't trusted him, not with Lucas, not with Parish and the baby, perhaps not even with her own heart.

What does it look like for her to truly give her heart away and allow someone else to keep it?

In a past life, Larisa had sat on the bench where he now sat, in the house of a man she'd worked so hard to escape. Despite her best efforts, he still haunted her. Quinn reread what he'd written and felt the truth of it. Even though he hated how she kept things from him, in her mind, she'd done it out of love. Maybe it wasn't fair of him to demand something of her that she simply could not do.

She loves me.

He picked up his phone to text Sid.

Quinn: Will you send me Parish's number?

Sid: I'm starting to worry about you.

Quinn: I'm fine.

Sid: You'll regret talking to her.

Quinn: Do you have it or not?

A few seconds later, the number appeared on the screen. Quinn put it into a new message.

Quinn: I'm sorry about the baby.

A thought came to him about the maze. He wrote it down, then drew some lines connecting other thoughts as they bubbled up and began to pop. It was as though the one central thought was rising in pressure, creating a cauldron of ideas. A thrum of electricity coursed through his bones, the joy of it, the plunge!

His phone was vibrating.

"Hi, Parish. Yeah, it's been a while. Look, I heard what happened. I wanted to say I'm sorry."

It was a short conversation, his mind had been captured by his work and not even Parish with her bubbling, overcaffeinated enthusiasm could pull him out of it. Mostly he listened. He remembered that he liked the way Parish talked, as though the world was a good place. And even though that would never be his mindset, it was nice to exist in a simpler world for a few minutes.

All through the call, one part of Quinn's mind stayed in his story. He took stray notes as placeholders for thoughts he wanted to remember to develop, and as soon as Quinn got off the phone, he dug in, pen in hand, to explore a mist-shrouded garden and a ghost trapped in a statue who looked a lot like the woman he loved. He worked until midafternoon when Hannah invaded.

"Walk with me?" She leaned over him and yanked the pen out of his hand. "You've been sitting here too long."

"Give it back."

"Twenty minutes."

"Haven't you ever heard you don't interrupt writers when they have momentum?"

"You've already lost it because you have no pen."

It's not a mystery to me why you're single, thought Quinn as he leaned out of the breakfast nook to try to grab his pen back. Hannah stepped just out of his reach.

"It's cold," he said, on his way to defeat.

"No excuses. Come on."

She found him a giant wool scarf and a shawl from the mudroom, then dragged him out the front door like they were friends off to have a lark in the Italian countryside. This lasted only until they were out of sight of the house, then her energy flagged, and she detached herself from him.

"I'm running out of time," she said. "The CIA says I'm not doing a good job."

"Hard to say what 'doing a good job' means in this case," said Quinn.

"They didn't find anything at the bakery."

Why did you tell them about the bakery? When?

He wanted to shout at her. It seemed too much of a coincidence that Lucas had left on a mysterious trip when he was supposed to be preparing for the artists' retreat. Instead, he fought to keep his voice even as he said, "Maybe you should just go home."

"Why? Are *you* going to find the nerve gas?"

Quinn gave her a look.

"I know I'm close. I went in and searched the office this morning. There's something in there. It's where he has all his meetings and phone calls."

"And?"

"No false bottoms or extra drawers or anything."

"Maybe there's nothing to find unless you know what you're looking for."

"Like?"

Quinn shrugged. "In my movie, they go after the guy's accountant. But that wouldn't work in real life because if you did that, he'd be able to trace the leak and know it was you."

"The CIA will help me with that."

Quinn smiled grimly to himself.

"You think I'm wrong for trusting them, don't you?"

"I think you should go back to Minnesota and call Larisa so she doesn't have to worry about you anymore."

"Then she'll just worry about you, eh?"

"I know what I'm doing."

"What exactly are you doing?"

"Dancing." Quinn slid his feet across the road, a glide, a two-step. It felt good to stretch his legs.

"Why are you so happy?"

"I'm not really." Quinn flexed the hand that he'd been using to hold the shawl closed, his writing hand, with a nice round callous on the middle finger. But he did feel something that looked a little like happiness, the bright spark of possibility that marked the beginning of a new project, an idea he wanted to chase until he wrapped his greedy little fingers around it and pulled it apart to see how it worked. "What's your favorite story?"

"I dunno. *Anne of Green Gables*, I guess."

"Why?"

"Because she's impulsive and allows herself to be angry. Or something."

"You identify with her?"

"No, I just like the idea of it, even though she hates herself afterward and has a lot of doubts. She's just like Larisa." Hannah kicked at a pebble. "Does first, regrets later."

"Like what she did with your boyfriend?"

"Oh that." Hannah bent down and grabbed a fistful of rocks from the side of the road, then began to toss them. "She can't help herself, you know. Always has to be everyone's number one. I don't even think she knows what she does. She just thinks she has something to offer to everyone, and people read that the wrong way. I mean, could I ever trust a guy who wasn't interested in her? She's just so bright. She makes everything around her look gray."

Quinn couldn't argue with that. It was probably one of the things that made him feel so safe with her. He could exist in her shadow, circulate that bright sun, and be happy forever knowing he'd rarely be the one to carry a conversation, or make the right joke at a party, or impress people with his growing knowledge of Renaissance and medieval architecture.

"I miss her," he said.

"But you kinda hate her right now, right?"

"I'm working on it."

Chapter 19

Hair on Fire

Larisa and Sid stayed out all night driving. They ate breakfast together at the same diner where she'd sat with Ana before New Year's. Sid talked about his little sister's college search, and how uncomfortable his mother was with the whole thing because Sid had failed out and none of the siblings who came after him had even tried. In the hour they sat there, Larisa learned more about Sid than she had in all the months they'd known each other. They didn't talk about the coming out moment Larisa had narrowly avoided at the hospital, or how her friends were processing yet another dark revelation from Larisa's past.

"Long time since I pulled an all-nighter with a girl," said Sid as they drove back to her apartment.

"You and Quinn do this a lot?"

"Oh yeah, when he's on a project, he barely sleeps. And he doesn't like being alone because he verbally processes a lot of shit, and he likes to have someone answer him when he talks."

Her phone buzzed with a picture out of Umbras's kitchen window, a gloomy, rainy scene. Seeing it, Larisa felt a stab in her chest. "I still can't really believe he's over there."

"It's not really a typical situation, is it?"

"We could argue that neither are very typical." She frowned as she read Quinn's next texts. "He says Lucas has gone out of town and maybe came here."

Sid's focus on the road diverted as he stared at her. "You think it's the stuff with Pam?"

"Hard to think it's a coincidence. But all the way here without calling to question me first?"

"Not a good sign."

They pulled through the gate into Larisa's complex. "I don't like dropping you off to be by yourself if he's in town," said Sid.

Larisa barely heard him. Her apartment door stood open. The lights on inside.

They looked at each other. "Sabrina," said Sid.

Together, they dashed out of the car, across the courtyard to the door. Inside the apartment, a man lounged on Larisa's couch. His skin was the particular burnished color of someone who spent a lot of time in the sun and didn't bathe. His jeans appeared stained if not soiled from use. He wore a jacket without a shirt underneath.

He was laughing at Ana who'd trapped Sabrina on the far side of the living room and was chasing her from side to side with a lighter. Lines of angry red scratches on Ana's hands showed that this had already been a long fight.

"I'm calling the police," said Sid.

Maybe Larisa said no, which was always her default response. Avoid publicity at all costs. But she wasn't thinking about that. Ana had brought a stranger into her home. Ana was torturing her cat.

She lunged forward with a feral scream fed by all the moments that night when she'd wanted to scream but held herself in check. She grabbed the back of Ana's flimsy shirt and yanked her back.

"Yeeee!" laughed Ana as she swung wide, hands flung out, in one, an open flame. "Larisa you're home!" The lighter brushed against the scarf Larisa kept draped over her lamp as a decoration. It caught fire.

The guy on the couch sat up. "Oh shit, is that a real fire, or—"

"So pretty." Ana reached for the scarf. Larisa grabbed her hand and yanked her back.

"What the fuck do you think you're doing?"

Ana pouted, then lost herself to giggles. "Why upset?"

The fire had spread to the lampshade. The smoke detector began to howl. Larisa squinted up at the ceiling trying to remember if there was updated fire suppression in her unit. Barely audible beyond the noise, was the far distant wail of police sirens.

"Good party, babe, I'm outta here."

"No wait, you have to meet Larisa. She's my friend."

Larisa pulled Ana toward the door, then turned to look for Sabrina. Smoke was filling the room. "Sabrina," she called, not for a moment thinking it would do any good. The cat never came when called unless it was Quinn calling. She knelt on the floor, looking all around from cat level. Finally, she spotted Sabrina cowering at the side of the couch. Larisa scooped her up just as Sid rushed past her. He knocked the lamp onto the floor, threw the sofa blanket on top of it, and began to stomp it with his feet.

"Evil cat," said Ana.

"Who was that man?" asked Larisa.

"He's been hooking me up. We're friends."

"I see."

"Are you angry because I know you're lying?"

"What?" Sabrina squirmed in Larisa's arms, little chest pumping with panic. Larisa held her tighter.

"You didn't kill the man Lucas said to."

"Why do you think that?"

"I don't think, I know." Ana leered at her with an unfocused gaze.

"Did you tell him?" asked Larisa.

"He told me."

"Is he coming here?"

Ana shrugged. "He doesn't tell me this."

The sirens were growing louder. Larisa had a choice to make, and she needed to make it fast.

"You need to leave."

When Ana didn't move toward the door, Larisa motioned for her to follow. They walked out together.

"Don't come back here. If you do, I'll have you arrested."

"For what?" The girl appeared confused, but then she was distracted by the dog in the unit across the way barking at the window. "Puppy."

"Ana."

"Yes?"

"I'm sorry."

The girl blinked up at her. "We're all sorry. What good is this?"

"Please go."

"Okay, fiiinnne. Bubye for now!" She blew Larisa kisses as she skipped out of the courtyard and squeezed herself through the gap between the security gate and its post.

"Is she okay?" asked Sid.

Larisa shook her head, then realized he meant Sabrina. She turned so Sid could examine her cat. There were scorch marks on the long fur of her tail, and one of her nails had been pulled out, probably caught a bad angle when she'd attacked Ana.

"We should take her to the vet."

"Yeah."

"You can't stay here."

"Yeah."

"Larisa?"

"I know. I'll pack after we talk to the police. I was just thinking."

"You can't trust anything she said. That girl was high as a kite."

"But we have to consider it might be true. Lucas knows I lied to him."

"You just heard from Quinn. He's fine. You're the one who isn't fine."

"But he could—"

"What?"

"I don't know. I can't think."

An LAPD squad car pulled up outside the gate. A neighbor opened his door and peered out, then another.

"Fire?" he called.

"It's out now," said Larisa.

And then she heard it, the rapid-fire click of a telephoto lens.

Hours later, huddled on the balcony off the master bedroom of Quinn's house, Larisa was surprised to find it wasn't even noon. She'd found Quinn's old Tibetan prayer bead bracelet in her bag, and she'd come to sit and move her fingers over it in meditation, a halfway attempt to organize her mind. There'd been no reason to know the time. Every task had flowed from the other, talking to the police, then packing her and Sabrina's bags. Calling her parents to warn them of what they'd probably see in the papers the next day, an emergency vet appointment, then Sid deciding she'd stay at Quinn's house instead of her parents'.

She hadn't been sitting on the balcony very long when Quinn called, and that's when she saw the time. In the back of her mind, she'd thought it was past time when he would've called before going to bed.

"Any sign of Lucas?" he asked.

"Since I'm practicing honesty, I'll say there are signs of Lucas everywhere. But no actual sign of him. Sid brought me over to your house, just in case."

Silence. She knew Quinn was thinking that they'd avoided spending time in his house because he'd lived there with Parish.

"I talked to her today," he said.

"Oh yeah?"

"It felt like the right time. If there's ever a right time to talk about that stuff."

"How was she?"

"Same old. Getting out of the clinic soon, worried about her dating prospects. She put on a good face, but I think she's pretty upset."

"I'll try and make it over to visit her this week."

"You'll take Sid with you?"

"Sid's with me all the time now. Except for the college visits."

"Did he tell you about the cockroach graveyard?"

"Ew, no?"

He laughed softly and she felt small, damaged pieces of her draw together and mend at the sound. "How was your day?"

"Good. Your cousin is obnoxious. Rifat could be my friend if not for, you know." A pause. "And I've been writing."

"Writing?"

"Yeah. It's something Lucas has me doing. I dunno. Is it weird that I miss him? I mean, I hate him. Every day there are at least three times I want to punch him in the face, but . . . fuuuuuck."

"I'm sorry."

"This isn't your fault."

"I knew what he was like. I stood by, made excuses—"

"Saving yourself counts for something, you know."

"What if part of me was also saving him?"

"I'd say that's pretty par for the course. You save people, Larisa. That's what you do. Even when they don't deserve it."

Larisa swallowed down the lump clogging her throat. "Please come home."

"Soon," he promised.

Chapter 20

A Distracted Venus

Lucas reappeared at breakfast the next day. His mood was unreadable, but Quinn thought he seemed to struggle to concentrate on the music—a selection of work from Max Richter. As they ate, Lucas found reasons to touch Quinn's hand, when he reached for the sugar, the butter, to correct the way he held his fork. And Quinn found it easy to receive.

They spent the morning together in the study. Lucas asked philosophical questions about storytelling, and Quinn felt less judged than before, as though Lucas's absence had softened his awareness of Quinn's faults and now they were having a conversation as equals.

"I've been thinking of quieter conflicts," said Quinn as they sat together on the study sofa. He sat in the middle with Lucas on his left, sitting sideways, his interior leg stretched down the length of the sofa behind Quinn's back. "Like how difficult even small things become when two people want different things."

"The villain is always a matter of perspective." Lucas reached out and curled Quinn's hair around his finger. "Unless the writing is terrible and has some kind of moral purpose."

"If it's a story of man against man, does one of them have to be a villain?"

"Is that what you're writing?" Lucas leaned toward the coffee table, reaching for Quinn's journal. Quinn nudged it out of reach. "I'm not ready."

"You've had two and a half days."

"I'm slow, remember?"

"A true submissive would mold their desire to mine." He said it playfully, almost with respect, instead of judgement.

"I'll tell you that I've done a very Renaissance thing," said Quinn.

"How's that?"

"I'm building the story and its world from ancient times."

"Brava. Look at you go. That deserves a reward. Get up."

"Where are we going?"

"The Uffizi. But you can't go out in Florence wearing that." He pointed to Quinn's long-sleeved T-shirt and the flannel sweatpants Larisa had bought him for the Minnesota trip.

"Are we at the point of matching outfits?" asked Quinn.

"You are truly horrifying." Lucas led the way to his office and on into his bedroom.

Quinn allowed his gaze to drift around with apparent carelessness, pretending to be a man interested in another man's bedroom because of what might be done there. *Hannah thinks this is where it happens. There's a safe or a file cabinet or something hidden.*

But there wasn't even a desk, and the room struck him the same as before. Modern and almost sterile compared to the rest of the villa.

He doesn't do anything in this room except sleep.

"Did you know that in Florence, during the Renaissance, police monitored what people wore?"

"Don't we still have those?" Quinn followed Lucas into his closet. While he was occupied browsing clothes, Quinn scanned the walls for anything that didn't look like it belonged.

"If you were of a certain social standing, you could only have so many buttons," said Lucas. "And your outfit could only be one or two colors. Truly good people only wore one color so as not to display wealth."

"Huh."

"They knew something we've forgotten." Lucas held up a blouse and pants with buttons instead of a zipper on the fly. "Buttons are erotic."

Quinn took the clothes and glanced around wondering if Lucas expected him to change right there, which he would do, he decided. It no longer felt like such an invasion for Lucas to see his full suit of skin.

"Button yourself in." Lucas stepped back and closed the closet door. "When we come home, I get to button you out."

Heat rose on Quinn's cheeks at the thought of a complicated undressing and all the possibilities hinted by it. Would Lucas play at a slow and delicate revealing? Or would he be fast and rough? Quinn thought he might like a little of both. As he struggled to get into the clothes and fasten them, he imagined a slow unbuttoning would only last so long before both of them were so turned on, fabric would necessarily be ripped from his body.

"Are you done yet?"

Quinn laughed. It was quite a process getting into the clothes, which ended up being not only the pants and shirt, but a vest and jacket all fastened with buttons, at least a hundred in total.

Larisa would take scissors to me if we ever played this game.

Deep breath, rearrangement of his face into something he thought looked open to possibilities as he stepped out of the closet. Lucas stood a few feet back checking his phone, not at all holding his breath in anticipation of Quinn's grand entrance.

"What do you think?"

Lucas's head jerked up, then was followed by a long appreciative look as he tucked his phone away. "Perfect. Let's away."

In the car down to the city, Lucas told him things about the villages they passed. They were like little suburbs but with more character, each with their own history and unique perspective. This one featured a famous monastery, that one a vineyard, the one where so and so owned a villa and threw very loud parties.

Through it all, Lucas's hand rested on the middle seat between them, just close enough in Quinn's peripheral vision that he kept turning to look at it, to see if it was coming closer, to see if perhaps he might place his hand beside it.

I feel like I'm in high school again, he thought.

"What do you think?" asked Lucas apropos of nothing.

"About what?"

"Anything, everything." Lucas's smile was irritated, almost condescending.

Quinn shrugged. "I like it here."

"Why?"

"Why what?"

"Why do you like it here?"

"It's pretty?"

"What exactly is pretty in your eyes?"

"All of it," said Quinn.

Lucas turned to the window. A few seconds later, he pulled out his phone.

At the museum, Lucas bypassed the long line of tourists by waving a card at the security checkpoint. Then they were inside, not a building built as a museum, but a palace that had once been a person's home. Quinn could hardly imagine it.

"What do you want to see?" asked Lucas with more than his usual undertone of impatience.

Quinn pushed back his own irritation. It felt like Lucas asked these questions just to watch Quinn fail to answer them. He didn't *want* to see anything. Lucas had asked him to come, Quinn had agreed. It was what a submissive did, right? Be agreeable. But Lucas seemed to want Quinn to *want* what Lucas wanted, and Quinn didn't know anything about how to fake that. He certainly didn't have enough feelings to make real expressions of interest. He'd already forgotten the name of the museum.

"You vex me," said Lucas as they walked through the first gallery. "I really don't know what to do with you." Quinn felt

Lucas giving him a considering look, which seemed different than the considering looks he'd given him before. Not that Quinn was an expert, but those looks had felt like suspicion. This look was something else, a kind of smoldering.

I'm getting to him.

Instead of encouraging the smoldering, Quinn decided to be vindictive.

"Well, you won't have to worry. I'll be leaving soon."

"You've just arrived," said Lucas.

"I have the London premiere at the end of the month, and all the prep work for it starts next week."

"Prep work?" asked Lucas like he thought Quinn was making excuses.

"Marketing meetings, distribution reviews, logistics, fittings."

"I see."

Lucas looked so surprised that Quinn laughed. "Did you think I was just going to live here indefinitely like Hannah?"

"Hannah's staying until Carnevale." Lucas frowned. "Well, I'm not done with you. I don't see how you can leave." They had paused before an oil painting of some bloody ancient scene, a man's torn and bleeding back, an archer poised for the killing shot unseen from the shadows at the edge of the scene. Lucas's frown deepened as he gazed at it. "Are you going back to her?"

"If she'll have me."

"You're not right for her." For once the insult didn't sting, as though the arrows Lucas was firing that day had been blunted.

"Can I ask you an honest question?"

Lucas waved his hand through the air and almost smacked a passing tourist in the head. "What does it matter? You're already moving on. You don't care about what we're doing here."

Before he knew what he was doing, Quinn reached out, caught Lucas's hand midflight, and held it still. "I care," he said, perhaps too forcefully. "But I have responsibilities."

For a moment Lucas studied him, trying to mince his words,

then he shrugged. "What's your question? It better not be boring."

"Why do you think she left you?"

"She didn't leave me. We agreed to take time apart. I was a distraction from school."

"Is that your final answer?"

Lucas slanted his eyes at Quinn. "You think you know a better answer?"

"I'm asking what you believe happened."

"Why would what I believe not be the truth?"

"What is truth?"

"Don't even. Your capacity to reason using philosophical theory could be unmanned by an ant."

They walked up the stairs to the second-floor gallery where the very famous Venus painting lived. There was a crowd of people all around it so Quinn could only see the top from a distance, a naked woman with a very crooked neck and wild red hair that had nothing on Larisa's.

Is it famous because it's really better than all these others, or is it famous because someone said so a long time ago and now everyone recognizes it? Quinn kept the thought to himself so Lucas couldn't judge his small mind.

Finally, Lucas said, "We didn't want the same things. And neither of us was willing to give up what we wanted for the other person."

"A tragedy then."

"The difference between the love stories of the old compared to the young is that the old become attached to things. Our quest for love is no longer the all-powerful engine, it's a sidecar."

"So you understand why I have to leave."

"I understand why you *think* you must leave."

They moved on to another painting, then another. A Madonna and child with halos, a Medici celebrity in his red hat and cloak, another scene of ancient violence, Caesar betrayed by Brutus. Lucas's silence began to grate on Quinn's nerves. Why did he feel like he needed Lucas's permission to leave? More importantly, why did he want it?

They drove back to the villa in silence. It wasn't a long drive, but Lucas pulled out his pocket watch twice to check the time. Sometimes, with the way he looked out the window, Quinn thought he was thinking about something entirely separate from Quinn's planned departure. It should've made Quinn feel better. Instead, it just reminded him how he was failing. Quinn ran his fingers over the buttons on his vest. *Not failing entirely*, he thought. *Not yet.*

In their absence, the villa had descended into chaos. The front drive was filled with delivery trucks. Both the front door and the side doors of the old carriage house stood open. People rushed in and out. Lucas checked his watch a third time.

"They should be done by now."

Rifat came out of the breezeway with a stack of pastry boxes bound in twine in one hand and waving a phone in the other. "Phone!" he called.

Why can't he just be a baker's son? thought Quinn as he eyed the phone. It looked like the burners used in cartel movies, the ones with easy-to-access sim cards and pay-in-advance network plans.

"I need to step away," said Lucas. "Why don't you get dressed for the night?"

"What about the buttons?" asked Quinn.

But Lucas was already walking away, phone pressed to his ear.

"Have a good time?" asked Rifat.

"Who's on the phone?"

"Just a friend. Something about this weekend."

"You're a terrible liar."

"Yeah, well." Rifat clapped him on the back. "Don't take it personally."

Excellent advice, thought Quinn. But still, he stood watching Lucas's retreating back, feeling abandoned. *I need to know who he's talking to.*

Quinn thought if he rushed, he could change clothes and go eavesdrop at Lucas's office. The only problem with this was the buttons. The rush of Lucas's exit, then Quinn's subsequent rush to his room, had made him jittery, which made it nearly impossible to do the fine motor work of unbuttoning himself. In bitter urgency, Quinn yanked the clothes off wholesale and pulled on the outfit that had been laid out on his bed. The fabric of the matching jacket and pants had the sheen of velvet but not as heavy. Under the jacket, a paisley disco shirt with buttons that didn't start until halfway down his chest.

He was waiting for that call when we were at the museum, thought Quinn. Maybe they'd only gone to the museum because Lucas had wanted the distraction. Maybe he didn't care at all that Quinn would be leaving.

It was all a lot to think about. He took the back stairs up to the second floor and jogged down the central hall of the southern wing to the palazzo only to find Lucas with Rifat at the top of the stairs about to descend. Quinn slowed down and shifted to the left side wall so he would be out of their field of vision as he approached.

"I'm not convinced it was Agent Smith." said Lucas. "The timing's too close. Call in your closers. See if they can dig up any contacts."

"Sometimes things are just what they look like," said Rifat.

"Ana isn't that sloppy."

"Send a message to Lava. Not now, wait a few hours so it doesn't look like a reaction. Tell them to start moving the stock."

"You think they're on the secure lines now?" asked Rifat.

"I think we should act as though there's a leak beyond the one I patched."

Quinn was almost upon them. It felt like he'd heard too much, and he didn't want them to know so he flapped his arms as though testing the limits of his new jacket. "What do you think, Rifat? I'm old school tonight."

Their heads both snapped to the side so quickly Quinn knew he had to cover for their surprise or he'd be in trouble. "It's just me," he laughed.

Rifat recovered first. He reached out and touched the sleeve of Quinn's jacket. "People are going to be stroking you all night."

Quinn gave Lucas a devious glance that he hoped looked authentic. "I think that's the idea."

For a moment, Lucas looked annoyed, then he motioned Quinn to his side. "Come along then."

They descended to the square where Lucas's wait staff rushed around erasing evidence of the last minute delivery truck chaos. Hannah drifted among them in a modest, brown cocktail dress. Quinn accidently met her eyes as he was trying to process what he'd heard. He saw her expression change, felt her home in on him in a way that felt too obvious. *She could be the leak*, he thought. *They'll be watching her.* If she was too friendly with him, would suspicion also fall on him? A spike of panic shot through him, made him want to brace for impact, but before they reached her, the doorbell rang. The guests had arrived.

The painters were a mixture of members from a Florentine artists' collective and local hobbyists who thought they might like to become painters. They were accompanied by three master instructors and three subjects. Not surprisingly, all three subjects were exceptionally beautiful women who didn't look older than eighteen.

Quinn had assumed that since Lucas had dressed him and he was Lucas's special guest, that he would have a place at Lucas's side the entire night. But just like on New Year's Eve, Lucas didn't introduce Quinn to anyone. After the third circulation to a new group of people who all ignored him, Quinn gave up his invisible place at Lucas's side and prowled the walls of the piazza with Rifat.

"Did something go wrong with his work today?" asked Quinn.

"Why?"

"He seems distant."

"Maybe you did something to upset him."

"I said I'd have to go home soon."

"That would do it, don't ya think?"

"You tell me. Doesn't he tell you everything?"

Rifat laughed. "He doesn't. And I don't want him to."

Fair enough, thought Quinn. He pointed down at the brand-new basketball shoes Rifat was wearing. "Nice shoes."

"Thanks. They're Villains by Li-Ning."

Over dinner, a man who was apparently the Florentine chief of police complained loudly that there was more to art than the nubile female—no offense ladies—and what was he expected to look at all weekend? This was related by Rifat who translated as he and Quinn stood in the corner of the dining room and watched.

Perhaps something was lost in translation because the man, who everyone called Commissario, had brought along a fair-haired companion with dark, soulful eyes and visible nipple rings under his thin satin shirt.

The Commissario's complaints were met with equal vigor by Marchella, the leader of the artist's collective and one of the master instructors for the weekend. She argued that the retreat had been canceled three times, once solely due to a conflict in his schedule, so she'd brought what she'd brought, and please don't be insulting to her daughter—one of the subjects—who'd given up her time to fill in for a last-minute absence.

Among the true artists, two were students; one was from France, which Rifat found funny because the French had a reputation for not thinking there was any art worth studying in Italy. The hobbyists included a real estate manager and his wife and a pair of newlyweds whose honeymoon had been canceled because of a severe cold front in Poland.

After dinner, they moved to the drawing room for the opening lecture and exercises. Lucas worked his way through the guests, chatting with a stilted formality that showed his distraction.

"Why is he doing that?" Quinn asked Rifat. "He already met everyone."

"It's a thing he does," said Rifat.

Yes, Quinn had seen similar glad-handing at the film society meeting. "But why these people?"

"It's what you do when you want people to like you, right?"

The idea that Lucas would care if these people liked him surprised Quinn. *He's lonely.* Quinn knew all too well what it was like to be in a room full of people and feel terribly alone. *Do not pity him.*

"The set up looks good," said Rifat, pulling Quinn out of his thoughts. He saw how easily the guests navigated the set he'd designed. The easels had been set up in pairs around a pedestal draped with a damask shawl and topped with a vase of fresh-cut calla lilies. The idea being that the more experienced artists would guide the less experienced artists. He saw that the lighting was just as he'd expected, no glare or shadow. And that when there needed to be a shadow, the instructor could create one by turning off one lamp.

"Lucas doesn't seem to have noticed." Quinn searched the room for Lucas and found he'd gone out the glass door to the patio and was on the phone again.

A deep voice called out across the room. "Aha, c'è qualcosa di bello per me da guardare."

Beside Quinn, Rifat chuckled. "You've been spotted."

Quinn followed his gaze to the Commissario headed straight for them.

"Come ti chiamano ora che sei venuto sulla terra?" He petted Quinn's sleeve as he took his hand and kissed it.

"Questo è Quinn VanderVeer. È un regista Americano," said Rifat.

"American?" The Commissario sighed. "I suppose you are one of those tight asses."

"I am," said Quinn, trying to look as cold and straight as possible.

"Allora, we want you anyway. I like to practice English."

Quinn looked back at Rifat for help as the Commissario took Quinn by the hand and led the way to his painting station. Rifat mimed that he wasn't getting involved.

The Commissario and his paramour had Quinn sit on a stool between them and give them nonsense advice on their painting as they followed the master's lecture. Every comment they made came with their free hand touching his arm or his shoulder or his back in a way that unnerved him at first. He didn't like being touched in public by strangers. But when Lucas came back inside and Quinn caught him watching, he decided it was a reasonable price to pay to remind his host that other people found Quinn desirable.

At the end of the lecture, after they made him decide which of them had done the better still life, they invited him to go back to their room. He politely declined but couldn't manage to escape an end-of-the-night top off of hot brandy, which he only pretended to drink.

By the time he'd detached himself from the Commissario, Lucas had disappeared again. Quinn found him alone in the small den where he'd watched Larisa's live stream. A fire had been built up. Lucas lay on a sofa staring at the ceiling, fingers interlaced across his chest, lost in thought.

"Mind if I join you?"

"Why would you want to join me?"

"That's a surprising amount of self-loathing for a Friday night." Quinn picked up Lucas's feet and settled himself at the end of the sofa beneath them. "You don't like the painters?"

"I don't like the Commissario grabbing at you."

"No?"

"He's not worth your time."

"But that's not what's bothering you. Would you like me to guess?" Quinn quirked his mouth in that suggestive way he knew Larisa liked. She said it lit up his whole face with an unspoken promise.

Larisa. Quinn's heart ached.

"You think I'm a monster," said Lucas.

"How much did you drink tonight?"

"There are people whose lives have made death common, then there are those where it's so uncommon, the timely deaths of aged relatives will haunt them for years. You're the latter. You can't possibly understand me."

I know you're lonely, thought Quinn. *You believe you're too unique for public consumption so you hide even when you're with people.*

"In my experience, when people say something like that, it's more about how they see themselves than what others actually see."

Quinn watched the shadows of firelight play across Lucas's dark expression. The undertone of malice that usually marred his features had faded. He appeared soft, vulnerable in a way Quinn had never seen. *He's really upset about something,* thought Quinn.

"Goes back to storytelling, doesn't it?" mused Lucas. "When you build a character, you ask, How do they make sense of their choices? Is it different than how the reader makes sense of them?"

"And it varies from reader to reader," said Quinn. "But you're not a character in a story."

"You judge me. I see it when you look in my eyes. You see, I have that in me. Monster is a plausible story because I'm one of those people."

What were they really talking about? Monster was a particular word to put out into the world without context.

"What would you think if I said Larisa had killed someone to protect you?"

Sharp cold clamped down on Quinn's chest. For a moment he lost awareness of his place in the room. One word wrapped itself around his brain stem. *No. No. No.* Somewhere, some other part of him knew he was supposed to answer. When he dug them out, the words didn't sound like they came from him. "She would never do that."

"And yet sometimes it happens," mused Lucas. "So many movies with that unlikely person trapped in circumstances beyond their control."

No. No. No.

Quinn gathered himself, placed his awareness back in his body, his feet, his hands, his lap with a pair of wool-socked feet resting on it. "You asked Larisa to kill someone?"

"Why do you think I'm part of it?"

"That's the most plausible narrative. Every movie involving Washington, DC has told me that political people find it useful to commission murders."

In Quinn's peripheral vision, he saw Lucas smile. Then, just as quickly as it'd come, the expression vanished. "You should go to bed. The forecast isn't good for tomorrow. You might be called on to entertain our guests."

"Don't I get to know what happened?"

"She lied to me. I just have to prove it."

"She's not your hitman. Lying was probably the only option you left her." Quinn paused for breath, then couldn't stop himself from adding. "I don't want to be your pawn."

"Then you should've stayed in Minnesota." Lucas yanked his feet up from Quinn's lap and pointed toward the door. "Go. I'm done with you tonight."

Quinn stood, panting, halfway between panic and picking a real fight. He wanted to burn all his painstakingly constructed bridges, tell Lucas exactly what he thought of him, demand straight answers. Instead, Quinn fled the den. In the hallway, he pulled out his phone.

The call went straight to voicemail. It was the middle of the afternoon in California and Larisa's phone was off.

"Larisa, it's me. I just heard—I'm sorry. I didn't mean for it to be like this. I didn't think he'd—it doesn't matter. I'm an idiot. But you knew that already. I'm coming home. We'll figure this out I promise. Just . . . I love you."

Chapter 21

A Body at the Country Club

"Do you know where Lucas is?" asked Larisa.

"Florence. But he was recently in Germany." Pam wore a frown like a disgruntled monarch. "It's likely he's responsible for the disappearance of a man who was working as one of my informants within Lucas's organization."

"Did that person know John's death was staged?"

"Not exactly."

They were sitting by the window overlooking the putting lawn at the Los Angeles Country Club. Pam had chosen the location for their meeting, which had been a mistake, and made Larisa doubt her qualifications as a criminal mastermind. She hadn't thought about how crowded the restaurant would be at noon on a Thursday, which was Swiss steak day. And while crowds did sometimes make meetings innocuous, Larisa being at the club was the opposite.

She'd dressed down, put her hair up in a bun, wore a conservative, cowl-neck sweater with a jacket that smelled like smoke. They'd already been interrupted three times by people coming up to ask about her parents or express sympathy over the fire, which had made the front page of the *LA Daily News* and *Deadline*.

"The thing we're looking for wasn't on the island," said Pam.

"You're sure?"

"He hired transportation. We bought some people on the crew who reported that they only loaded munitions and anti-tank rocket launchers."

That's not nothing, thought Larisa. The next time she saw Agent Osna she was going to give him an earful about the hypocrisy of the CIA only caring about nerve gas.

"Where did it go?"

"We made sure the boat was intercepted by Indonesian coast guard." Pam smiled faintly. "I think I've proven worthy of your information."

"Unless he's testing us." Larisa tried to think, but everything in her head felt murky. "A raid on the winery will be obvious now."

"What winery?" asked Pam.

A man in a sweater vest approached their table. "Sorry to interrupt. Larisa, I'm so pleased to see you out and about."

"Hello, Mr. Cerner."

"I think you're old enough now to call me Frank, right?" He patted her shoulder. "Please tell your father thank you again for his support. We've had the best response. Oh, and lunch is on the house today. So sorry about your apartment."

Larisa forced a smile. When he'd gone, she savagely cut a piece of her steak and shoved it in her mouth. "My dad gave money for the new carriage house."

"There's a carriage house?"

"For the equestrian club."

Pam took a moment to process this, then returned to their conversation. "What winery?"

"Not now."

"We can make it look like it came from someone else."

"Like my cousin?"

Pam backtracked. "You're right. There's some time. I haven't seen a listing for the gas yet. But it's possible he acquired it for a specific buyer. If he moves it—"

"I know." She didn't point out that her time was limited if Lucas knew Hagan was alive.

"And the CIA is getting restless."

"What do you know about the CIA? Shouldn't you two be

like oil and water?" Larisa took another bite of her steak. Two tables over, a woman was watching her with that look Larisa knew too well. *She's going to come over and say something.* Her hand jittered as she reached for her water. *Too much coffee today, Larisa.* Sid had been watching out for her eating and drinking schedule, but today he was out of town, and she'd sunk back into that unsettling blur of time. It felt like he'd been away for a week and also just a few hours.

"What else do you have that we can act on now?"

"Money."

For a moment, Pam stared at her, nothing moving except her eyelids doing a slow, disbelieving blink. "How?"

"He has an accounting firm."

"I mean, how could you have walked out of his life with that information?"

"He trusts me." Something bitter overwhelmed the steak in Larisa's mouth, a bad peppercorn that tasted like guilt. *Lucas deserves it,* she thought. But the demon side of her descended from the brain fog and said, *But he doesn't deserve to be betrayed.*

Which is exactly what he's counting on. More bitterness, not the guilty kind.

"What's the name of the firm?" asked Pam.

The woman had left her table and was on her way. *I really can't today, lady,* thought Larisa. And then, because why not? She raised her voice and said, "It's called the Striped Blossom." Larisa made two circles in the air with her hands to illustrate a luscious backside, then mimed her hands cupping them.

"It's a bondage club south of the river. Very clean. Expert staff. They have an exotic Scandinavian domme who learned how to whip at Harvard."

Pam was staring with her mouth open, half-masticated salad visible inside. Larisa had just enough time to flash her a winning smile before she turned to face the oncoming woman who was now red in the face and fuming, drawing all kinds of attention so that the tables around were already watching when she said, "You should be ashamed of yourself, young lady. This is a family place. Children could be led into darkness by seeing you."

"The darkness of the passion that created them? Or the things they think about at night when they're alone in their beds?"

The woman's hand lashed out and slapped Larisa across the cheek. Later, Larisa would regret what she did next because her mother found out. But in the moment, it felt like a win. Also, being slapped in the face was a level of assault that gave Larisa permission to stand and present her ass to the woman.

"These are the cheeks I like to have slapped, ma'am."

The woman's eyes went wild. Her rage consumed whatever she might've said next. Larisa moved to sit back down, but Pam was gathering her purse, clearly more embarrassed by the attention than Larisa.

They walked out with Pam in the lead and Larisa trailing because she didn't want to appear like she was retreating from the fight.

"You're unbelievable."

"I try."

"The idea is not to be memorable."

"I don't think anyone will remember you."

"But it will be talked about. And someone will inevitably wonder, what was Larisa de France-Kahn doing at lunch? Who was she with? Senator Hagan's widow. That's strange. How do they know each other?"

"We met through Kahleah. Your husband was supporting her husband's campaign, remember?"

Pam deflated. "Yes, that's right. Fuck. This business." She shook her head, then began to laugh. "You have balls though. That woman. Is the accounting firm really a bondage club?"

"I think the direct translation is cave of pleasure."

"And I'm looking for a Scandinavian who went to Harvard."

"But you're going to be discreet."

Pam pulled out her phone. "We already have people in place in Florence. I'm sure they'd love to go to a club and do research."

As Pam was dialing, a man who looked just like a secret service agent approached her and said softly, "We have a situation."

"And?"

"Security breach."

"Here?" Pam glanced around the parking lot, every visible stall full. People in polos and sport coats and golf shoes walked in and out of the club's front doors.

"This way," said the agent.

The two of them began to walk down the lot. Not entirely sure that their meeting was over, Larisa followed.

Then she wished she hadn't.

They stopped at the back of a black SUV. The agent moved to the back door and opened it. Ana lay across the backseat, her neck a swollen mass of bruising from the giant hands that had crushed her windpipe.

"Oh fuck," gasped Larisa.

"Caught her snooping around Dr. de France-Kahn's Bentley."

"And you just killed her?" gasped Larisa. Her demon ego-voice added, *He called you doctor,* as a side note.

The security agent glanced at her, then at Pam as though he felt it unnecessary to explain himself. But Pam nodded.

"She took some photos of the two of you through the window just there." He pointed toward the lawn. "When it appeared like she was going to send them, I intervened." He handed Pam Ana's phone. "The threat was contained."

"You know this woman?"

"She works for Lucas," said Larisa.

"Did you tell her we were meeting today?"

"Obviously not."

"How did she follow you?"

"I don't know. She showed up—"

"Give me your phone," said Pam.

"What?"

The security agent yanked Larisa's bag off her arm and held it open for Pam.

"Excuse me. You can't just—"

Pam dug around inside and found Larisa's phone. She cracked off the cream and gold Lancôme cover, popped open the battery cover, removed the battery, the sim card, then snapped it in half. The sound the plastic made was like one of Larisa's bones being broken.

"That's my life you just destroyed," said Larisa.

Pam handed the security agent Larisa's keys. "Make it look good."

"What? No. I need that car. You can't do that."

"We can't have him tracking you."

The agent had already started down the line of cars toward Larisa's Bentley, her bag crunched under his arm.

"That's a Gucci purse, you asshole." He didn't stop. Larisa could've chased him, but it seemed unlikely she'd be able to change the trajectory of the situation. "This isn't happening."

"How long has he been tracking you?" asked Pam.

"Are we sure that's the reason? Ana could have just—"

"You weren't followed here. My people would've seen it. Do you think it's been since Christmas? That would mean he knows you met John at that dinner."

Larisa opened her mouth to protest that she was sure Lucas had better things to do. She closed it when she realized how silly that would sound.

"You should ask him for money."

"What?"

"Ask Lucas for money to pay the men you hired to kill John."

Larisa reached out and braced her hand against the taillight of the SUV.

"Actually, it's probably too late for that. He'll already be wondering. And wondering is as good as the truth. You should probably go underground."

"Underground," repeated Larisa. *What about Quinn?*

"He could come after you for deceiving him," Pam sounded

like she was talking to herself, making her own plans. "He'll want the truth."

Larisa pressed her hand against her mouth to suppress a sob. "You have to fix this. I can't—I have to warn him." Larisa looked around for her bag to retrieve her phone, then remembered they were gone.

"Warn who?" Pam's voice became prickly with suspicion, which Larisa barely noticed.

Oh, right. I didn't tell her about Quinn.

"What's going to happen to my car?"

"Larisa, are you lying to me?"

And that right there, the super intense look on Pam's face, told Larisa all she needed to know about trusting Pam with Quinn. She pulled herself upright, tried to look like the world didn't feel like it was unraveling around her, and gave Pam her best clinician's face. "If you're talking to the CIA, maybe you could tell them you're getting close to the gas. That way they don't make a mistake and drop a bomb on Umbras."

"Bomb Tuscany?" Pam laughed. "They're not planning anything that extravagant."

"What then?" *And how do you know?* Larisa's throat ached. She wanted to scream. She was so, so tired of secrets.

Poor Ana.

"I want you to come with me."

"Where?"

"My house. We'll set you up there until this is over."

"I have a home," said Larisa. Then, realizing she had no phone, no car, and that no one knew where she was, she began to walk backward. Her eyes skittered around the parking lot looking for more of Pam's security agents.

Pam followed her. "You're a liability. I need you with me."

"That's why I have the phone. Call me when you have something." Larisa turned and not quite ran back into the club. The concierge smiled to welcome her back and she returned it, sidling up to him as she watched the door.

"Do you have a member directory?"

"Of course."

Pam didn't follow her inside but stood under the breezeway watching through the window.

"Will you call Jaden Valdez?"

This request seemed to amuse the concierge, but he woke up his computer and opened the directory app to look up Jaden's number. Besides her parents, who she would not call, Jaden was the only one Larisa knew for certain kept an active membership at the club; her husband Adrian liked to play golf. Of course it was Jaden.

The ringer on the phone was loud enough for Larisa to hear it. *Pick up, pick up, pick up.*

What was Jaden normally doing right now? Mid-afternoon. Was it Thursday or Friday?

Thursday, thought Larisa. The worst Thursday of her life. She craned her neck to see the far end of the parking lot. Her beautiful, cherry red Bentley was gone.

Did I love it because Lucas gave it to me?

The ringing stopped and Jaden's voice broke through the handset speaker. Larisa snatched the phone from the concierge. "Hey Jaden, it's me. I need a ride."

"It's okay if you want to yell at me," said Larisa.

"Some other time." Jaden looked furious, but she'd come. Larisa could barely believe it. "What happened?"

"I think Lucas has been tracking me since we broke up," said Larisa.

"Wow," said Jaden.

"That's all you have to say, wow?"

Jaden scrunched up her nose so her sunglasses rose and covered her eyebrows. "What's the right answer?"

"It's invasive."

"Yeah, but . . . I mean, he cares about you?"

Larisa braced her arm against the door as the Land Rover screeched around a corner.

"He bought me that phone when I graduated."

"You haven't upgraded your phone since college?"

"He knew I was with Steven that night."

"Remind me, who is Steven?"

"My cousin's ex."

"Oh right, the cheater."

"He died in a car accident."

Jaden turned to look at Larisa. "I'm thinking something dramatic. Wanna know what?"

"What?"

"He's your one true love."

"Lucas? No."

"A burn down the world, don't care what other people think love that I could've had with Shane if you hadn't ruined it."

"Jaden!"

"I'm just saying—"

"Car!"

"Yeah, yeah." Jaden yanked the steering wheel to avoid t-boning a convertible.

"I bet he told Parish where your wedding was. That's how she knew to come find Quinn. And he would've known my routine at the club, so he could've told Parish that too. He knew when I went to New York." Larisa sucked in a breath and held it. She felt dirty. Like her entire adult life had been a lie. *I was never separated from him. Not in his mind.*

"This is big," said Jaden. "We should take it to happy hour."

"What?"

"Tomorrow, happy hour. You need to update the girls on all this."

Tomorrow felt like a long way away. "Can I stay at your place tonight?"

"I was already thinking that. Good thing it's only four. We have plenty of time to set up for your event. Can we add a note in your introduction where you say, 'Streaming from the gorgeous living room of—'"

"What event?" asked Larisa.

Jaden gave her a look.

This is shock, Larisa told herself. *You're in shock.* But the timing seemed strange. After so much had happened, why now? The fact that she was having this problem at all was surprising. She thought she was beyond shock. She'd always taken pride in her ability to handle whatever came. Not the dead body of a girl who'd never had a chance. Not Lucas secretly monitoring her life.

I believed we'd come to an understanding.

Even with Jaden's harrowing driving, Larisa was able to collect some vital fragments of herself as they drove up the mountain. By the time they arrived, she knew hosting her BDSM live stream discussion would be impossible. The first thing that needed to be done was contact Teale and ask her to handle it, but without her phone, the process became insurmountable. Larisa dragged herself into the great room, collapsed on the sofa, and didn't move until Jaden's little dog came and began to lick her arm.

"You should hydrate," called Jaden from the kitchen.

"Does it come with Xanax?" Larisa knew it wasn't a good idea to medicate. She already felt too slow and unfocused. But at the same time, there was this strange, jittery feeling in her legs like they wanted to spring up and run.

When did I eat?

Sid will be worried.

Ana's dead.

Ana's dead.

In another life, we could've been friends.

In another life, I could've been her.

Larisa managed to turn her head and look down at the dog. It gazed up at her expectantly, tongue hanging out, panting, slobbering quite a lot for such a little mouth. *I've turned into a cat person.*

It was too much work to push the dog away.

Jaden came in with a tray and brightly colored glasses with straws built into them, the adult version of something Larisa was sure she'd ordered from a cereal box as a kid.

"Adrian has some Valium left over from his surgery. Would that help?"

Larisa shook her head. "I just need you to . . ."

What? There'd been thoughts, next steps in her head, now they were gone.

Does Quinn think I've killed someone?

He'll be worried when I don't answer his call.

"You have a laptop?"

"Yes, uh, I think so. Not quite sure where." Jaden handed her a glass. "You just sit tight."

Larisa's fingers curled around the glass, felt its strangely smooth texture and how it wasn't as cool as she expected. The drink inside wasn't chilled. It looked like water but tasted like chemicals.

I could have saved her if I'd known.

Lucas did this.

She reached out beside her for the phone that wasn't there, thinking she'd call him, she'd say the things she'd been holding back, and somehow, they'd turn him into a different person. The force of his love for her would shame him.

Or something.

No phone.

But Jaden had returned with a laptop, the power cord spilling off the top and trailing on the floor. The dog jumped off the couch to yip at it.

"I think it's dead. When are you supposed to start?"

"Later," said Larisa, answering a different question, or maybe the same question in a different version. It didn't matter. Her mind was doing strange things. There was Lucas on a stone-covered beach with waves that sounded like a landslide, pant legs rolled up so he could wade out to a dark space that looked like a cave. He'd promised to retrieve a treasure and bring it back to her.

Lucas in Vienna in the thin hours of a New Year's Day whispering in her ear that she had ruined him. She could feel his lips on her neck, the soft brush of them like a magnet pulling her backward in time. And how she longed to go back to that time, when she didn't know, when nothing else had existed except Lucas and whatever they were doing together next.

An entirely different way of living. An impossible dream.

"Can I see your phone?"

The weight of the unfamiliar phone made Larisa's fingers clumsy. She almost dropped it before she managed to activate the screen, and almost dropped it again shifting it to one hand so she could open YouTube.

What's it called?

Larisa stared at the screen, straining to pull together two halves of a thought, an impression. Lucas, the record player. Him saying, "She's praying to the goddess for the war to end because so much has been lost."

An opera with a woman's name.

Maria.

Joan.

Ana.

Larisa squeezed her eyes shut, fingers typing. When she opened her eyes, she found the name on the screen, *Norma*, scrolled until she found the famous aria Lucas had argued was the aria that defined all others: "Casta Diva."

"What's this?" asked Jaden, who wasn't an opera person.

"A prayer for peace."

It has to end.

Chapter 22

Night Visit

"What do you mean you're in San Diego?" asked Quinn as he slammed his door closed and turned the key in the lock.

"The second college visit," said Sid. "What's wrong with you?"

"I need you to find Larisa."

"Didn't know she was missing."

"Her phone's off. I don't—I think something happened." A breath that felt like there was glass in Quinn's lungs. But he took another one in the hope that the dark spots encroaching around the edge of his vision would dissolve. The hand holding his phone was going numb.

"Did you call her?"

"Of course I called her. The phone's off."

"Okay, yeah. Let me finish up, and I'll call you from the road."

"Sid."

"What?" The note of impatience in Sid's voice was enough for Quinn to bite back what he would've said next. He had to be reasonable. Whatever had happened, Sid rushing up from San Diego wouldn't fix it. Putting him in the middle of an unknown situation might just make things worse. He had no idea what Larisa's life had been like while he'd been gone.

She's been talking to Lucas.

Quinn realized Sid had hung up, but he was still holding the phone to his ear. He stumbled to the bed and let it drop there, a black dark box. All he wanted was for it to light up, a message, an incoming call. Larisa always had her phone.

Slowly, his breathing became less painful. He drummed his fingers on his knees, his thighs, his chest. This was his body. These were all the parts, alive and well and of value even if he felt the opposite. When he felt able, he moved to the armoire and pulled his bag out of the bottom.

Packing.

And when that was done, and he still hadn't heard from Sid, Quinn made his nest of a bed on the floor by the window and sat with his back against the wall, the duvet wrapped around his shoulders to keep off the chill.

First he called Larisa with the same result.

Then he called Sid. No answer.

He Thought about who else he could call and decided against it. He had Kahleah's number, but he didn't know what he could say without having to explain too much. And Larisa might never forgive him for pulling one of her friends into her mess. *Their* mess.

He fell asleep but dreamed of sitting awake, watching the door to his bedroom, the shadows of moonlight and wind-whispered trees scattering across the floor. And then he was awake, and Lucas was there, kneeling directly before him, watching.

"Agh!"

"Shh," whispered Lucas. "The house is asleep."

For a moment, Quinn thought he was dreaming. But his heart was pounding, and all the smells of Lucas were coming up to him in a rush, so he thought not. No dream was that vivid.

Lucas reached out and pressed a finger against Quinn's lips. The pressure became a stroke against the shape of Quinn's mouth, which he'd never thought about until now, under the pristine line of fire marked by Lucas's fingernail.

"You think badly of me," said Lucas in that same soft whisper.

Quinn tried to shake his head, but the rest of Lucas's fingers expanded out and cupped his chin.

"What did you tell her?"

"Nothing," said Quinn.

The cupped fingers dug in, pressed skin to bone, insistent. "What did you tell her?"

"She didn't answer when I called. Her phone's off."

The hand released Quinn's chin, retracted. Lucas shifted his knees, straddled Quinn's legs, and edged closer so they were almost nose to nose. Lucas peered at him.

"Do you know what I could do to you right now with just my hands?"

Quinn swallowed. As he did, an inflection of memory came to him, the way his throat had ached after Lucas had almost strangled him. He imagined that had been the smallest taste of what Lucas could do with those hands.

A voice that certainly wasn't his own murmured, *Play the role.*

"I have imagined some things," said Quinn.

Lucas blinked at him. Then, as though taking up the challenge, he grasped the bottom hem of Quinn's shirt and yanked it up over his head in one smooth motion.

"Tell me." Lucas's voice rumbled down Quinn's spine, a growl. "What things?"

"As quiet as tea leaves unfurling their edges. As loud as a bugle call shattering the first mists of morning."

Lucas went still, almost as though he'd forgotten both his original threat and the course correction Quinn had laid down, and now they had stepped over an invisible threshold into some other place. *Where did those words come from?*

From the look on Lucas's face, he seemed to be wondering the same thing. He appeared stunned, as though, instead of poetry, Quinn had slapped him across the face.

"Write it down," said Lucas as he pushed up onto the balls of his feet. "Write more, write everything."

He stood and retreated to the door.

"Wait," said Quinn, also struggling to his feet. "Why did you come in here? You thought I'd said something to Larisa."

"It's probably nothing," said Lucas. "She canceled her discussion."

Chapter 23

Cloud Nine Crashing

The sisters, plus baby Maria Josephina Raphaella, were already in the usual booth when Larisa and Jaden arrived at Cloud Nine. *The last time I was here, I wore jeans,* thought Larisa. But she couldn't for the life of her place that day in a time relative to this one. Had it been the previous week? The past month?

"Why is it all so exhausting?" Krissy was asking the universe as they sat down. "Oh look, they're friends again. Did you hug it out?"

"Risa had an emergency," said Jaden.

"Don't even talk about exhausting," said Rosa, continuing the previous conversation. "This child will not sleep."

"But she's so cute." Krissy held Maria up to Kahleah. "Isn't she cute?"

"Adorable." Kahleah looked across the table at Larisa as though she'd come to happy hour with a different agenda than everyone else. *Are we fighting?* wondered Larisa. This felt like a thing that'd happened, but the details were unclear.

"Is your emergency why you're ignoring me?" asked Kahleah.

This seemed a difficult question. Larisa wanted the answer to be no, but she did go through periods of strategically ignoring people. She opened her mouth to answer, but Jaden cut in.

"She broke up with her phone because of Lucas."

"*Lucas*, Lucas?" asked Rosa. "Is he—?"

"No," said Larisa.

"Yes," said Jaden.

"Remember what we told you about New Year's? Quinn went over there to try to convince Lucas to fuck off," said Krissy.

"Right, right, but what does that have to do with Risa's phone?"

Someone opened Cloud Nine's front door and Larisa glanced over to watch who was coming in. *Maybe it'll be Quinn,* she thought, even though there was no reason to think Quinn had come back to LA. In that microcosm of a moment, as the door stood open, she needed it to be him. He needed to be home and safe.

He has no idea what Lucas is capable of.

This has to end.

Those four small words had been playing over and over in her head since she'd left the country club. Each time they came with a dip in her gut like the floor had dropped out and she was plummeting through empty space. She'd tried to do the reasonable thing. With Pam she'd even tried the unreasonable thing. And still nothing. She felt even more fatally linked to Lucas than before.

He'll find out I'm feeding Pam information.

He'll kill Quinn just like he did Steven.

No, thought Larisa, not like Steven, the disposable, not worth her time cheater. It'd be worse than that because Quinn mattered.

"So . . . what's going on?" asked Rosa.

"He put trackers in her phone and the car," said Jaden.

"No!" gasped Krissy. The horrified look on her face made Larisa feel a little better. At least one of the sisters understood the violation.

"Since when?" asked Kahleah.

"Since always," said Jaden. "Isn't that amazing? She thought they'd broken up, but like, they hadn't. He's been secretly waiting for her to come back to him."

"Uh, Jaden, I don't think—"

"So, he knows you were at my house with Senator Hagan?"

Kahleah was pulling out her phone. Larisa wondered who she was going to call about that damning little detail.

There's no one to call.

"Larisa?"

Larisa couldn't remember the question Kahleah had asked so she said, "I saw a dead body."

Krissy laughed. "Like at Madame Tussauds?"

"In the parking lot of the country club."

"Oh." Another Krissy laugh, less certain this time.

"Why are you laughing?" asked Larisa.

"I don't know. I mean. It seems funny?"

"Seems like there's a lot of bodies these days," said Rosa. "Hagan on New Year's and now this one. How many people are you supposed to fake kill?" She gave Jaden a knowing look, but Jaden said, "I think this was a real dead body, not a fake one."

They seemed to really see Larisa then, to look closer than they would've otherwise, and in that looking, realized she wasn't quite right. Larisa wanted to say something to erase their concern but formulating a coherent sentence that wasn't going to end in tears seemed unlikely.

"Well, that's what happens when you're . . ." Krissy stopped, focused on her drink.

"I'm a what?" asked Larisa. "Sexually adventurous? Famous? Asking for it?"

"I was going to say obsessed with someone," said Krissy. "Because you were. I mean, even last year weren't we joking that we liked the Larisa-with-Lucas version better than the Doctor-Larisa version?" She looked around the table. No one returned her look. "I'm just saying."

"He was fun," said Rosa. "Remember when life was fun? Now it's like, schedules and money and debt and this school or that school or calls from school. Some asshole actor's kid called Yasmin the c-word on the playground yesterday. How does a six-year-old know the c-word?"

"You're saying I shouldn't have broken up with the terrorist who asked me to kill a US senator?"

"I'm saying we're old," said Rosa.

"Speak for yourself," said Kahleah. "If Cade doesn't get his shit together, I'm ditching his ass and moving to the Bahamas."

"Hurricanes," said Jaden. "Spotty bandwidth."

"Would you really leave him?" asked Krissy. "I mean, that seems like a lot if he's just, you know." On the table, her phone chimed. A moment later, Jaden's echoed it. And then, from somewhere in the depths of their purses, Kahleah and Rosa's.

Krissy was first to her phone. "It's an SOS from your mother." She showed Larisa her screen.

> Risa's Momma: WHERE ARE YOU? HANNAH
> IS HERE TALKING ABOUT BOOBS AND
> SECRET AGENTS.

"Does your mother think of us as extensions of you?" asked Jaden.

"I'm strangely okay with that," said Krissy. "I mean, she invited us to Italy."

"And we declined because we'd never go on a trip with your mom without you," said Rosa.

"I think there's an autocorrect problem here," said Kahleah. "I've met Hannah, and that girl doesn't know anything about boobs."

"Do you want me to call her?" asked Krissy.

"I'm not sure."

"Call her," said Kahleah.

"Hi Suzette, this is Krissy. Yeah, I—"

The phone's earpiece erupted in indistinct yelling. Baby Maria started to cry.

Larisa reached over, took Krissy's phone, and hung up.

"Risa, you okay?" asked Jaden. "You look kind of yellow."

"I just want quiet for a minute."

"Your mom sounds—"

"She'll be fine." *Nothing's fine.* "I can't have that conversation on the phone."

"I'm confused," said Krissy. "What conversation?"

"Hannah has told them Lucas is a terrorist."

A beat of silence, then Kahleah nodded. "Yep, that's an in-person conversation." She pointed at Rosa. "You're sober right? You're driving."

Around her, the sisters slammed back the ends of their drinks, then began to pull on jackets. Someone took each of Larisa's arms, then she was out in the cold and looking down at her feet walking along the pavement thinking how long her legs seemed even though she was wearing flats.

She thought of her father who'd always believed in Larisa's ability to make good decisions. Last spring they'd joked about how, even when things looked dark, she found ways to draw everything together. He'd said she and Quinn didn't have to follow a relationship blueprint laid out by Suzette or the tabloids or anyone else.

He's going to be so disappointed in me.

Larisa had expected her mother's incoherent yelling, but it took her a moment to realize she was yelling about the woman at the country club—who'd ended up being someone important—and not Larisa's questionable choice of boyfriends. What she didn't expect was Sid charging across the foyer of her parents' house demanding to know where she'd been. Kahleah put up a hand to stop him before he exploded on her.

"Whoa, she's here now. Everything's fine."

Everything's not fine, thought Larisa.

"Quinn said I had to find you, and I couldn't."

"I'm sorry," said Larisa. "I lost my phone." Someone's arm was around her back patting her.

"It wasn't her fault," said Kahleah in a voice that told Sid he'd better back off. In the background her mother had stopped yelling and was cooing instead. Rosa had shoved Maria into her arms.

They drifted into the living room. Hannah sat on the love seat picking her nails. At the fireplace, Gunter stood looking at the family portrait that hung over the mantel. *No eye contact,* thought Larisa. It felt like a bad sign. One of her least favorite things was entering a room where the conversation had already started.

The sisters filled up the sectional. Larisa didn't sit down but stood before Hannah, daring her to look up so she could ask with her eyes, *What did you tell them?*

"Alright, now." Gunter moved from the fireplace to take charge of the room. "We're all here. I think this is an excellent opportunity to firmly establish the salient details of the situation. Who would like to start?"

"How's Quinn?" asked Larisa.

"He was fine when I left," said Hannah.

"So why did he think I was in trouble?" *How did he know?* Larisa corrected herself with a better question. *What did he know?* Then she realized anything Quinn knew must have come from Lucas.

Hannah hitched her shoulders up to her ears and let them drop like she didn't know, and she didn't care. Larisa knew this was a performance, that Hannah did care and this scene was probably murdering her in her head, but the performance still made her blood boil. It wasted time they didn't have.

"He was planning to leave." Sid glared at Hannah. "But he sent her in his place because she messed up. Left him to take the fall for it."

Angry tears flooded Hannah's eyes. "I didn't mess anything up! He said he wasn't ready to leave."

"He said that because you didn't give him a choice," said Sid.

"That's not it." Hannah finally looked up, her face full of righteous rage. "You should be happy, Larisa. Your exes like each other so much it was like I didn't exist. I went to help, and it meant nothing."

"You should've stayed out of my business."

"When your business endangers everyone else, you don't get to make that call."

"Notice that nothing went terribly wrong until you decided to play hero."

"I did it for Steven!"

Larisa blinked. And then, because there wasn't anything to say to that except nonsense born out of the fear rushing through her veins, Larisa sat down beside Kahleah. She wrapped her arms around a pillow and concentrated on sitting still. She was just going to sit still. She was just going to be quiet and listen and try to understand all the possible interpretations of 'your exes like each other.' Because she was sure they didn't. Not really. They were both pretending to like each other so they could get what they wanted. *Me.*

"The last I heard from Quinn he was trying to call Larisa. I think he thought Lucas was looking into Hagan," said Sid. "Maybe he didn't buy it? So, I dunno, it seems like we should do something about that?"

"Senator Hagan?" asked Suzette. "What does he have to do with—"

"Different Hagan." Larisa looked to Sid. "I'll call him now if you let me use your phone."

"You can't. Quinn gave his phone to Hannah."

"So he's cut off?"

"That sounds bad," said Krissy.

"But I mean, if he's happy, maybe this is a sign?" asked Jaden.

"Jaden, you're not helping," said Kahleah.

"So what now?" asked Rosa. "It feels like there's just bad things. Bodies in country clubs, dead phones, lost phones, trapped in an Italian villa with a hot, rich—okay, that doesn't sound really terrible."

"Whose body at the club?" asked Suzette.

Larisa opened her mouth for a lie and realized she didn't have any left. Her father had shifted his position at the fireplace, a signal that he was beginning to put things together. Maybe not a complete picture, but enough to know that all the younger people in the room were operating from the knowledge that Lucas wasn't exactly who Larisa had said he was. And unlike her mother, Gunter would've noticed the tragic death of a state senator in the news.

"Now we've had the opening round, I think we should start from the beginning," said Gunter.

"The beginning?" Krissy scrunched up her nose. "Well, it was junior year, right? Summer?"

"We just went over this," said Jaden. "It was October on the train."

"Right. She met Lucas at a party on some sex train thing, and we were all very jealous."

"Even those of us who weren't single were jealous, if we're all being honest here," said Rosa.

"And it turns out he's a terrorist," said Kahleah. "Not like the Vanguard variety we've got here. More like a James Bond villain type terrorist, moves the bad stuff around to bad people, holds meetings in exotic tropical locations, has a secret club."

"I'd like to hear this from Larisa," said Gunter. Finally, he'd looked at her. Larisa could hardly bring herself to meet his gaze, to see the shock there. She'd never given him reason to be concerned like that. She'd always been good, the kind of kid her parents didn't need to worry about. And now he knew it'd all been a lie. She'd gone so far over her head, the only option had been to lie to him. Lies and more lies piled on top of each other. Her dashing lobbyist boyfriend was the one addictive pill she'd allowed herself to swallow. And she was still trying to cut the habit.

Chapter 24

Blood in the Paint

Yesterday, Italian Time

A knock on the door jerked Quinn from a sleep that'd ended up deeper than he'd thought possible after Lucas's invasion and abrupt departure. The time spent afterward had been filled by pouring words onto the pages of his journal by the light of the moon.

Sid hadn't found Larisa. Now it was morning and one of Lucas's staff members had entered his room and was buongironoing him as she hung an outfit on the door of the armoire and said he would be pleased to wear it that day so he could help with the art.

No messages on his phone while he'd slept.

Where did Lucas go this week?

Did he see Larisa?

"Stay calm," Quinn told himself as he began to dress. "There's nothing else you can do right now except what you've been doing."

The new outfit looked like what a high fashion critic would describe as toga-inspired; a tube of violet fabric fastened over one shoulder with three fragile-looking linked chains and gathered at the waist by a matching belt.

If this were a scene in the movie of his life, Quinn thought the scene could be interpreted two ways. The first: His character had officially become a paramour whose body would be on exhibit for Lucas's guests. The second: He was being punished. And what an excellent way to punish a man who best liked to lurk in the shadows of the wallpaper than make him parade in front of strangers?

Both can be true, he thought. It didn't matter. He was done playing games. He texted Sid.

> Quinn: Get me the first flight out of Florence.

> Quinn: Tell me you found her.

Five minutes passed without a notification that Sid had read the messages. Quinn called. The line rang through to voicemail.

Quinn dressed in his own clothes, shoved the rest of his stuff into his bag, and was just starting toward the door when another knock sounded. He opened the door to find Hannah standing on the other side in a toga similar to the one he was supposed to be wearing, except hers had two shoulders and a slit down the front all the way to the belt.

She blushed when she saw him looking. "I didn't think it would be quite like this." She laughed. "But hey, you only live once. For all I know, this will be the high point." Her eyes swam around the hallway in an unfocused way that made him think she was drunk.

"Why aren't you dressed? The session's starting in like twenty minutes."

"What session?"

"It's raining. They can't go outside to paint the garden so we're going to be models. They're doing the girls as nudes this afternoon." Hannah shuddered. "I don't think I could do that. I mean, I know art has its own morality, but really, it's pornographic."

"Hannah. What's—?"

"I'm fine. Or I'm as fine as you. What's up with you?"

"Lucas asked Larisa to kill someone for him. And either she did it or she lied about it."

"WHAT?" Hannah pushed into his room and closed the door behind her. "Talk fast. Actually, better get dressed while you talk."

"She's not answering her phone."

"Since when?"

"Last night."

"When's the last time you talked to her?" Hannah pulled her phone out of a pocket hidden in the skirt of the toga and dialed. "Get dressed," she hissed. "You have to do this with me before you leave."

It was easier to obey than argue. Quinn was already going numb, segments of his awareness shutting down like lights in a storage facility, a cascade of plunging darkness. But Hannah thrust the toga into his arms and pushed him into the bathroom, closing the door. A few seconds later she yelled, "She didn't answer."

The toga was comfortable to the touch, a soft fabric he might've liked as a blanket. Wearing it was an entirely different matter. He wasn't yet numb enough to ignore how it exposed his arms, one shoulder, some of his chest, his legs past the knees.

"What's taking so long?"

Quinn came out holding the toga in place. The chain fastener had eluded his shaking hands. Hannah did it for him. "I'm going to call Aunt Suzette. She'll know if anything's happened."

"Larisa wouldn't want you to do that."

"Well, she doesn't get a vote if she's not answering, does she?"

"Can we just . . ." Quinn held up his hands, waving them in front of Hannah like he was a magician trying to transform a wild thing into a calm thing.

"She wouldn't kill for him, would she?"

"I'm more concerned what he'd do if she tried to fake it." Quinn lowered his voice. "Ask your handler."

"Why?"

"Just ask."

"But why?"

Quinn sighed. *There's no way Lucas doesn't have some kind of surveillance in this room.* He pulled Hannah out into the hallway. "Larisa might have asked the CIA to help her," he hissed in her ear. "They'd know if something happened."

Up ahead in the hallway, the Commissario's paramour called, "Giorno, Quinn! We're ready for you."

"I don't have time for this," Quinn muttered.

"We have to pretend," said Hannah as she dragged him down the hall toward the drawing room. That morning's instructor beamed a smile so bright Quinn thought everything was okay. They would tell him there'd been some mistake. Larisa was fine. Lucas wasn't the demon he sometimes seemed.

But no, the instructor was just excited about art. And because they were excited, Quinn didn't manage to detach himself from Hannah and walk out of the room.

"How long will this take?" he asked.

"Finché l'arte ha bisogno."

Quinn searched the room for Rifat to translate. The artists were filing in, but no Rifat. The instructor set Hannah up on a stool wrapped with the scarf from the night before.

"Can't you get someone else?" asked Quinn. "I need to go." He tried to walk away, but the instructor gently pushed him into place standing at Hannah's side. He was about to protest more forcefully when Lucas came strolling in with the Commissario. His eyes lit up when he saw Quinn.

"Ciao, bello! I will love to study you all morning," he called as he walked to his easel.

"Would you relax?" hissed Hannah. "You're not leaving me."

Quinn was about to argue. He thought the instructor said it would be hours. He wasn't going to stand for hours while people stared at his body. *How big is the airport here? What if there's only one flight out each day?*

Lucas circulated through his guests. At the end of his circuit, he came up to the instructor to say hello. He gave Quinn a nod of acknowledgement as though nothing was wrong, as though the night before he hadn't said, 'Larisa is lying to me' in a voice that mirrored film versions of historical dictators passing judgement on the people who challenged their rule. *If only he'd become an actor,* thought Quinn.

As he passed them, Lucas reached out and squeezed Hannah's shoulder with an extra weight as though to press her into place and keep her there. After he'd moved on, she wiped at her skin like he'd left a residue.

The instructor began their lecture, moving around Quinn and Hannah, pointing to this or that part of their bodies, the drape of the togas. It seemed they used a great many words for simple things. But what did Quinn know about painting? In those first minutes, his skin prickled with hyperawareness of so many eyes evaluating him. It felt as though they were all deciding if he was worthy, if he was doing a good job, if he was going to make it.

The heat of his rush through the house with Hannah dwindled, replaced with a damp chill. He thought Larisa would find it funny, and so very typical of him, that when he finally made up his mind to do something, he was stalled by other people's expectations. He didn't want to be doing this, and yet he hadn't refused. Maybe this was Hannah's secret superhero skill—she guilted people into helping her. He resented that she was using her 'nice girl from rural Minnesota act' to keep him from leaving.

Or I don't want to leave. The thought came as though from someone else, the version of himself who'd looked at Lucas sitting alone by the fire and thought, *He's fine once you get used to him.*

Better than fine.

"My handler wants account numbers and a list of properties where the gas could be held." Hannah was whispering, but Quinn still glanced to the instructor to see if she'd been overheard.

"Are you seriously talking about this now?"

"Help me think. We're running out of time."

There's no 'we,' thought Quinn. "You're staying for Carnevale," he snapped.

Hannah looked hurt. "Not if he pulled Larisa into something bad."

"They won't be anywhere you can find them without getting caught."

The Commissario's head poked out from the side of his canvas. He gave Quinn a sly look. "Your storm is a beautiful expression."

Quinn tried to retract his face into blank neutrality.

"Have you been in his bedroom yet?" whispered Hannah.

Against his will, memories of the bath came back to him, fed by that other side of himself, the side that wanted to stay. In memory, his mind played tricks on him, painted Lucas in softer tones, made him seem strangely considerate. Quinn didn't need the errors of memory to picture the long line of Lucas sitting on the side of the tub, casual but elegant. Suddenly, Quinn wasn't cold any longer.

"Did you see any computer or flash drives or anything?" asked Hannah.

"No."

"Will you cover for me if I go look?"

"No."

"Why not?"

"Because you won't find anything."

She stuck out her lower lip and turned her head a fraction of an inch to give him a pouty glare. "You haven't fallen for him, have you? He's not a good person. He's selling nerve gas to terrorists."

"Would you keep your voice down?"

Lucas was across the room consulting with a painter on her work. As though he felt Quinn's gaze, he shifted his eyes. Cold. Unreadable. All knowing.

If you've hurt her . . .

"You. Are. Supporting. A. Terrorist."

The instructor was speaking again. Quinn closed his eyes and focused all his senses on that gentle flow of words. He imagined it as a physical river washing over him, warm and scented of basil and thyme like Francie's kitchen, which he wanted to take back to California with him. He imagined the great truths of painting were hidden in those words, how the artists' minds were being filled with inspiration.

His grasp at peace only lasted a moment before he lost it. And thought instead, *What can I do?*

"Leave with me today," he whispered.

"What?"

"Tell him you feel guilty. I've convinced you to come to LA with me and make amends with Larisa."

"But I can't leave with nothing. My handler—"

"You gave them the bakery. They should be able to do their job without you. This is too dangerous."

Hannah fell silent. He could feel heat radiating off her back into his left arm as she argued with herself.

Have I fallen for him?

I thought he was going to teach me how to be a submissive. Aside from the fake sex worker, there hadn't been a hint of the bondage lifestyle that Quinn had expected.

He doesn't even have a bondage room.

Which couldn't be true.

He has to have a bondage room. Why didn't I ask Larisa about it when I had the chance?

"What did you mean before, when you said you were afraid of being caught in the office?" he asked Hannah.

"When?"

"When he's with the prost—the sex worker. You tried to sneak into the office, but you thought he'd catch you."

"Because they were in the bedroom."

It still didn't make sense. There was no bedroom door. She would have heard if they'd stopped. And she wouldn't have been caught because there would have been a delay while Lucas released any restraints that'd been used.

Hannah's a virgin, he thought. "What did you hear when you tried it?"

"Nothing," said Hannah. "They were so quiet it was scary. Like he knew I was coming, and he was hiding to pounce on me."

Which didn't make sense, even knowing the woman wasn't a real sex worker. Because there was no door. Because whatever they were doing, Hannah would've heard them. But Quinn had listened to that same silence.

"You're sure they go into the bedroom?"

"Both times I've snuck in, the office was empty. But it creeped me out, so I left, and later they were all sweaty and . . . you know."

"But you've never heard them in the bedroom?"

"What's your point?"

"There's another room."

The Commissario's head appeared beside his easel again. "I cannot see the eyes. Will you?" He made a gesture with his hand for Quinn to lift his head.

"Another room?" echoed Hannah. "Where?"

"Probably behind a soundproof panel."

"We should go look."

"It probably has a security code."

"But if we find it, then we can tell my handler—"

The instructor walked up to them to conclude their lecture. Again, they indicated various parts of Quinn and Hannah's bodies and parts of the togas, then they smiled at Quinn and Hannah. "Va benne, gratzie mille." They were free to go.

Across the room, Lucas was withdrawing to answer his phone.

"Come with me," said Hannah as she hounded Quinn back to his room.

"I'm leaving." *If I don't leave now, I might not have another chance,* he thought.

Hannah took up her position on the other side of the bathroom door as he changed clothes.

"I thought you wanted to help Larisa," she said.

"I *am* helping Larisa. I'm going home and removing myself from Lucas's reach. She wouldn't have allowed herself any communication with him if I wasn't here."

"You're delusional if you think that."

Quinn threw the toga against the wall. Never again would he wear anything like it. Never again would Lucas dress him. He savored the comfort of his layers of long sleeves as he walked out and faced Hannah's pouting frustration. His duffle was on the floor where he'd left it, his phone resting on top. He had three missed calls from Sid and one message with a screenshot of flight information. Quinn pulled up the number for a taxi service that spoke English, then realized he didn't have an address to give them.

"What's the house number here?"

"I don't know."

"How do you get back when you travel?"

"Lucas has a car service. I just call them and they take me wherever, then bring me back."

"Call them for me."

She pulled out her phone and stared at it for a moment.

"What's wrong?"

"My handler says the mafioso Sforza is coming up from Naples to meet Lucas. They think maybe he's the buyer for the gas. I'm supposed to find out."

"Hannah, look at me. You can't do this. You're a phlebotomist from Minnesota. Call the car. Come with me to the airport."

For a moment Hannah stood frozen and Quinn felt the familiar summoning of his old rage. He wanted to shake her, to command her by all the phenomenal cosmic powers to just do what he said. But he held himself back, if only so he didn't scare her into not helping him.

Hannah dialed the car service. "Hello, yes . . . Airport, as soon as you can get here. Thirty minutes is good." Then she hung up. "Happy?"

He nodded.

"Okay, then I guess I'll go pack."

They walked together to the stairs. She went up to her room. He continued walking into the central part of the villa. Lunch was being served in the palazzo. He stopped in the doorway, partially hiding behind the students who were chatting up the girls who'd be models for the afternoon session. Lucas stood beside the fountain holding a velvet-lined case the size of a shoebox. Round white things—maybe stones or cameos or coins—rested on the velvet. The two instructors with him looked impressed.

I should say goodbye, thought Quinn.

He could stop me.

To stop you, he'd have to show his cards.

In some ways that would be a relief. Quinn was tired of not knowing the difference between pretend and real. He hated the guilt welling up, as though he owed something to Lucas for teaching him, for the journal, and the encouragement to write.

This has all been a dream. And when I leave, the dream will end, thought Quinn. Maybe what he felt wasn't guilt but the sinking realization that he'd failed to do what he'd come to do. Now it felt like a fool's errand. Lucas remained just as attached to Larisa as before. He still saw her as his own.

Movement in Quinn's peripheral vision drew his gaze upward. There, to his horror, was Hannah, creeping along the library shelves on her way to Lucas's office.

Oh no. No. No.

A quick glance across the room told Quinn Lucas hadn't seen her. His head was bent over his box, cocked to the side as he listened to one of the instructors. Before Quinn thought about what he was doing, he'd turned and was sprinting back to his room. He shoved his bag in the bottom of the closet, dashed to the bathroom, stripped, pulled on the never-again toga, and ran for the stairs as he fastened the belt.

Upstairs, down the hall, back into the palazzo. There, a pause to suck in air. He crouched down and squat-ran along the closed study doors, around the corner and along the library wall to Lucas's office door. It stood open. Just an inch, but still, details. *Do better, Hannah.*

He heard the crunch of something heavy landing on the floor. With a glance over the railing to make sure Lucas was still occupied, Quinn slipped through the door. Hannah was at the wall on the left side of the desk, the strangely-stretched painting of Samson and Delilah wilting in its cracked frame at her feet. She was struggling to push it aside so she could open the door that'd been hiding behind it.

"Help me," she hissed.

Together, they cleared the floor. From the outside, the door looked ordinary, which was probably why Hannah didn't hesitate to turn the knob and open it, heedless of alarms.

Like she's never seen a heist movie, thought Quinn. This woman didn't make sense to him. What kind of person volunteered for the CIA without at least having a cannon of movie examples to help her think through what she might encounter?

"Oh wow," said Hannah.

The room was black, the floor, the walls, the ceiling, a solid void if not for the twin black light bulbs which illuminated stark white rubber furniture that glowed purple—a four-poster bed, a chaise lounge chair, a desk and its chair—all equipped with rings for ropes or other restraints. The floor gave way under Quinn's feet as he entered the room, a spongey, industrial rubber material with holes, and a grate underneath.

"Look."

He followed the glowing line of Hannah's pointing arm to a long narrow cage at the base of the bed. There was another, larger one, attached to the wall in the far corner. Unless Quinn was seeing things, there was also another door there. He tripped on a pair of chains left on the floor as he went to investigate.

"What is this place?"

"Check the desk." Quinn moved along the wall until he felt the seam of the door, then the handle. It turned with an ill-used groan. He pulled the door open just enough to see out into the comparatively bright light of the north wing's central hallway.

"There's a laptop here. I bet it has everything they need." Hannah's excitement sounded too young, too bubblegum to be safe. If this was the scene in a horror movie, Quinn knew what would happen next.

"If you take it, he'll know it was you. Think. If the CIA can't use it. If he continues running free. Can you live with him knowing it was you?"

"Nerve gas," she whispered fiercely, her eyes almost cartoonishly large as they glowed in the black lights. "Doesn't that mean anything to you?"

There will always be someone selling weapons, he thought. *There will always be people killing other people.*

But she wasn't going to back down. And that meant his options had gotten smaller.

For Larisa, he thought.

"Are you ready to go?" he asked.

Hannah nodded.

He steered her toward the door and pushed her out. He handed her his phone. "Once you're in the car, call Sid, tell him the ticket needs to be in your name. Don't contact your handler until you're out of Italy."

"But—"

"Put yourself first. He won't."

"You're not coming?"

"You need to watch more movies, Hannah. Go." He closed the door in her face and took in his scene. The laptop had been in a drawer. If Lucas was sufficiently distracted, he might not think to look for it right away. The plane left in two hours, an eternity filled with ways Hannah could be caught.

Quinn lined himself up with the interior door, came forward into the center of the room, and knelt. When he'd met Larisa at

Club D, he'd been taught to keep his back to the door. But he'd never thought about if this request was specific to Larisa or standard practice.

"I'm supposed to be an imperfect submissive anyway," said Quinn as he sat back on his feet and folded his hands in his lap. It was too scary to sit with his back to the door; the carpet in the office was thick enough to mute any approach.

"You can do this."

Should have tried those butt plugs, he thought.

Maybe he'll be gentle.

Quinn focused on slowing his breathing. A submissive' s greatest desire was the will of their master. He needed to at least seem like he wanted this.

In through the nose, out through the mouth.

In through the—

Quinn's breath caught. The air in this room was different than the rest of the villa. Instead of cooking herbs or rosemary-infused woodsmoke or even the scent of cold old stones, this room smelled like the iron of blood. Standard bondage rooms had solid floors so they were easy to disinfect. They had no need for a grate.

People have died in this room.

Quinn had been kneeling just long enough for his feet to go numb, but not long enough to steady his racing thoughts when Rifat appeared in the doorway. Quinn kept his head bowed, chin to chest, but he could see Rifat's Villains, saw him stand still for a moment as he swore in Arabic, then left.

Whatever happens, thought Quinn. *Larisa will forgive me.*

Time stretched. Sometimes Quinn thought he could hear the din of conversation filtering in from the palazzo. But he knew that was impossible. By now the afternoon painting session would've started.

The grid of circles in the floor had become a permanent imprint on his legs by the time Quinn heard Lucas coming. He was surprised to hear him. And even more surprised to hear him speaking Italian. His voice was low with a tone of intimacy, the promise of a secret. Two pairs of feet appeared in the doorway. Lucas's real leather loafers and an elegant pair of heeled boots, which he didn't quite recognize until he heard the Commissario's reply to whatever Lucas had said.

Oh fuck.

They entered the room. The conversation continued. The Commissario's hand grazed Quinn's bare shoulder, fingers trailing down along the top of his spine.

"Bellissimo."

A drawer opened and closed. Not the desk drawer, one in a cabinet Quinn hadn't noticed. Lucas knelt before him and fastened a leather collar around his neck, then hooked a lead to the ring in the front. In a very low voice, he said, "You will do exactly as I say. You will be silent."

Despite himself, a shiver of anticipation rippled down Quinn's spine. He hadn't realized how much he missed being commanded. Already he could feel his body coming alive, rearranging itself in anticipation. When Lucas motioned for him to stand, Quinn stood. Head still bowed, he followed Lucas over to the chaise. As he did, Lucas continued to speak to the Commissario. He pointed out the lubricant on the little side table and gave a small laugh as though making a joke. The Commissario also laughed.

Lucas settled himself against the back of the chaise, his legs together down the middle. He pulled on the lead to guide Quinn forward over him, his knees on the outside of Lucas's, his hands holding himself up on the chaise's armrests, the crown of Quinn's head level with Lucas's face. Down below him, a bulging tent in the center of Lucas's trousers.

He's getting off on this and nothing's happened yet.

At Quinn's other end, a draft. The Commissario had flipped back the edge of the toga. Suddenly everything was real. Quinn reared back against the lead. "I can't."

Lucas yanked on the lead to keep him in place. "Hold your form," he whispered.

The lube was as cold as the Commissario's hands, careless with routine as they slid along Quinn's line, then parted him. No slow build up, no prelude, no apparent awareness of how small Quinn's entrance was or what he might need for this to be a mutually-enjoyable experience.

"Un momento," said Quinn, though not loudly enough that he had a prayer of the Commissario hearing him. "I'm not prepared."

"Quiet." Lucas braced his palm against Quinn's shoulder to keep him from pulling forward, away from the Commissario's reach. He leaned the side of his head against the side of Quinn's head, his breath a cool ribbon of air against his ear as he said, "Breathe." Then, "Don't disappoint me," in that voice that offered no space for argument, no option to do anything but obey.

A last desperate, "Please," dropped from Quinn's lips as the Commissario entered him. With it, a rush of fullness so surprising that for a moment Quinn didn't feel the pain. But the Commissario kept coming in and coming in and finally it was too much; Quinn cried out.

The Commissario froze. A stream of distressed Italian was directed to Lucas. As an important man, the Commissario was used to having what he wanted. Along with it, he was used to the illusion that whoever he was with wanted what he had to offer: his large dick, which felt slightly bent to the left or else he wasn't lined up. It was that pressure on the left that had turned from fullness to pain, as though Quinn was being torn open.

Lucas spoke reassuringly, the Italian version of *He's inexperienced. He's fresh for you. You're breaking him in for me.* The exact meaning didn't matter as much as the result, the Commissario starting his work again. When he reached the end of his length, he began pumping.

"Please," Quinn gasped. "I can't—" He clenched his jaw against another scream.

Lucas released the lead on the collar, used his thumb to pull Quinn's chin up, straining his neck so they were eye to eye. The whites of Lucas's eyes glowed in the black light like the eyes of another man, a man Quinn had known existed but had yet to meet. He gazed at Quinn with a quiet satisfaction, indifferent to his pain.

But then the expression softened. Lucas reached up and drew Quinn's head forward, allowing him to rest on Lucas's shoulder, to bite down on the thick layers of his sweater and mute the cries he couldn't suppress. Lucas held him firm until the end, one hand on the back of his head almost tender, the other against his shoulder, pushing Quinn back into the Commissario whenever he tried to pull forward to protect himself.

When the Commissario was finished, he patted Quinn's ass and said cheerfully, "Not too bad. A little wormy for me."

"He'll be punished for being a disappointment," said Lucas as he pushed Quinn back on to knees he could no longer feel and slid out from under him. Too quickly, Lucas was pulling on the lead for Quinn to get to his feet. He sat still, ignoring the pulling on his neck. His arms had fallen to his thighs and lay there like deboned fish, trembling so hard his eyes were out of focus.

"Come!"

The word cracked against Quinn's frozen shoulders. He told his legs to move and, somehow, they did, off the chaise and across to the foot of the bed where Lucas pulled open the top of the cage. Quinn stepped into it and sank down. It was only a few feet high. When he laid down, Lucas brought the top down over him and his shoulders pressed against the bars on both sides. It didn't matter. As the padlock clicked into place all Quinn could think was, *He can't touch me in here.*

Lucas and the Commissario left the room the same way they'd come in, chatting casually, as though nothing out of the ordinary had happened. One of them laughed. That laugh rang through the space between his ears, mocking him with its carelessness. He didn't matter beyond his role in their stray moment of pleasure. He hadn't done anything that would've made either man respect him. In every way, he had failed.

The sun had come up, but it remained hidden behind the clouds. Out the kitchen window, half of the garden had been eaten by the mist.

Quinn adjusted his pen for a better grip. His hands remained unsteady. Grasping small things like his toothbrush, buttons, the handle of the teacup had become a challenge. His body temperature, a subjective thing on a good day, had become a tempest, shifting between extremes without any apparent trigger. When Rifat had come to help him out of the cage, he'd been shivering so severely his chattering teeth had given him a headache. But that had passed. Now, he wore his own clothes and had wrapped the kitchen shawl around his shoulders. He kept thinking of scenes of shell-shocked soldiers from World War movies.

In his journal he wrote, *What's the difference between a villain who believes he's a hero and a villain who can't help doing what he does even if he hates himself?*

On the oven side of the kitchen, Francie and Carla were talking softly, studiously ignoring him. The music playing over the villa's speakers was something suitably moody. The artists had gone back to Florence. In their absence, the weather had determined to turn everything into a messy watercolor.

He's trapped by fate. Or by one wrong decision. Or where he was born.

Quinn drew a line through what he'd just written.

Carla came and refilled his tea. She pulled a bottle of pills out of her pocket. "For the pain?" she asked.

"So you do speak English."

She laughed softly, then left him alone.

He wondered how she knew he was in pain. Sometimes, even he forgot. If he found the right position, or didn't move for a period of time, he felt almost comfortable. He wondered if everyone in the house knew what had happened to him.

This was the right way to think about it, a thing that had happened 'to him,' but it didn't feel quite right in his mind. He could've fought back until the Commissario was repulsed. He'd been allowed that freedom and not used it.

Why?

Lucas had commanded him.

Now he knows I'm not enough for him.

When did that become something I wanted?

A flash of memory focused on a wolfish smile, a red coat, and a top hat. *From the moment I met him,* thought Quinn.

As though summoned by Quinn's thoughts, Lucas slid onto the bench opposite him. "You missed breakfast."

"I'm sorry." Quinn kept his eyes down on his journal to hide his resentment. "I'm not ready to eat."

Lucas twisted around and called to Carla for tea of his own. "You understand why it had to be done, don't you?"

Quinn drew a circle in his journal and began to draw lines to turn it into a maze.

"You broke into my room," said Lucas. "Then you expected me to tend to your needs in the middle of an event."

"I know."

"You broke one of my favorite paintings."

"I didn't," said Quinn softly. "It was like that. I came up to surprise you in the bedroom and I saw the door open." This was a gamble, one Quinn believed would fail because he was certain Lucas had security cameras in the house. But it was the only story he could tell that would protect both him and Hannah.

"Already open?"

"I went in to check for you. And I was overwhelmed by what I found." Quinn hazarded a glance up and found Lucas staring out the window, putting the pieces together that Quinn had laid out for him. He waited for Lucas to mention the missing laptop and missing Hannah.

Instead, Lucas said, "What did you think of my dungeon?"

"It's much nicer than the club in LA."

"Of course it is. I've spent years on it." Lucas paused to receive his tea from Carla. "I hope your first experience hasn't soured you on it."

Quinn swallowed down tea-flavored stomach acid. "The Commissario said you work with him. So I thought that's why—I know he was interested. It makes sense that you'd offer me to him." Quinn stabbed the nib of the pen into the page, then quickly covered the gash with the side of his hand. "I'm glad you were there with me."

"You did better than expected."

No apology.

He's not even going to ask if I'm alright.

The rain continued its inarticulate precipitation. The music drizzled slow circles through its measures. *I could stab him in the neck with this pen.*

Nerve gas.

An entire terrorist network.

My future with Larisa.

I want him to like me.

I'll be okay as long as it doesn't happen again.

I wish it had just been the two of us.

"I know you were planning to leave," said Lucas. "But given what's happened, the progress you've made, I think you should stay longer. I've begun some arrangements with your studio. And I—"

"Did you rape me because I said I was leaving?"

Lucas sipped his tea, eyes glittering as he debated a response.

"—a friend of mine is an up-and-coming star in Altuzarra. He's sending down some designs and his best people to work with us on your clothes for London." A pause that felt like consideration cloaked in calculation. "I think a trip abroad will be good for us."

Quinn drew his pen across the page until the ink bled and caught, causing another gash. "Us?" he asked.

"Of course. Now we've had this bonding, I'm not letting you out of my sight. Shall we invite Larisa to join us?"

"I thought you were upset with her."

"I was, yes. But I jumped to conclusions. There have been some things happening with my work that were clouding my judgement."

"She's involved with your work?"

"Just a small thing, schmoozing politicians. She's so good at that, you know. And she—well, it's over now."

"Did you really ask her to kill someone for you?"

Lucas smiled a smile with just the hint of threat lingering behind it. "What do you think?"

"Politics are beyond me." Quinn held his breath until Lucas laughed softly. The right answer.

Play the game. You're in now. Don't waste it.

The pen was shaking in Quinn's hand. He tried to tell the muscles they could relax even though he knew there was no reason for them to believe him.

"Come now." Lucas left his side of the bench and sat down beside Quinn, took hold of his shaking hand, and began to massage it. Those hands, that touch, possessive, confident, as though they'd already spent years like this together, as though Lucas was the kind of partner who tended to suffering instead of observing it. "Don't be dour. You're exactly where you're supposed to be. I'm going to make you into something magnificent."

And I'm going to break your heart, thought Quinn.

Lucas's phone began to ring.

Chapter 25

Living a Soap Opera

Larisa hadn't been able to sit still through Hannah's story. Hannah, of course, made all her actions seem reasonable, everything she did serving the cause of helping the CIA bring down a wanted man. But Larisa could read between the lines enough to see that her cousin had done something impulsive, been unable to follow through on it, dragged Quinn into the mess, then let him save her without any thought to what it would cost him.

"You have the laptop with you?" asked Gunter.

He'd asked very few questions during Hannah's story, and now, hearing the deep gravel of his voice strained with the kind of fatigue he hadn't had since he'd retired, Larisa couldn't help but feel this was all her fault, which made her internal rage at Hannah even larger.

"We should get it to the authorities as quickly as possible. Then we'll see about Quinn." Gunter glanced at Larisa without quite looking at her, but her heart thrilled at the promise. Now her father was involved, things would happen. They would rescue Quinn. This nightmare would end. Happily ever after.

I don't deserve that, she thought.

And she knew even her father wouldn't be able to fix the mess she'd made.

Rescuing Quinn is only half of the ending.

"There's nothing to be done about Quinn," she said. "He chose to be there. We have to assume he'll choose to leave when it suits him." Her voice wavered at the thought of Quinn with Lucas, knowing choice was a word that changed meaning in his villa of shadows.

"I think we should call your mother," said Suzette to Hannah. She waited for someone to weigh in; when no one did, she left the room. Hannah watched her go, mouth open as though she wanted to argue, but didn't have anything left.

Foolish, foolish, foolish, Larisa wanted to scream at her.

Was Quinn really planning to come back? she wondered. *Does that mean he's forgiven me for hiding the baby?*

"I'm going to step out for a moment." As Gunter left, he gave Larisa a warning look as though he knew she was contemplating the bloody murder of her cousin. To prove worthy of his trust, Larisa retreated to the library alcove off the living room and plopped down on the window seat.

Sid came in and sat down in her father's oversized armchair. "Did you go home at all yesterday?"

"What was yesterday?"

"You went AWOL, lost your phone and car?"

"And I witnessed a murder. Don't forget that part."

"Your parents are really calm."

"They just know how to perform for guests. When you all are gone, I'll get it. They thought last spring was bad, but if this leaks, none of us will recover." She turned to face him. "How are you doing?"

Sid reached up to scratch his bald spot. "Guess I'm glad you're not dead, cause that's what I was thinking when you didn't answer any of my calls and didn't answer for Quinn either."

"I'm sorry."

"Seems like you had good reasons."

In the living room, a more composed version of her mother floated in with a cart full of gift baskets. Every year, Suzette gave the sisters the advance samples of the new products for her beauty and whole wellness line, which Larisa had always thought were a not-quite concealed bribe to stay friends with the wayward, difficult daughter. "I know these are late, but its tradition, isn't it?"

"They're wonderful," said Krissy.

"I'm sorry I don't have one for you, Hannah," said Suzette, not sounding sorry. "I didn't know you'd be here."

"What did Mom say?" asked Hannah.

"Oh, she didn't answer. I'll try again later."

Larisa listened to the soft rustling of activity as the sisters received their gifts, how very normal they all sounded, each playing their expected roles. Rosa was effusive in her thanks. "Thank you so much, Suzette." Kahleah was practical and interested. "Oh, I've been looking for a new overnight mask." Jaden said something not quite right that she didn't realize was off. "The bottles are so cute. They're smaller than last year, right?" And Krissy, groveling. "I read about this one in *Vogue*, didn't you go all the way to the jungles in Kyrgyzstan to set up farms for the base?"

She wants a job, remembered Larisa but couldn't think of how she knew that or how long Krissy had been looking or why.

"Can I say something I know you won't like?" asked Sid. "I think you should go see him."

"He chose to—"

"Fuck that, Larisa. You're hiding behind that like you don't know the man couldn't make a good choice for himself if all he had to do was pick one of three and all three were good. He'd find a way to pick something else if he thought it'd be good for someone else."

Tears burned Larisa's eyes. She fought them back. If she started crying now, she wouldn't be able to stop. Sid was looking at her like she was the luckiest girl in the world but also cursed.

"He thinks you're the best thing that's ever happened to him, so he's gone off to fight for you in the worst possible way. It's not going to occur to him to come home until it ends. But he can't end it, can he? Only you can do that." Sid took a breath. "Please."

"I don't know how." Her voice caught. "I don't know how."

"Call Eddie. He'll get you on the carpet in London. Just be there, see what happens."

"What if Lucas is there?"

"I don't understand the question. Why does it matter if he's there or not?"

"He'll—" Larisa struggled to locate the right word. *Catch me,* she thought, even though she knew that wouldn't make sense to Sid.

Sid gave her a look like he wanted to argue.

"How did he sound?" asked Larisa. "When you talked to him?"

"Before the bit where he thought you were in danger, and I was turning the city inside out trying to find you? I think he was okay. I mean, it's not like he'd say if he wasn't."

"But you'd be able to tell, wouldn't you?"

In the living room, Rosa pointed excitedly at the TV. "Look, its baby Henry Cavill!"

"No way," said Jaden.

"It's *him.*"

"What movie is this?" asked Kahleah. "I'm looking it up."

On the screen, a Hollywood version of Venice Carnevale as actors in historic costumes and masks staged a street scene, creating obstacles for a young man in a cape making eyes with a mysterious masked woman.

From the love seat, Hannah sighed.

She's probably thinking she was going to go to Carnevale until Quinn ruined her plans, thought Larisa.

"He felt he wasn't being pushed as much as he'd expected. It was bothering him, I think. Like he was trying to figure out Lucas's plan," said Sid. "It's almost worse when you feel you're supposed to be scared but you aren't, right?"

"It's impossible to keep your guard up with Lucas."

"That thing he staged at Christmas—do you think he knew Quinn would come with him like that?"

Larisa shook her head. "I have no idea."

"But what do you think?"

In the living room, Kahleah said, "This is an adaptation of *The Count of Monte Cristo* and that is, in fact, Henry Cavill when he was—"

"I knew it!"

"Is it adultery if you have sex with a masked stranger in Venice?" asked Krissy. "I mean, it would just be like thrill seeking, right?"

"Like a roller coaster?" asked Rosa.

"If you plan to do it, definitely cheating," said Jaden.

"It doesn't matter," said Kahleah in a warning tone. "We're not going to Italy."

"And even if we were, it was Milan, not Venice," said Rosa.

Suzette laughed. "There's one in Milan, actually. Winter Duryea hosts a masquerade the night of the last runway show. She invites all the models, all the designers. Larisa and I based my fall gala off that event, though the Italian version is much bigger, more formal."

"That sounds so fun." Krissy guiltily glanced around for Larisa.

"If only Larisa wasn't such a party pooper," said Suzette, doing a passible imitation of a petulant teenager.

Larisa pretended not to hear her. She was trying to find an answer to Sid's question. It was so difficult to think, especially about this. She'd spent so much energy trying to get Lucas out of her head.

"Remember what you said about why I didn't want to go to Italy?"

"Yep."

"It's true. I mean, not in an obvious way. But I—I don't know what I'll do if I'm exposed to that world. It's not just him." Larisa waved her hand toward the living room. "That woman, Winter? She's one of Lucas's friends. They plan the masquerade together every year. Even if he isn't in Milan, she will be. She goes to almost every show, she knows all the Italian designers. I was with him in

Milan for a month, we rode the streetcar, we shopped at the Galleria, sat in coffee shops and read books."

"So what? It was extra romantic? American girl in Italy?"

"No," said Larisa softly. "It was him. I'd never been with anyone who only wanted me. Everything about my life to that point had been as the daughter of my parents. I was a teenage reality TV star who went off to college and was asked for autographs when I went to World Civ."

"Poor you."

She slapped his knee. "What I'm saying is I didn't fall for Lucas. I plunged all the way off the cliff, and I didn't feel the pressure changing in my ears, didn't see the rocks coming up out of the sea. I'd been waiting my entire life for a chance to be my own person without knowing that was the thing I wanted. He became the only thing I wanted."

"Not super surprising given you don't seem to have any emotional boundaries whatsoever."

"I have some. With my mother, kind of. And with my friends."

"The friends who're still secretly thinking of going to Italy without you?"

Larisa looked out at the living room wondering if any of the sisters had heard what Sid had said. They were here supporting her, but they didn't feel the catastrophe the way she did, which wasn't their fault. Even to Larisa, it didn't quite feel real.

"I thought we were analyzing Lucas, not me," she said.

"Right. So we think he wants you back? He thinks he'll sabotage your relationship with Quinn. He tried a couple of ways. They didn't work. Then at Christmas—can we call it passive aggressive kidnapping? Like he didn't give Quinn a choice, except for the one he wanted Quinn to make."

"If I go try to rescue Quinn, I'll just make things worse. He responds when he thinks people have strong feelings.

"He wants you to come to him because it's obvious he's the one."

"But he's afraid Quinn might be the one."

Sid snorted. "This is a soap opera."

"Lucas loves the opera," said Larisa. "He loves balls and games and extravagance and larger-than-life everything."

"Why make you play assassin?"

Larisa glanced into the living room again. The sisters had coalesced around her mother, their heads all bent together, plotting. *They're going to ask me to go to Milan,* she thought.

"I don't think it was about Quinn as much as it was about trying to get me involved in his world. Our last big fight was about me needing my life with him to have meaning. So maybe he wanted to see if I liked being part of what he does?"

"Twisted. But really, when you think about it, how many people have job satisfaction?"

"True. I mean, he—"

"Wait, back up. You didn't leave him because you found out he was an arms dealer?"

"That. Is. Correct."

"Huh. You know, I like your parents, but this raises some serious questions about what you were taught growing up."

You don't know what he's like, thought Larisa. "I just told you, cliff diving."

"But feelings die down. Those—what do you call them— hormones wear off."

"These didn't." Larisa let the words hang in the air as she continued to watch the sisters. Krissy was giggling. Jaden had this mischievous smile on her face. Even Kahleah looked happy, a little less fierce than the resting 'don't mess with me' expression that'd become her new norm.

They'll be with me, she thought. *We could do it.*

We, she thought.

"So you're not likely to kill him. But you gave Pam what she needed, right? And Hannah has that laptop, so the CIA might get off their asses and do something. It's just a waiting game."

"Not a long wait if you trust what the CIA says."

"But we don't want Quinn to be trapped."

"Or killed when those people decide to act."

"Riiiight." Sid crunched up his face. "When you say it like that, I'm wondering what we're still doing here."

"We're still here because Hannah's scared and probably doesn't know how to contact the CIA."

"Lucky for her, you do."

"I don't have my phone."

Sid lightly punched her in the arm. "Figure it out, Doctor Larisa."

She pushed him away so she could stand up and return to the living room. "Everyone, I've made a decision. We're going to Milan for fashion week."

A stunned silence. Kahleah looked suspicious, like she wanted to lodge a protest in Larisa's defense. But then Jaden let out a, "Whoo, Italy here we come!" And the moment for protest passed.

"Thank you, Larisa," said Rosa.

"Thank you, Suzette," said Krissy.

Suzette looked flustered by the abrupt change but more than pleased once she realized it'd actually happened. Seeing her mother happy almost made Larisa feel like a good daughter. She waded into the living room and stopped beside Hannah on the love seat. "Get the laptop. I'll drive you." Larisa kept walking to the far side of the room where she picked up the house phone where her mother had left it and continued walking until she reached the back patio.

A deep breath in, then its matching deep breath out. She dialed the number she would never forget. It rang four times before the line clicked open.

"Hello?" asked Lucas.

Another deep breath. Larisa's hand flailed through the air, then caught on the doorjamb.

"What's the occasion?"

"I'm calling about Ana."

"Yes?"

"I want to talk to Quinn."

"What about Ana?"

"I'll tell him."

"Don't play games, Larisa."

She dug her nails into the doorjamb's white painted wood and waited. If Lucas wanted to know that badly it meant no one else had told him about Ana already, which meant he probably didn't have other people in LA. It meant she could tell him anything and it'd sound like the truth because he'd heard it from her first.

There was a shuffling over the phone speaker, then a familiar high tenor throat clearing. "Hello, Larisa," said Quinn.

The tears came then, hard and fast, so that Larisa couldn't answer right away. Silence filled the line. "So," she stifled a sniffle. "Lucas's friend here had a run in with some bad people. If he knows about her cocaine habit, he'll understand."

"Are you okay?" The way he said it broke her heart. Like he knew what she'd been dealing with. And then she thought, maybe he did know something, because he'd called Sid panicking.

"I'm okay."

She wished they had code words so he could tell her all the things he wanted to say without Lucas knowing.

"We're such terrible bondage people," she laughed. "We don't even have a safe word."

She heard Lucas grumble something in the background.

"Yes, we do," said Quinn. "It was in the contract."

Contract, thought Larisa. *For our fake relationship? Really?*

Not wanting to admit that he remembered something she didn't, Larisa said, "Well, it wouldn't really apply here, would it? Sounds like you're having fun."

"I am, but it's harder than I thought to be away from Penelope."

In the background she heard Lucas ask, "Penelope?"

Then Larisa remembered the apparently random name Quinn had chosen for their code word so that in social situations, if one of them was uncomfortable, they could let the other know.

He'd never explained why that name. At the time, she'd thought it adorably quirky.

"I'll give her lots of extra pets," said Larisa. *And I'm coming to get you.* "She's been scheming ways to get out of her situation."

"Situation?" asked Lucas.

"Tell her she didn't know how good she had it with your parents."

"I will."

Somewhere, on the other side of the house, the doorbell was ringing, a thing that almost never happened at her parents' in the middle of the day.

I'm coming, Quinn. Hang on.

"Does Lucas have any other questions for me?"

A soft voice, indistinct so Larisa couldn't hear.

"He says he hopes you won't have any trouble with your work even though Ana's unavailable. Otherwise, he'll be very disappointed."

"Tell him not to worry." Larisa sounded braver than she felt. That threat, even with Quinn translating Lucas's words with his softer voice, reminded her of the last time Lucas had been disappointed.

Someone was calling her name. Larisa turned and saw Sarah, her parents' house manager, hurrying down the hall from the front of the house.

"I need to go now."

"Maybe when we have time, I can meet you in Paris," said Quinn.

"Paris?" asked Larisa, staring as Sarah started making exaggerated gestures for her to come inside.

"I've heard it's always a good idea."

Larisa swiped at her face as fresh tears surged. How just like Quinn to quote her favorite movie when they both didn't know what else to say. She hung up and opened the sliding glass door. "Sarah, what's wrong?"

"The police are here. They want to ask you questions about a dead person."

Pam, thought Larisa. *Pam sent them.*

Larisa surveyed the yard. Running was an absurd idea, but she didn't have any other good ones.

"Tell them you couldn't find me."

Sarah's eyes widened.

"Tell Sid to feed Sabrina."

Without waiting to see if Sarah was going to be okay with this new, marginally criminal, level of responsibility, Larisa sprinted across the back lawn and into the hedges that led down into the canyon.

Please Leave a Review

So glad this book found you! If you enjoyed reading it, please leave a review on Goodreads and Amazon if you use them. Please also tell people about this book. Books are sold by people talking about them.

    - Cheers, Jaye

You're welcome to post about Casta Diva all you want on your own socials, but if you want a dedicated place to discuss this, and my other books, with your fellow readers, join my private, member-only reader group on Facebook.

Homme Fatale

The Final installment in the Elaborate Lives series

Larisa commits to coming to Italy to rescue Quinn, but first she must complete an errand for Lucas in Las Vegas. In the meantime, Quinn and Lucas's entanglement takes on a new level as Quinn is pulled fully into Lucas's criminal underworld, role playing for a mafia godfather, and trying not to be caught in friendly fire as the CIA closes in.

Sign up for my mailing list to receive early offers and announcements.

Acknowledgements

Land Acknowledgement

Casta Diva was written on the ancestral land and traditional territories of the Omaha, Oto, and Pawnee Nations. They are the original custodians of the land on which I have lived and worked while writing this novel.

Special thanks to my intrepid beta readers Hannah Gage, Lisa Albright, Heather Leighson, and Emma V, who all agreed on several important things that caused me to rewrite a large portion of this book.

Thanks to Sarah McGuire my editor who fixed all the commas and also caught several continuity errors, to Damonza Designs for the great cover, and to Clara at Author Tree for taking my Word doc and making it look like a book.

About the Author

Jaye Viner lives on what used to be the plains of eastern Nebraska with a tall human and three fur bombs. She knows just enough about a wide variety of things to embarrass herself at parties she never attends. Her short fiction has been published in Drabblecast, Everyday Fiction, The Rumpus, and Others. She is the author of *Jane of Battery Park*, the *Elaborate Lives* series, and the Afternoon Delight romantic shorts. Find her on Instagram and TikTok @Jaye_Viner or her website JayeViner.com

Social media links for ebook
https://twitter.com/JayeViner
https://www.instagram.com/jaye_viner/
https://www.facebook.com/JayeViner
www.jayeviner.com
https://www.goodreads.com/author/show/7107386.Jaye_Viner